ANACONDA

A SEXY ROMANTIC COMEDY

LAUREN LANDISH

Edited by VALORIE CLIFTON

Edited by JOHN HUDSPITH

Photography by ALEX WIGHTMAN

Edited by DONNA HOKANSON

ANACONDA

A SEXY ROMANTIC COMEDY

They say size doesn't matter...

Football star and internet sensation Gavin "Anaconda" Adams is the *biggest* celebrity our little town has ever seen.

But I had *no* idea who he was when I accidentally walked in on him naked.

I was shocked, seeing *all* of him, a cocky grin on his face. I didn't know what to do.

So I *ran*.

Now I'm in a world of trouble. No matter what I do, I can't get *that* image out of my head. **His strong muscular thighs. His washboard abs. His big, throbbing, toe-curling... Jesus!**

To make matters worse, Gavin wants a date with me. He's seen the lust in my eyes, and he's not taking no for an answer. I should tell him to get lost. He's nothing but trouble, and he's only here for a week.

But with one look, I go weak in the knees. And whenever I hear his deep, rich voice, I feel my defenses crumbling.

It's only one night. What could it hurt?

❋

Want the FREE Extended Epilogue? Sign up to my mailing list to receive it as soon as it's ready. If you're already on my list, you'll get this automatically.

Irresistible Bachelor Series (Interconnecting standalones):
Anaconda || Mr. Fiance || Heartstopper
Stud Muffin || Mr. Fixit || Matchmaker
Motorhead || Baby Daddy

CHAPTER 1

BRIANNA

"*T*his is fucking disgusting," I mutter with revulsion, looking around the hotel room and barely able to hold back the nausea twisting my stomach from the foul stench. I clamp a hand over my nose, trying not to breathe the acrid air in through my mouth and shaking my head at the horror before me.

Actually, disgusting is an understatement. The room looks like a frat house after a night of binge drinking and wild orgies. There are pizza boxes, crushed beer cans, and dark stains everywhere.

Jesus Christ.

No wonder the smell is so bad. These guys are pigs. My eyes continue to roam and I spot at least one smashed bottle of vodka before...

"Oh, hell no!" I croak, almost dry heaving and turning away from the revolting sight of several used condoms. I can even see something white and sticky nearby. I grab the top of my uniform and pull it up over my nose, no longer able to bear the stench. "They don't pay me enough for this shit!" Holding my breath, I beeline for the door. I gasp as I exit the room and enter the hallway, letting go of my shirt and sucking down a lungful of air. I normally can't stand the air in the smoking section of the guest rooms, but right now, this air is sweeter than a double-fudge chocolate chip sundae.

After a few grateful breaths, I pull out my walkie talkie from my side pocket and shake my head as I press the microphone button. "Maintenance, this is Housecleaning."

"Whatcha need, Bri?" asks a familiar scratchy voice, and I sigh, relaxing. It's Jimmy, an older man who still wears corduroy and thinks he's in the 70s. But besides his penchant for living in the past, he's pretty cool and will empathize with my pain. This isn't the first wrecked room that I've walked in on, and it certainly won't be my last.

"We have a problem," I tell him, letting the direness I feel seep into my voice. "A *big*, big problem."

"Is it that bad?" Jimmy asks. There's a slight note of hope in his voice. I know what he's thinking. He's hoping that maybe it's nothing a little bleach and elbow grease won't fix.

I feel sorry for him. And to think I didn't even step foot into the bathroom.

I shudder at the gross images that flash in my mind as I reply, "Yes! Your boys will have their hands full. Room 333. Bring steam cleaners, a sandblaster . . . and maybe a hazmat suit."

Jimmy groans over the radio. I hear him inhale as if he wants to say something, but the transmission cuts. He knows that he can't say much about it. Our radios aren't monitored like the police scanners, but they can still be listened to. And with what's going on, we can't take chances. A crackling sound pops my ears.

"If you guys get it done, I'll worry about the towels and sheets," I add.

"Grand Waterways Hotel . . ." Jimmy says forlornly. *"Grand Water Sewer Way would be a more apt name."*

I huff out a chuckle at that. Jimmy shouldn't have said that over the line, but it's the damn truth. "Can't argue with that," I say wholeheartedly. To the hotel's credit, though, it can't help what guests like a team of pro and collegiate ballers do to its rooms when they're hosting drunken parties. I've heard that they stay here instead of in the city to keep the players 'out of trouble'. But they still have their parties.

"I'll handle it, Bri. We'll be up in a half hour. Maybe you can catch the rest on the back half of your shift?"

A feeling of relief washes over me. The man is a lifesaver. There's no way I could handle these types of situations without him.

"Thanks, Jimmy."

"No worries. Maintenance out."

"Poor man," I mutter, tucking my walkie talkie back into my pocket.

Grateful to be free of that disaster, I make my way to the elevator, press the down button, and wait for the doors to open. Once inside, I mull over which floor I should go to, but my watch beeps, reminding me that I need a break.

I jam the button for the basement, leaning against the wall as the carriage starts to go down. My back aches, my feet ache, and I'm pretty sure that my skin needs to be scrubbed with something stronger than soap and water after just walking into that filthy room. The image of the used condoms on the floor flashes in my mind and my skin crawls.

I can't wait until I finish my degree and never have to step foot into this place again, I think with disgust.

I definitely don't feel like working the rest of my shift after that. I'm aching and sore all over. I'm seriously overworked, and I don't think I can take any more surprises.

But at least I'm mostly finished, and I've got the next thirty minutes to chill out, try to get myself back together, and maybe pop a Tylenol or two before I do the last set of regular rooms, the suites, and then the floor that I normally hate most because I never know what to expect, the penthouse suites. They can range from sparkly clean to a pigsty as bad as the room I just left... depending on who's been staying there. Sometimes, the ballers are too damn cheap and just trash a regular room.

The ding sound and opening doors pull me out of my reverie. I walk out of the elevator and head to the maintenance room. I wash my hands using rubbing alcohol and some germicidal stuff from the medicine cabinet in the staffroom before I apply two coats of lotion, praying that maybe this time I won't be bleeding from between my fingers like the last time I had to do this.

I look up in the mirror and sigh, shaking my head at the reflection that looks back at me. Bra-length, dark brown hair, tired eyes, and a grumpy countenance. I look like I haven't had a decent night's sleep in over a week.

I don't need this shit, I say to myself. *I can't wait to get out of this place. Hell, I'll take just about any job with benefits over this.*

But more than benefits, I need money. Doing twenty-nine hours of maid work in a hotel just doesn't cut it when you're like me—Master's degree student with no family, no credit cards, and about two thousand dollars left from a student loan. Somehow, I have to stretch this small amount of money to cover the gap in my living expenses for the rest of the year.

I shake my head again as I think about how close I'd been to that internship.

One computer error. That's all that kept me from landing a paid internship. One idiot at school who typed in my GPA wrong, saying I had a 1.8 instead of a 3.8. By the time I got it all sorted out, it was too late. All of the internships were already snatched up.

"Face it, girlie," I grumble to myself, "if this keeps up, you'll be going down to the food bank for canned goods by Christmas." I rub the last of the lotion into my hands. The sound of heels clicking against the tiled floor causes me to turn around, and I see my best friend, Mindy, holding a mocha latte in one hand and a cup of green tea in the other. She wiggles the latte at me.

I take it from her, feeling grateful for her thoughtfulness. "Tell me you put cinnamon in it," I say.

Mindy steps back to survey me, shaking her head, her dark brown hair that's cut into a side bob glinting under the lights and her large brown eyes flashing with a mischievousness that almost makes me smile. I have to say, she looks hot as hell in her uniform—a white dress shirt, open at the front, a short black skirt, an apron, and stockings, her feet adorned with black glossy heels.

"You bet your sweet ass I did," Mindy chirps before going over to the free table in the staff break room and kicking out a chair with her foot before sitting down. "Double cream, double sugar, double cinnamon, basically double everything I could get my hands on. Come on, I know your schedule as well as you do. It's the least I can do."

"You're a lifesaver," I tell her, raising the cup to my lips and taking a sip. I close my eyes as the warm liquid hits my tastebuds and I let out a groan. It really is sweet.

"You know, you keep moaning like that, and people are going to think you're up to no good during your coffee breaks," Mindy jokes, sipping her green tea. "I mean, I get it. You skipped breakfast like you always do, but damn, girl, should I leave you and the latte alone with a necktie hanging on the door?"

"You keep making drinks like this and bringing me scones, and you may just have to," I joke. "But how'd you know?"

"What? That you'd be tired?" Mindy asks, laughing. "Uh, in case you forgot, for the past two weeks, we've all been wiped out. I'm sure that V-man loves the money, but he's not the one busting his ass" —Mindy glances down at her thighs critically— "or in this case, big ass."

"Oh, come on, you're a size two!" I protest.

Mindy scowls. "A *big* size two."

"There's no such thing!" I scoff.

"Want to see my ass?" she offers.

"I'll pass." I chuckle. Mindy always does this, complaining about her weight when there's nothing to complain about. I just argue with her to get kicks. I take another sip of my heavenly latte before adding, "And if Mr. Vandenburgh hears you call him V-man again, you know he's going to blow his stack."

Mindy laughs and screws up her face, looking remarkably like John Cleese as she pitches her voice perfectly to match the hotel manager's. "Ahh . . . yes, Miss Sayles, we've noticed that you're taking your job far too seriously, and I'm going to need to make sure you don't have a broom handle lost inside your buttocks. Please bend over and spread your cheeks for me."

I laugh, barely holding onto the coffee in my mouth as I set my cup down, trying not to cough. I can't help it. Mr. Vandenburgh does look a lot like a very short but chubby John Cleese, and Mindy's got the voice down to a tee. Mindy lets up, and I swallow before sitting back, wiping at my eyes. "Girl, thank you. I *so* needed that. You don't even want to know what I had to deal with today."

"What, the production monkeys aren't appreciative of the fine rooms we've made available to them?" Mindy asks. For the past two weeks, The Grand Waterways has been rented out by a Hollywood studio that's producing a film in town. While the production team staying at the hotel haven't exactly been the cleanest guests, they've been a hell of a lot better than the sports team that just trashed that room.

"No, actually, it was that rowdy ball team." I shake my head. "And you don't even want to know what I saw in their room," I say, pinching my face into a disgusted scowl.

"Sure I do," Mindy says, her eyes flashing.

"No. You don't," I say firmly. "Trust me."

"Tell me!"

"No."

"You suck."

"Let me just put it this way. I had to call Jimmy and his team to handle it."

Mindy makes a face. "Oh, it was one of those, huh?"

"Yeah. One of *those*."

"I bet it smelled like toe jam and ass crack." Mindy grins.

"Actually, it was worse." I laugh, remembering the acrid stench that made my eyes water. "There were like stains . . . everywhere. It was so gross!" I don't even think about bringing up the used condoms.

Mindy grimaces. "Good lord, what the hell were they doing in there? Having a golden showers competition?"

I snort, nearly gagging on my coffee, and then I start coughing so hard I nearly choke.

Mindy stares at me with concern, half-rising out of her seat. "Jesus, you okay, Bri?"

I motion her to sit back down. "Don't do that!" I gasp when I'm able to recover.

"Do what?" Mindy asks innocently.

I wipe at my eyes. "Make me laugh when I'm drinking coffee. I nearly gagged to death."

Mindy grins impishly. "Wouldn't be the first thing you gagged on."

I scowl at her. "You're disgusting, you know that?"

"Oh c'mon, Bri, don't be such a prude." She pauses, nodding at the supply room. "So, what's left on your schedule?"

"Too much," I reply. "But at least the penthouses should be easy. One of the suites is being used by some film crew, so they don't want us in there. One is empty until a guest arrives tonight. So, that leaves just one."

"Then perhaps, Miss Sayles," a stern voice says from behind me, "you should look at making sure you have that room prepared for our VIP guest." I turn to see Mr. Vandenburgh, all five foot four inches and about two hundred plus pounds of him, standing in the doorway. He's in his tailored suit, of course, looking like a thousand bucks from the neck down while looking like a grumpy ass disorderly from the neck up. "That is, unless you want to pay for that coffee you're holding."

Oh, God, please save me.

I shake my head. "No, you're right, Mr. Vandenburgh." I glance over at Mindy, who is barely hiding a smirk.

"Well then, get on with your duties," he says acidly, his scowl hard enough to curdle milk.

Please let me find another job so I don't have to deal with this shit anymore.

Seriously, after that bullshit upstairs, I'd almost be ready to tender my resignation if I were offered a job at McDonald's sweeping the floors. I'm just so over this.

Vandenburgh opens his mouth as if to scold me further, but I hold up a finger as I drain the rest of my coffee.

"I'm going!"

I give Mindy a thankful nod as I pitch my empty cup into the trash. She flashes me a sympathetic look as I turn and walk out, making my way to the service elevators. I really can't stand Mr. Vandenburgh's presence for more than a minute, and I just want to knock out the rest of my shift and go home.

As I head up the hall, I can hear Mr. Van start in on Mindy.

"What the hell did you do to the machines, young lady? I got complaints about the coffee this morning..."

I crack a smile as I imagine the look of consternation on Mindy's face.

By the time I finish the regular rooms, I'm nearly about to pass out as I push my supply cart toward the service elevator.

"Just a little while longer," I tell myself, "and I'm free."

By some miracle, a lot of the rooms on the next floor aren't that bad. In fact, I'm feeling like salvation is near when I make it to the penthouse suites. My first stop is room 601. It's reserved so I skip it.

Room 602 is occupied, with the 'do not disturb' sign on the doorknob.

So, that leaves Room 603, which should also be empty. The guest isn't checking in until this evening. Before I step inside, I check the guest list. It just has '**ANACONDA**' scribbled on the sheet. I frown at the name as I stare at the big bold letters. What the hell kind of name is Anaconda?

Shaking my head, I open the door and hold back a jealous grumble at the sight before me. Seriously, the living room of this penthouse is bigger than my entire apartment. Two thousand square feet, a master bedroom and a smaller bedroom-slash-office, and a sitting room. The damn thing even has a chef's kitchen.

My grumble turns into a hiss of anger when I see that someone's been up here, and it sure as shit wasn't Goldilocks.

"None of this should be here," I mutter as I take in the mess, frowning at a jacket that's been thrown over the Italian leather sofa and a bag that looks like it was carelessly tossed into a chair and knocked it over.

Puzzled, I check my sheet again. Nope. No one's supposed to be here. I step into the room, leaving my cart outside.

"Housekeeping?" I call tentatively. "Anyone here?"

Silence is my only answer.

"Hello?" I dare again. When I get no response, I walk over to pick up the chair that's been knocked over. I figure that maybe someone has checked in ahead of the guest and left in a hurry. I'll straighten things up and just leave.

A sound behind me causes me to spin around, and my breath stills in my lungs.

Holy fuck!

My heart skips a beat as my eyes take in the naked . . . *god* standing before me. Well, ok, he's not totally naked. He's got a towel over his head and he's drying his hair.

But the way he's built . . . sweet Jesus. He looks like he's chiseled out of granite, with big muscular arms, breathtaking broad shoulders, a proud chest, an eight pack, and . . .

"Anaconda . . ." I whisper as I see what's hanging between his legs, my pulse pounding in my ears. He's got to be at least seven inches long already and he's not even hard. My skin prickles as I gaze at his thick cock, my nipples hardening, my breath coming out in short pants.

The man freezes when his eyes fall on me, and I feel like I'm going to melt into a puddle on the floor. I have no words for how hot this man is. He's not just hung like a horse. He's *fucking gorgeous* too. Shaggy blond hair hangs down over his forehead, with startling blue eyes that seem to glow from the inside and a face that would make artists drool. He's staring at me, his mouth, with full, sexy lips, hanging slack, the towel dropping from his hand to the floor.

Neither of us says anything for what seems like an eternity but has to be just a few seconds before he recovers and grins, his eyes boring into me with an intensity that makes me weak at the knees. "Hi, I'm Gavin," he says easily, as if he's not standing in front of me with a monster-sized dick dangling between his legs.

He's not doing anything to cover it up either. Given what he's packing, I understand why. It's like he's proud of it as he stares at me with a confidence that borders on gross arrogance.

Heat rises in my chest as he steps forward, a cocky smirk turning the corner of his lips, and I take a half-step back, my pussy clenching around nothing. It's an effort to keep my eyes on his face as my heart hammers in my chest and my cheeks burn with embarrassment.

"You all right?" he asks. Even his *voice* is sexy, a low baritone that causes my pussy to clench again.

I open my mouth to reply, but my eyes stray back to *it*, and my heart skips another beat. *Shit. Shit. Shit.* I can't deal with this right now. I tear my gaze away from it, my eyes darting this way and that, looking for a way out as he closes in on me.

I want to run away. But I can't move. It's like my legs have filled with stone. Against my will, my eyes flicker back to *it*.

Sweet Jesus! It's swaying with each step, swinging back and forth like a giant pendulum, almost putting me into a hypnotic trance.

When he gets close enough to touch me, I'm suddenly free of my paralysis. Heart pounding, I spring forward, nearly tripping on my way to the door. I'm only able to mumble, "Sorry," as I run from the room with a flaming red face, trying my damnedest to not glance back for one last look.

CHAPTER 2

"*A*naconda! Anaconda!" the reporters yell in my face after a particularly rough game, jamming microphones and cameras at me. "Do you have anything to say about what happened?"

God, I hate that fucking nickname.

I blink several times as rapid flashes of lights go off in my eyes, fighting down the exasperation that flares inside me. They're herding me like a fucking zoo animal, each one of them fighting one another to stick a mic in my face.

A fraudulent smile spreads across my chiseled jawline as I wink into the cameras and prepare to formulate an answer. I'm trying to appear unruffled by the question, though I want nothing more than to tell them all to get the fuck out of my way. I know how they'll spin it if I do. And I can already see the headlines now.

Gavin Adams Flies into a Rage after a Bad Game Because of Scandal.

I know I should ignore the trolls, who are only looking for a rise out of me or a soundbite to try and get another five minutes of story out of what was a total mistake. But after dealing with the team, the league, and all the drama that ensued, I'm pissed off. Losing 20-0 against our biggest rival isn't helping much either.

"Mr. Adams has nothing to say," Miranda, my agent who doubles as my PR rep, says loudly over the ungodly clamor of shouting voices and clicking cameras, beating me to the punch. My eyes are drawn to her. She's dressed sharply, as usual, in her red designer dress that fits her shapely frame like a glove, the epitome of a middle-aged professional woman who's still getting some mileage out of her body as well as her brains. "So, if you all would just excuse us. He has more important things to attend to."

"Hold up, Miranda," I interrupt her, maintaining my fake smile. I figure I can use my charm to defuse this situation and be on my merry way. I raise my voice and politely say, "I'm sure everyone's heard about my little incident, but I want to let you all know it was just an accident. And that's it."

"There was nothing *little* about it!" a female reporter shouts, and then giggles ensue. I ignore her and the rest.

"So, you don't have anything to say about the footage of you circulating on the internet?" asks one of the other reporters.

I scowl at him. *That will teach you to stop for a photo op and try to smooth things over.* "What footage?" I ask flatly, knowing exactly what he's talking about.

He smiles, his freckles spreading across the bridge of his nose. "The one of you dropping your towel in front of Sara Jameson on live TV."

I hold in a groan, irritation flaring. These people are acting like I whipped it out and gave Ms. Jameson a lap dance. All I did was bump into her in the men's locker room after a game. It wasn't 'live TV', and she shouldn't have been back there in first damn place. It wasn't my fault the fucking towel fell off. But as soon as it did, I apologized to the wide-eyed Sara and put it back on.

I thought we were cool after that. She even told me the cameras hadn't caught my mistake and I had nothing to worry about. Until the cameraman with her, or someone at the network, decided to leak the unedited video dubbed *Anaconda* out to the internet. It's spreading like wildfire now along with my new nickname.

This whole thing has been a goddamn PR nightmare too. Miranda has spent a week of sleepless nights sending DMCAs to various websites to get the footage taken down. It's been an endless battle. When one goes down, another one pops up. Still, it's fewer of them than when this all started.

I just wish I hadn't been so careless.

"It's unfortunate," I say, keeping the smile on my face with massive effort, "but really, it was an accident. Now if you guys would please move out of our way, I have to get to—"

"What does your mother think about you flashing millions of people?" the same guy cuts in again, taking delight in my irritation.

Miranda winces next to me as I grit my teeth, no longer able to control my anger.

"Are you fucking deaf? I just said it was an accident!" I snap. Miranda is going to be pissed I lost my cool, but I can't stand any more of this shit. "Now, if none of you have a question that's actually related to my game, don't waste my fucking time!"

"Okay, that's enough! No more questions!" Miranda shouts, taking me by the arm and dragging me toward the exit. Miranda hisses out of the side of her mouth, "Dammit, Gavin, you know better than that! Now that little soundbite is gonna be all over the evening news."

She's right. I knew the second it left my lips. But I'm not going to admit that to her. I'm too fucking pissed right now.

We reach the door at the end of the hall and I practically kick it open, muttering, "Whatever. You try stepping in my shoes and tell me you wouldn't have reacted the same way."

Miranda wisely chooses not to answer.

❄

Present Day

"WHAT A SHITHOLE," I MUTTER AS I GAZE OUT THE WINDOW. WE'RE passing by rows of shops that look like they belong in some backwater town of a Midwest state. Fields, fields, a John Deere tractor, some barn that looks like it should be torn down, and a place called Stuckey's. The town's still up ahead, but for fuck's sake, I can see the water tower with the town name on the side. It looks like it came out of an old music video.

Then again, the place is clean. I can see kids playing in the front yards, and there isn't a hint of smog in the sky. And the streets aren't jammed with traffic.

Still . . . "They really want us to film here?" I ask.

Miranda nods. "It's the ideal location."

I would argue against that, but I decide not to. I just came from yet another press event teeming with hungry reporters and I'm drained from all the bullshit. "As long as I don't have to deal with any more paparazzi, I'll consider myself lucky."

"You shouldn't," Miranda says. "I've called ahead and made arrangements. No one should know that you're checking in."

"Good," I growl, rubbing at my eyes. "Because they bring up that fucking video every time." It's been two years. And still, this shit is all anyone ever wants to talk about. It takes everything inside me to not go off on them.

That's why I'm trying my hand at acting during the off season. Miranda thought it might go a long way in helping my image and getting people's minds off my . . .

"Please don't," Miranda begs. She's been through the wire these past couple of seasons, doing her best to temper my edge whenever I'm close to exploding. I have to admire her tenacity. If I were her, I would've quit on me ages ago. "I don't want any more surprises. We'll get you to the hotel and you can put your feet up until shooting starts tomorrow."

I relax back in my seat at her words. A shower and a soft bed sound nice. And maybe a kitten to share my bed with. I shift in my seat, not feeling the excitement that usually comes with such a thought. Normally, I'd be turned on by the thought of hooking up with a local honey, but now...

"Earth to Gavin," Miranda says, shaking me from my thoughts. "You all there?"

I turn back, tugging at my Italian designer t-shirt and blazer, nodding. "Yeah, just wishing I could wear something comfortable. What is it with Italians and skinny sleeves?"

"Makes your biceps look bigger," Miranda says with a cheeky smile, pulling her phone out of her purse. "Even with the blazer."

I shake my head as she gets on the line with the hotel. There's always an angle with her.

"Yes, this is Miranda Parker, personal assistant for Gavin Adams. You don't . . . oh, for fuck's sake, check under Anaconda!" she snaps, a scowl that can shatter glass spreading across her face. "Yes, Mr. Adams will be coming in this afternoon, and I want to make sure that the room is perfect for him. Huh? What do you mean, why? He's the second-highest ranked star in the movie, that's why!"

I sigh, wishing that Miranda wouldn't play it up so much. I get it, she thinks that my going a little more 'High Roller' will get me more endorsements, more media attention, more of everything. I mean, I don't play in New York or Los Angeles, so I'm not near the media centers. Then again, considering how terrible LA is football-wise, I think I'm glad I don't play for them.

But Miranda's taken that idea and run way over the top with it. "Yes, he's supposed to have the Egyptian cotton sheets on his bed that I sent ahead, the minibar is only to be stocked with the glacial water and the exact liquor list that I emailed you . . .?"

"Oh, for fuck's sake, I drink tap water," I mutter.

Miranda reaches over, slapping my knee. I let her get away with it, though she's testing me with her antics. After all, she's been in the publicity game for athletes for a long time. She got me some of the endorsement TV spots I've done, so she knows her job. I just think she's taking my plunge into Hollywood a bit too seriously.

"Fine, fine, that'll be acceptable in the short-term," Miranda says into her phone, grinning. She's getting off on this, I swear. "And yes, there are to be two Toblerone chocolates on the kitchen counter. No, not those, one's supposed to be fruit and nut, the other crunchy salted almond. Well, I suppose you'll just have to find one, won't you?"

"Cut them a break, Miranda," I growl, but she's going with it. I mean, I get it. Ever since I showed that I'm in that upper one half of a percent of football players, things have been thrown at me. Money. Cars. Contracts. And women? Hell, I've never had to ask for one. They always ask for me.

But there's a difference between being a cocky football player and being a dickhead. Miranda's pushing that line, and finally, I reach over, taking the phone from her. "This is Gavin Adams. The room's clean?"

"Why yes, of course it is, Mr. Adams," says a snobby voice that grates my teeth. "This is Mr. Vandenburgh. I was just telling Ms. Parker that while we have the confectionaries you requested, we were unable to find the specific Toblerone that you—"

"I don't care about that," I say, cutting him off. "Just make sure the room's nice, and we can worry about the rest later. See you soon."

I hang up the phone and toss it back to Miranda, who's glaring at me now. "There," I say. "Problem dealt with."

Miranda shakes her head as she slips her phone back in her purse. "You know, you're not letting me do my job, *Anaconda*," she says half-jokingly.

"Your job is to make sure I look good in the press, not to bully hotel managers," I growl. She knows I hate the name Anaconda. Sure, she's tried to spin it as if it's a good thing, that I always find a way to 'snake through the defenses'. But everyone and their fucking grandmother knows why it's my nickname. It's been on the internet in 1080p for two years now.

"My job is to make sure you look the part," Miranda says pointedly. She reaches into her bag, pulling out her iPad and turning it on. "By the way, you made the press again." She tosses the iPad over into my lap.

I try not to groan as I look at the webpage she's pulled up, another of those half tabloid, half sports page sites that she likes to track for mentions about me in the offseason.

Anaconda Snakes Another One! the headline blares, showing me walking with a girl. She's got her knees splayed out and a **pained** look on her face, the caption reading, *Anaconda Adams earns his nickname again with yet another young lady as the star running back and soon-to-be actor leaves a hotel in New York the night after appearing on a radio show.*

I read a few more lines and sigh in disgust and turn the tablet off, throwing it back over to Miranda instead of chucking it out the window like I want to. "That site is a fucking disgrace. They're saying I barebacked her with no lube."

"You didn't?" Miranda asks, her smile disappearing when I glare at her. "What, Gavin? You know your reputation says that you've got a groupie in all thirty-two cities you've played in. And it's funny. I thought you'd laugh after the rest of the problems you've been dealing with."

"Maybe that had a little truth to it in my rookie year, but that was then," I grumble, shaking my head. Sure, I went out with the girl, but I didn't fuck her. I just wasn't feeling it. I have no fucking clue why she looks in pain in the photo. They probably snapped until they finally got one with a weird-looking expression on her face. Fucking scoundrels is what they are.

"Whatever the case may be, any press is good press," Miranda says, putting her tablet away. "Just relax."

"Relax, she says," I mutter sullenly, watching as the limo hangs a right and a hotel that actually looks like it belongs in a ritzy section of Vegas comes into view down the street. Grand Waterways Hotel. "Relax for what?"

"Because you need to be calm, cool, and collected for your upcoming interviews," Miranda says as the limo starts to slow down. "You can't start getting annoyed and chewing out the reporters on camera just because they ask you about your anacon . . . umm, romance life."

"The hell I can't," I growl. "My personal life is no one's business."

"These are different times, Gavin," Miranda says softly. "The days where people only want to hear about your talent are over. They want to hear about what you're wearing, who you're dating, who you're thinking about sleeping with. And considering that there's a . . ." her words trail off, but I catch her meaning.

The video. It always comes back to that goddamn video.

"It's bullshit."

Miranda shrugs. "It's just what it is."

I sigh, leaning back and unbuttoning the blazer. "The next time a reporter asks me about my sex life or my dick, I'm walking off. I don't care if it's on the red carpet of the fucking Oscars. It'll be better than giving them another sound bite. At least during football season, they ask about the game first sometimes."

"You'd better not," Miranda warns.

I clench my jaw, wanting to reprimand her for scolding me like a child, but I resist the urge.

"Tell me again why they picked this place?" I ask, changing the subject.

"Because it's a little podunk city," Miranda says. "Remember, you're supposed to be this badass who plays around with the main heroine for some of the movie. You two have known each other since you were kids, and they've got to get some background scenes."

"Oh yeah. The big dying scene," I say with a grunt, remembering the script. At least my character goes out with a bang—literally. A hit squad rattling my car with machinegun fire before they blow it up with a rocket? Guess I'm tough to kill. Too bad I won't do much for it. It's all stuntmen. "When are they filming that?"

"Umm, I'm not exactly sure," Miranda says. "But you'll have time to practice and get your lines down at least."

I grunt noncommittally and then ask, "How detailed are these love scenes supposed to be?" I know I'm supposed to have at least one bedroom scene with the leading lady of the movie, Leslie Hart.

"It'll be shot in darkness with blue light, according to what I saw from the studio," Miranda says. "Don't worry, the Anaconda isn't going to be making his big screen debut. Who knows? They might use body doubles for a lot of it."

I shake my head in disgust as we come up on the hotel. "Fuck," I mutter, seeing the paparazzi parked outside, irritation causing me to clench my jaw. "Figures. I can't go anywhere without these vultures showing up."

"Pull around the side!" I yell to the limo driver, who's kept his mouth shut the whole time we've been bickering. The guy's a pro. I'd have jumped out several stop lights ago if I had to sit there and listen to us.

He just nods and waves, pulling around the corner and driving a bit farther before pulling over. I grab a hooded coat, pull it on, and throw the hood over my head. "I'll see you tomorrow, Miranda," I tell her, flashing a wink.

I slam the limo door and slap the roof before Miranda can reply, and I walk away, ignoring the people on the sidewalk. I'm through a side entrance within two minutes, easily evading the vultures with cameras waiting at the entrance.

I head up to the front desk, keeping my sunglasses and hat on. Thankfully, the manager's on duty, and while he trips over his tongue a few times, probably still worried about the chocolates, I slip off to the elevators and up to the top floor. Room 603.

I unlock the door and head inside, yanking my coat off before throwing it at the sofa. I don't even pause to take in the opulence of the room or the breathtaking view of the skyline through the floor to ceiling windows. It's nice and all, but I've stayed in plenty of five-star penthouse suites and I'm used to luxury.

There are several bags waiting for me on the floor. Miranda must have sent them ahead.

I pick up one of them to see what's so important inside, and when

I do, I see a dress and some stilettos. Someone sent up the wrong bag.

Annoyed, I sling the bag at the table and into one of the chairs, not caring when the chair falls over onto the floor.

I check one of the other bags. This one has my clothes. I set an outfit out on the bed, dark slacks and a white dress shirt. I'm supposed to be having dinner in a few hours with Miranda and a big movie exec to go over a few things before shooting. And I can't go to the meeting if I smell like cigarettes and musk.

After I've made sure I've picked my most dapper attire, I walk into the bathroom, slide out of my clothes, and enter the shower stall for a quick rinse. As the cool water hits me, my mind wanders to the possibility of picking up some ass tonight. I could see myself easily picking up some chick from the event I'm heading to. Hell, maybe even someone from the hotel lobby. But once again, I'm unable to get excited at the prospect of sharing my bed.

I shake my head as water runs down my forehead and into my eyes. What the fuck is wrong with me? There was a time where I'd been happy to share my bed with one or even two. But the thought just doesn't excite me anymore.

I guess I'm getting tired of sex that doesn't mean a damn thing.

My mood sour, I finish rinsing off and step out of the stall. I'm in the middle of drying off when I realize I left my pants on the bed. I walk into the room while rubbing the towel against my head.

"Anaconda," I swear I hear a sweet voice say as I'm about to pull the towel from my eyes.

Goddamn, I think, seeing the sight in front of me, then my inner voice groans. *Oh, no. Not again.*

25

The towel slips from my fingers as I see a woman dressed in a maid uniform, her eyes as wide as a doe's as she gazes at me. Fuck. She's beautiful. Rich brown hair frames big, brown, soulful eyes, a slightly upturned button nose, and ruby pink lips that are soft and plump. The sort of lips that I'd love to have wrapped around my cock.

My dick twitches as I look over the rest of her. Her uniform has a French maid vibe to it, showcasing her figure and legs that stretch on for days.

I'm used to seeing beautiful women, but there's something about this girl that makes my blood heat in a way it hasn't in a long time.

"Hi, I'm Gavin," I say, stepping forward and then stopping. I feel stupid as fuck introducing myself while I'm butt naked. But it can't be helped. The snake is already out of the bag. There's no use covering him up now.

The girl doesn't reply, her eyes as wide as saucers, her legs trembling. Jesus, she looks like she'll need a respirator, her chest heaving as her eyes flit to my face, back between my legs, and then back to my face again.

Her mouth works for a moment as her eyes play ping pong, and I can't help but grin at the effect I'm having on her. I don't know why I'm enjoying this, but I am.

I boldly take a step forward, though I know I shouldn't. She's fucking petrified. "You all right?"

Her cheeks burning red, I hear her mumble, "I'm sorry," before she turns and runs from the room without looking back.

For a moment, I'm tempted to go after her, but I don't. After all, I *am* naked, and I don't know where the fucking bathrobe is. But

I'm pissed I didn't get her name. She was gorgeous. And I could see the way she looked at me. I know *that* look.

And the image of her looking up at me with those eyes while I push into her body is going to be in my dreams until I make it a reality.

But she ran from me. I clench my jaw as I think about her plump, pouty lips and her wide eyes as she took in my naked body. My cock twitches again as I remember the lust that flashed in her eyes.

I decide right then and there that I'm gonna find her. And when I do, I'll have those sweet lips wrapped around my cock in no time.

If it's the last thing I do.

CHAPTER 3

BRIANNA

"*G*irl, you're not gonna believe this," I hiss, dragging Mindy into the back of the coffee shop after fleeing Anaconda's room. She was in the middle of cleaning a coffee machine when I practically ran up, but I can't wait to speak with her. I have to tell what I just saw.

Hell, I can't believe it still, and I saw him . . . I saw *it* from less than ten feet away. Even now, my heart pounds when I think about, my pussy clenching at thin air.

"Won't believe what?" Mindy asks, her eyes burning with curiosity as she notices my breathlessness. I'm literally hyperventilating. "You walk in on an old couple 69ing or something?"

"Hell no!" I say, grimacing at the thought. Leave it to Mindy to come up with something like that at the drop of a dime.

"Then what was it?" she demands impatiently, glancing back to the front of the shop. "I've got coffee to make!"

"You know that penthouse, the one I said was supposed to be empty?" I ask. "Well—"

"Yeah, the one V-man busted your tush about," Mindy says, nodding. "Why, was it *occupado*? Walked in on two guys doing the pile-driver?"

"Will you cut it out and let me finish a sentence!" I growl.

"Sorry," Mindy mutters, even though I know she's not.

I shake my head at her silliness, then give her a serious look. "What's the biggest dick you've ever seen?"

Mindy pauses, staring at me before catching my meaning. "No way!" she blurts.

I nod. "Way."

"How big?" she asks, her eyes wide.

"Big, big." I shake my head, my blood heating as the image of what was hanging between those incredibly muscular thighs flashes before my eyes.

Mindy stares at me. "We talking ruler big or Louisville Slugger big?"

"I'm talking this guy could knock it out of Fenway big," I joke, my cheeks burning.

Mindy whistles, impressed, and blushing a little herself. "And you got to see him naked?"

"The whole nine yards," I say, still not able to believe what happened. *Or twelve yards might be more accurate.*

"And why aren't you up there right now then?" Mindy asks,

leaning in and playfully nudging me with her shoulder. "You wouldn't be the first maid to have a little fun on the clock."

"Come on, Mindy, you know I'm not like that!" I protest, trying my best to hide my desire. "I'm not going to just screw a guy 'cause he looks good and is some sort of VIP prick." I pause and shake my head in wonder, the image emblazoned on my mind. "Still, no wonder they wrote *Anaconda* on the room sheet."

"No. Fucking. Way!" Mindy half squeals suddenly, causing me to jump. Grabbing my hand, she says, "You really met Anaconda Adams?"

"Who?" I ask, shaking my head. Mindy is practically shaking, she's so excited. "Who's Anaconda Adams?"

Mindy slaps her forehead dramatically, shaking it back and forth as if she's looking for heavenly guidance to cure my stupidity. "Gavin Adams, you bimbo! You know, the whole reason there's a production in town filming a movie?"

"What movies has he been in?" I ask, thinking where I could've seen this guy before but drawing a blank.

I can't believe this. I actually walked in on a naked movie star.

Fuck me. I'm *so* fired.

Mindy gapes at me like maybe I grew a third eye or a second head or something. "Movies? He's a sports star, but he's more known for a viral video that hit the web a couple of years back." She shakes her head as if embarrassed for me. "Jesus, Bri, you've really got to get out of the hotel or the classroom more often," she says, grabbing her phone out of her pocket. She quickly taps the screen and then shoves it in my face. "You saw this guy?"

My heart skips a beat at the instant recognition. The hair's different. It's styled and gelled perfectly, but those blue eyes are the same and the face with the powerful, sexy jawline is the same.

I read the information underneath. It's from some football website. "Gavin 'Anaconda' Adams, running back. Six foot one, playing weight of two hundred and twenty-nine pounds, says his birthday's in November. Yeah, this is him."

"You lucky bitch!" Mindy says a little too loudly, tugging me up front as a customer dings the bell. I follow her and she begins filling a guy's order. "Take my phone and check him out. The video will probably pop up when you type in just a few letters of his name." She chuckles and mutters under her breath to me. "It's funny because he's trying to be like a real actor now, too. Though he'd probably be better off performing for porn fetish websites."

I ignore Mindy's giggles and begin typing in Gavin's name on the phone. Sure enough, a video pops up on Google before I can even finish typing. When I click on it, it takes a second for the hi-def video to load.

I see Gavin standing in a locker room and a female reporter talking animatedly to one of his teammates when he suddenly turns around and bumps into her . . .

Ohhhh. My heart skips a beat as I watch the towel fall away from his chiseled hips, revealing huge, muscular thighs and that same huge cock I saw several minutes ago. The reporter in the video jumps back, her hand flying to her mouth, her eyes going wide with shock as she stares at Gavin's monster. A blush comes to Gavin's cheeks as his cock sways from left to right.

Mindy finishes the guy's order just as the video ends. It's short.

Less than ten seconds. Gavin was quick to pick up his towel at the end, but it was too late.

"Crazy, ain't it?" Mindy asks, winking at me.

"Yeah," I whisper, a flood of arousal going through me, my eyes on the last frame of the video.

"I'm so jealous you got to see that in person!" Mindy pauses and then nods at the phone. "But that's not the only thing he's known for. Go look at the other stories they have on him."

I flip back on the phone and look through other search results. Some of them are just a mix of sports stories. Apparently, Gavin's pretty good. He's been All-Pro four out of the past five years, but there's also a lot of gossip sites that have nothing to do with the sports or the video. There's a picture of him at a rock concert with a Victoria's Secret model and one in Cancun with some other hottie. No matter what picture I see of him, there's always a beautiful woman on his arm.

Money. Fame. Big cock. He has it all. My heart sinks as I realize this dude must be a major player. I guess it's not surprising, given his profession. The stories about his sex life are absolutely sala-cious. Headline after headline talks about either the Anaconda video or his sexual escapades.

I shake my head, whispering, "This dude must get more ass . . ."

"Than a Burger King toilet seat," Mindy cracks, finishing my sentence for me.

I roll my eyes and continue scrolling through the photos. Anger twists my stomach at all the photos of him with smiling women. I don't know why I'm getting upset. Gavin's not my boyfriend and I'm sure as fuck not his girl. But still . . . there's just something about it all that pisses me off. Maybe it's just the fact that there's a video of his junk on the internet with probably millions of lusty women watching it.

"I bet he heard me come in and was just waiting to pull the whole surprise naked man gig again," I fume, handing her the phone back.

For some reason, I'm convinced Gavin thought I would just fall to my knees and service his big cock because he was some famous celebrity. Arrogant prick. Heat infuses my throat, and I bring my hand to my neck unconsciously and swallow back a mix of anger and . . . "Seriously, I—"

I freeze as Gavin strolls into the coffee shop, moving with a swag that steals the breath from my lungs. He's dressed in black pants and a white dress shirt that's opened at the front, showcasing the tanned skin underneath. And he looks *damn* good. Not as good as he did standing in front of me naked. But still good.

For a moment I freeze, unsure of what to do, but then I quickly duck down behind the counter before he can see me.

"What the hell are you doing?" I hear Mindy demand in a whisper from above me. I give her a shushing gesture as I hear the sound of footsteps approaching.

"Hi, welcome to the Beangal's Den," I hear her say pleasantly. "How can I help you?"

"I'm looking for someone," I hear Gavin say. I close my eyes and hold in a groan at his deep tone. God, that voice. I feel like I'm lying on a bed of velvet whenever he speaks.

"Sure, sir . . ."

Mindy Price, you bitch, you'd better not give me away.

"Gavin Adams."

"It's a pleasure, Mr. Adams. I'm Mindy, the assistant manager here at the shop," Mindy says flirtatiously. "We here at Grand Waterways are happy to host D-town's *biggest* celebrity." I have to roll my eyes at her audacity of putting emphasis on *biggest*, and if I weren't hiding, I'd give her a good smack to boot.

"Nice to meet you too, Mindy," Gavin says, seemingly ignoring her play on words. "I'm looking for one of your co-workers, one of the maids. She's about my age, maybe a little younger?"

"Gonna need a little more than that," Mindy says, and I bite my lower lip, hoping she's not about to play a prank and betray me. "There's a lot of part timers here. The hotel has a work assistance deal with the university. Do you have a name?"

"No," Gavin says. "She ran out on me before I could get it."

Thank God he didn't get a good look at my name tag.

"Ran out on you?" Mindy says, a note of humor entering her voice.

My heart pounds in my chest as I wait for his response. If he's here to find out my identity so he can report me to my asshole boss, I'm screwed.

I hold in a groan as hear Gavin clear his throat. "Um, yeah, I bumped into her in a vending machine room on the top floor," he lies.

Relief sweeps through me and I close my eyes in gratitude. Good, he's not here to find out who I am so he can report me and make a big deal out of it. My eyes pop back open and go wide a second later as what he's really here for hits me.

No way.

"Oh really?" Mindy hums innocently, making me want to smack her upside the head. She's enjoying this a little too much. "How about you tell me what she looks like?"

"Well, she's about five eight or so, with rich brown hair and big, beautiful brown eyes," Gavin says, a slight catch in his voice. "And a face that's just . . . perfect."

My breath stills in my lungs as I listen to his description of me, and I have to wonder if he's talking about someone else. I've got plain brown hair and there's nothing special about my eyes.

"Damn, I'm jealous. You're making me wish I were this chick with the way you're talking about her," Mindy jokes. "She sounds absolutely gorgeous."

"She *is* gorgeous," Gavin says, his voice heavy.

I nearly choke, I'm so flattered. I *wish* I looked like the girl he's describing. I almost feel like he's lying, but it's obvious he's not. He came all the way down here just to find me. I bite my lower lip, my heart racing. It's just so hard to believe.

Mindy taps a finger to her lips. "Hmm . . . now that I think about it, I might know who you're talking—" Mindy begins to say, but before she can complete her sentence, I pinch her leg as hard as I can. "OW!" Mindy squeals.

"What's wrong?" Gavin asks as Mindy glances down at me, rubbing her thigh while I shake my head, mouthing *no, no, no!*

"A sudden sharp pain," Mindy says smoothly as if nothing

happened. "You know, one of those *annoying*, pesky things that just seems to stab you out of nowhere?"

Gavin chuckles. "You kidding? I play football. I'm used to—" A pounding on the window interrupts Gavin and he lets out a loud groan. "Fuck. Sorry. I didn't realize they followed me here."

"Anaconda, Anaconda!" someone yells, and then the door to the coffee shop bursts open, a crowd of people rushing inside. "How about some pictures!"

"Yeah!" someone else shouts. "Show us what you're packing!"

Mindy lets out a disbelieving laugh as the cameras begin to flash. "They can't be serious!"

"Sadly, they are," Gavin growls, letting out a loud groan, the cameras flashing so hard I can see flashes on the walls in front of me. "I have to deal with shit like this all the time."

"That's gotta be a pain in the ass," Mindy mutters in sympathy, raising her hand to shield her eyes before yelling over the tumult, "All right, people, if you're not ordering anything, please leave! Hotel policy!"

"I'll take care of them," I hear Gavin say, his voice laced with embarrassment. Then he raises his voice, a note of anger entering it. "All right, you vultures want your pictures? Let's go."

"Hey, I want an autograph the next time you come in here!" Mindy yells after Gavin. And then she lowers her voice and mutters, "preferably next to Anaconda."

I wait a minute until I hear the crowd exit the room before I stand up, brushing off my skirt.

Mindy is scowling at me.

"What?" I ask.

"What?" Mindy growls in disbelief. "Why the hell did you pinch me? You damn near broke the skin!"

"You were going to give me away!" I growl, half ignoring her as I look through the big plate glass windows of the coffee shop as Gavin talks with the media. My heart flutters as I watch him talking animatedly to the press, and I cross my arms across my chest.

"I wasn't! I was just messing with both of you!" Mindy shakes her head, her gaze going out the window to the crowd of clamoring reporters. "Did you hear the way he talked about you? God, you should be on your way to his room right now!"

"Please. He doesn't really want me," I say, my eyes still glued on Gavin as several people rush up to ask for his autograph.

Mindy shakes her head. "You should have seen the look on his face while he was describing you." She turns back to me with a wide grin. "He wants to pin your legs behind your ears, girl."

I scowl. "That's not happening and you know it." I try to sound as convincing as I can, despite the desire I feel inside.

Mindy returns my scowl, rolling her eyes. "What's wrong with you, Bri? I mean, I get it, you don't want to be easy, but he's a freaking legend! And hot as fuck!" And then she adds under her breath, "With a big cock to boot," but I hear it anyway. "You know what I'd do!"

She has a point. But I'm too stubborn to concede. Besides, so what if he thought I was cute? After reading those articles about him, I'm not even sure if I care that he's a celebrity or that he's hot as hell with a big dick. The man is just one big manwhore. "So?"

"So? When's the last time you got laid?"

I make a face, wishing I could pinch Mindy again. "Six months maybe?"

"More like a year, I'm betting," Mindy says, chuckling. "I'm not saying you need to whore yourself out to every hot guy who comes in here, but what's wrong with dusting the cobwebs off the muffin?"

"How long is he supposed to be here?" I ask, ignoring her crudeness.

"How should I know?" Mindy says. "But from what I've been hearing, they've got major shoots going for a week. He should be here for at least that long."

I bite my lower lip as my gaze wanders back out the window and I see Gavin putting on a fake, pearly-white smile as his picture is taken with a group of rowdy fans. A week? I have to try to avoid this incredibly sexy man for a week?

Lord help me.

"I'm in *big* trouble," I mutter.

CHAPTER 4

GAVIN

"*I*'ll suck yo dick, man," the toothless bum mumbles as he stumbles up to me, scratching himself all over his arms. Moments before, he'd asked me for some spare change, which I declined. Now he looks at me with his desperate, rheumy blue eyes, faded from being in the sun for far too long.

"What?" I ask with a scowl and an arched eyebrow.

The bum grins, displaying stained gums and broken teeth, then repeats more urgently through his mush mouth while flailing his arms at my crotch, "Man, I'll suck yo DICK!"

I grab his hands, shoving them away from my waist, and then push the bum slightly to the side. He turns back to me, reaching for what looks like a box cutter on his belt. I lash out instinctively with my work boot, catching him straight in that sunken hole of a mouth, and he goes flying back onto the pile of boxes behind him.

"CUT!" someone yells behind me, shocking me out of the scene.

I turn to see a flurry of activity from the stage crew as the director, Jim Thompson, gives me an enthusiastic thumbs-up with a goofy grin on his face. "That was great, Anaconda! You nailed him good!"

I grit my teeth at the hated nickname. I've told everyone on set not to call me it, and they still persist on doing it. I swear I'm going to blow a gasket by the time filming is over with.

"No fucking shit!" Lance, the bum and stuntman doubling as an actor whines, holding his mouth as he crawls out of the pile of boxes with the help of a young stagehand. Blood is seeping between his fingers as he scowls at me angrily, "Fucking amateur, you're supposed to pull the kick!"

"Dude, I'm sorry," I apologize, stepping forward to offer him help.

Lance waves me off as he shoves the stagehand away and climbs to his feet. "You fucking suck, Anaconda." He removes the fake gum caps from his teeth, showing the crew of onlookers a blood-stained chipped tooth. "Look at this shit."

"Hey, Lance," Jim cuts in. "Cut Gavin some slack. It was a mistake. Let's get you fixed up and redo the scene."

Jim's words only seem to make Lance even angrier as he scowls at me with hatred, grabbing a towel from the stagehand he just shoved and pressing it to his lips. "Fuck that! How about getting a real actor in here? This dude needs to go back to being an over-hyped and overpaid football star."

I was sorry before, but now I'm irritated. I didn't mean to kick the guy, but honestly, this whole scene is fucking stupid. When I read the script, I was under the impression I would be taking down a bad guy and establishing myself as a hero, not beating down a toothless crackhead who was desperate for a hit. The whole movie seems like it's going to be one of those low-budget, shitty D-rate, straight-to-DVD movies instead of the blockbuster Miranda promised me.

Lance continues his rant, spitting blood-tinged saliva at my feet. "Arrogant prick!"

Keeping my expression neutral, I turn away from Lance and walk off before I do something I end up regretting. The guy is testing my patience with his ranting. I didn't mean to kick him, but I did feel a little off during the stunt sequence, finding it hard to focus.

It's her, I think to myself, the image of the hot maid flashing in front of my eyes. The way she bounded from the room, her hair flying like a banner behind her like . . . *Bunny. My little Bunny.* I don't know her name, so that's what I'll call her. Desire runs through my blood as I clench my jaw and make my way off the set. *She's in my head, fucking up my game.*

I'm still smarting from the way she ran from me. No woman has ever done that to me. Not when they knew who I am. And she has to know who I am. Doesn't she? And that sassy friend of hers, Mindy, knew damn well where she was when I walked into the coffee shop. I could see it in her eyes.

As I walk away, I hear Miranda yell from the agent seat, "God-dammit, Gavin, get back here! We have three more scenes to shoot!"

"They'll be lucky if I come back at all," I mutter, ignoring her, not really watching where I'm going.

I hear a short gasp as I bump into someone. Leslie Hart, the vixen who's supposed to be my leading lady, stumbles back a step before catching herself. Dressed in jeans and a red halter top that showcases her cleavage, she's pretty enough, with long blonde hair and a sultry smile, but she doesn't interest me at all. Not after *Bunny*. I'm already dreading the romantic scenes that I'm sure are loaded throughout the script. Nothing else seems interesting so far. They're going to have to fill it with *something*.

"Sorry about that," I tell her.

Leslie waves my apology off with manicured fingers, the scent of her woodsy fragrance filling my nostrils. "I'm fine." She frowns, glancing over at the raging Lance. "But do you think he'll be all right?"

"I'm sure he will," I say politely, walking past her and continuing on to my trailer. I need a moment to reset. To try to get Bunny off my mind. Or the rest of the day will be a disaster. "But I really don't care," I add under my breath.

❄

I SIT BACK IN THE LEATHER TUFTED CHAIR NEAR THE WINDOW OF MY suite, a cognac glass sitting on the small arm table beside me. I roll my neck until I hear a pop and let out a satisfied grunt, feeling the ache in the soles of my feet.

Filming was a bitch today. After the fuckup with the 'bum', I had to shoot an action scene with Leslie. I'd been hoping that we could be professional, and so far, so good.

Everything after that was a complete mess when it came time to act. Whenever I had to recite my lines, I stumbled over them, fucked them up somehow, or even forgot them altogether.

It's that damn maid. *Bunny.* No matter how hard I try, I can't seem to get her out of my head.

But I know exactly what I need to cure this problem. I need to be balls deep inside her. Shit, we both need it. I saw it in her eyes. She might've run away, but you can't hide lust like that.

I shift in my seat and take a sip of the fine brandy, relishing the burn as it goes down. I've been unable to focus even off set. Rehearsing my lines seems a waste of time. Doing anything seems a waste of time. Unless it involves . . .

"Get yourself together, man," I mutter. "There's nothing at all special about her." I recognize the lie as soon as it leaves my lips. I've never had this type of reaction to a girl before. *Ever.* But at the same time, I have no fucking clue why I'm so worked up over it.

I need to find out if this is just some sort of fluke. Some sort of anomaly causing me to act this way.

And the only way to do that is to get her in my bed.

I grip my glass tightly, trying to push the sexy maid from my thoughts. I'm still frustrated by how much I fucked up this morning. I want to be good at this. Not just because Miranda is hyping this for me, putting her reputation on the line, but simply because I want to be good at whatever I do.

And right now, I'm fucking it up.

My cell buzzes against the wood of the end table. I set down the cognac glass and check it. A slight grin plays across my lips. It's my best friend, Mark Washington. He rode the bench all four years in college, but he and I still became good friends. We call each other every chance we get. "The very best speaking," I greet.

Mark huffs out a laugh. "How're you doing, Anaconda?"

Mark's about the only person I know whom I don't get pissed at for calling me Anaconda. Mainly because he's almost like a brother to me.

"Not too bad, man. Just got done shooting a couple of scenes today. How's life in Florida?"

After college, Mark went on to law school. Then he became a lawyer in Florida, specializing in admiralty law. He met a girl down there, got married, and has a kid on the way.

A part of me is kind of envious. And I don't even know why. I've enjoyed my freedom to do whatever the fuck I want. But I'm getting older now, and it's starting to not have the same appeal anymore.

"I'm doing good. Wife's good, kids are good. Little Sarah is already talking and little Mark is having a fit over it. How's . . . where the hell are you again?"

"You won't find it on most maps," I tell him. "They've got a decent college football team around here, a hotel that's way too big for this place, and that's about it."

Mark says jokingly, "You find yourself some fine country girl yet?"

"Nah," I reply. *Yes. And she can't hide from me forever.*

"Seriously?" Mark asks in disbelief. "I thought you would've already plowed through a cheerleader squad by now or something."

I grit my teeth, but I realize I shouldn't be getting pissed. He knows most of my reputation is exaggerated by the media, and I know he's just fucking with me.

"Actually, I've just been busy trying to get my lines right. This acting thing is pretty new to me and it's going to take me a bit to get the hang of it." I grunt. "I just hope I don't give Miranda a stroke in the process."

"Damn. Anaconda, the action movie star." Mark chuckles. There's a pause before he adds, "Shit, man, why don't you just say fuck all that, turn in your retirement for football, and just become a porn star—"

"Hey, Mark, I'd love to talk more, but I gotta work," I tell him, no longer in the mood for discussion. Besides, I'd rather not talk about who I'm *not* fucking at the moment. I need to start trying to work on my lines even if I can't concentrate. Or it's gonna be hell on the set tomorrow.

Trying to muffle the disappointment in his voice, Mark says, "No worries, dude, you do your thing."

No sooner do I hang up than Miranda buzzes in. I don't want to answer, but I know if I don't, she'll be at my door quicker than a bolt of lightning to hound my ass. But that's what I pay her to do. Sometimes I don't like it, but I *need* someone like her. Holding in a groan, I answer the phone.

I make no effort to sound pleasant. I know what this call is going to be about. "Yeah?"

And Miranda does not disappoint. "What the hell was that today?" she demands. "I didn't exactly expect Shakespeare from you, but you performed like shit." I can practically hear her shaking her head through the phone. "I'm just glad you didn't knock that poor guy's teeth out and we didn't wind up with a lawsuit on our hands or something."

Judging by the anger Lance displayed, I still might.

I grit my teeth, not wanting to deal with any of this right now. "Sorry. I just was . . . out of it."

Miranda squawks, "Out of it? More like the studio is going to be out of a boatload of money if you don't get your act together! Every day that we have to film over costs the studio tens of thousands of dollars."

I almost huff out a laugh. Did she see the quality of the set? I doubt they were spending a fraction of that. "The entire production seems pretty low-budget, if you ask me." Miranda pitched it to me like it was supposed to be an A-list film.

"Hey," Miranda protests. "They probably had to cut back on the budget since they had to pay you more. But I still think it's going to be a hit."

I shift in my seat. It makes me uncomfortable thinking Miranda negotiated a seven-figure contract on my behalf, especially if it meant the cast and crew took a pay cut. I know it's just business, but I'm not going to be starving anytime soon. Not to mention, I don't really deserve it. I need to prove myself, but Miranda thought it was important for appearance's sake.

"And I think it's going to be good for your career, regardless of whether it's a blockbuster or not," Miranda continues. "Remember, you're just starting out and your acting talent is almost nonexistent. We're operating on your looks, your popularity as a football player, and . . ." her words trail off, but I know she was about to say.

That fucking video.

"Gee, thanks for the vote of confidence, Miranda," I say dryly.

"I'm just doing what you pay me to do, tell you like it is," Miranda says. "But I need you to start being on your game after today, Gavin. There's a lot on the line."

I hang up my cell, frustrated, toying with my cognac glass. Miranda's right. I need to do something, anything, to get my thoughts back on track. I can't go on like this for another week. I have scenes to shoot, even if I do think this movie fucking sucks.

My eyes stray to the dark brandy in the glass.

Drinking certainly isn't going to help.

I get up from my seat, walking over to the mini-bar. There's nothing inside. Not even a bottle of water. I frown. I don't even remember drinking anything last night. I try calling the front desk, but after ten rings, nobody picks up. "What sort of nickel and dime operation is this?" I grumble, irritated. I've always been used to the very best service, and so far, this hotel is failing to match up to what I'm used to.

Screw it. I'll just go to the fucking vending machine.

I grab my room key and head out the door. As I'm making my way down the hallway, I pass a maid wagon outside Leslie's suite. And I run into something. *Hard.*

There she is.

The towels fall from Bunny's fingers at my feet, her luminous eyes going wide with shock. Her hair's a little messed up and she's obviously been working hard. But fuck, she looks beautiful.

I bend down to pick up her towels before she can react and offer them to her. "So we meet again," I say, cracking a grin.

Bunny gazes at me for a moment, still looking like a wide-eyed doe lost in the woods, a slight blush flushing her cheeks. "I-I-I'm sorry," she stutters, her full, plump lips quivering. Lips that I can't wait to taste.

She reaches out and takes the towels from my hands, causing little sparks to shoot up my arm where our flesh touches.

Fuck.

Blood rushes down below, and my cock twitches inside my jeans as I hold in a groan. "No need to be sorry," I say, holding my voice steady. "It was my fault."

She doesn't reply right away, her eyes dropping to the floor. In the silence that follows, I swear I can hear her heartbeat.

I clear my throat. "Listen, about yesterday . . ."

"I'm sorry about that too," she says, bringing her eyes back to my face. "If I'd known you were in there, I wouldn't have . . ." her voice trails off and her cheeks flush even more. I imagine she's thinking about seeing my cock right now. And it only further turns me on.

"That was my fault too," I reassure her. It's getting hard to keep the strain out of my voice. "I shouldn't have walked out on you like that without calling out first."

"Thank you," she says quietly, seeming totally relieved.

I arch an eyebrow. "For . . .?"

"For not reporting me to my boss. He would've" —she swallows— "fired me."

I wave away her worry, though I don't doubt her statement. The hotel manager did seem like an ass from the little conversation we've had. "There's nothing to report. It wasn't a big deal."

"Thank goodness," she mutters to herself. "Because I frickin' need this job."

The thought of needing a job as horrid as this one is a scary thought. The fact that she feels she *has* to work at a place like this fills me with concern. Although it shouldn't. My only concern should be bending her to my will.

I look at the chest of her uniform. No name tag. She probably didn't wear it in case she ran into me again. "What's your name?" I ask her.

"Bri-Brianna," she replies shyly.

I extend my hand. I love her name. And what a coincidence. It starts with a B—like Bunny. "Nice to meet you, Brianna. Mine's Gavin."

She looks at my hand like she's scared of it before taking it. I marvel at how soft and supple her skin is as I shake hers and then let go. I regret letting go instantly, lust burning through my body like an inferno.

She's blushing furiously as I take a step closer and a pleasant woodsy scent fills my nostrils.

"Well listen, Brianna," I growl in a slightly menacing but playful tone. "You actually did do something wrong yesterday."

I almost grin at her reaction, her lips suddenly quivering and her hand flying to her chest. "What? You said I didn't—"

I move in closer, backing her up against the wall and placing both of my hands to either side of her head. "You ran from me," I tell her, my voice dropping low. This close up, she looks so vulnerable. So innocent. Blood pumps furiously down below. She's making my cock so hard it fucking hurts. "And *no one* runs from me."

Her breathing is coming out in short, ragged pants, her soft body nearly pressed up against mine. She obviously wants me, and I want her too. Her lips beg me to kiss her.

We're so close, I can almost feel the heat emanating from her core.

Brianna stares at me, not sure what to think, her mouth opening and then closing. "I—" she begins, before she's interrupted by a crackle at her waist.

"Hey, Brianna?" says a man's voice.

Brianna tears her terrified eyes away from mine and glances down at her hip.

I clench my jaw at the interruption. Fuck whoever this dude is. Seriously. I'm tempted to take her walkie talkie from her and silence it so we can continue our conversation. There's nothing stopping me. But I step away, letting her free, placing my hands behind my back.

Brianna is breathless as she grabs her transceiver. "Y-y-yes?" she asks, her voice unsteady. "I'm here."

"Hey, it's Jimmy. You all right? You sound out of breath."

"I'm fine," Brianna says quickly, her eyes nervously darting to me and then away.

"Oh, okay. I got that issue resolved. The room's clear for you when you want. You read me?"

"Yes, Jimmy, thanks. I'll be there as soon as I finish up here on six,"

Brianna says, her voice tinged with relief. She continues to avoid my gaze as she speaks. "Thanks."

Whoever Jimmy is, I'm kicking his ass if I ever meet him. I was one second away from feeling those sweet pouty lips crashing into mine.

Brianna puts away her walkie talkie and grabs ahold of the cart, her eyes finding my face. "I'm sorry, Mr. Adams . . ." There's a flush to her cheeks that extends down her neck. A neck that I want to devour.

"Gavin," I correct her. I'm expecting her to chew me out for being so bold and pressing up on her like that. Or to call me a cocky asshole. But she doesn't.

"Gavin," she says. Fuck, I love hearing her say my name. I want to hear her screaming it, though. "Sorry to disappoint, but I have duties to attend to. It was nice meeting you." Before I can reply, she practically runs away like a bat out of hell, pushing her cart up the hall.

I watch her until she disappears around a corner, enjoying the sway of her luscious hips as she moves, fire burning in my blood and one thought on my mind. *This is starting to be a problem.* She got away from me again.

I'll get her eventually, I tell myself confidently as I turn away and start making my way to the vending machine room, feeling a dull ache forming in my pelvis. On top of a drink, I'm going to need a bag of ice to numb my aching balls.

And when I do, she's fucking mine.

CHAPTER 5

BRIANNA

*T*he next morning, my fingers are shaking as I check my uniform in the mirror, my heart pounding like a war drum. He was *so* close to me. I could practically feel the heat radiating from him. As I stood there, sandwiched between his hard body and the wall, every bone in me screamed for me to run away.

But I didn't.

It's only by chance that Jimmy interrupted at that exact moment. He *saved* me.

I would have let Gavin do anything he wanted to me had Jimmy not interrupted.

And I'd be out of a job as soon as someone found out.

I shiver as I remember the intensity in Gavin's eyes, his warm breath on my face. It scares me how much I wanted him in that moment, how I almost lost control. No guy has ever been so aggressive, and normally, I would have slapped anyone who was.

But I found myself frozen, unable to even say a word, much less move.

My fingers clutch my neck as I suck in a deep breath. I'm mad at myself for not standing up to him. The guy is nothing but a player, and I should've let him have it. I don't care if he's a celebrity with a huge cock. He definitely deserved to be called out on his bull-shit, brazenly pushing up on me like that. But I just choked up, caught up in his good looks that I'm sure he's used to getting him whatever he wants.

Ugh. Anxiety squeezes my stomach as I gaze at my reflection. It's time to start my shift. And I'm worried that *he* is going to be up there. And I don't think I can handle him coming up to me again. Not after *that*.

And certainly not after spending half the night tossing and turning in bed with a burning need I haven't felt in a long time.

I want to believe that I can tell him no, to fucking get lost. But I know it won't be easy.

I'm not easy, I tell myself, trying to build my self-confidence in the face of my desire, a*nd I don't want to give in to temptation just to become some cocky jerk's one-night fling. Even if Mindy says there's nothing wrong with it. I say there is, especially with someone like him.*

Vowing that I'll be strong if I encounter Gavin again, I close my locker and make my way to the lobby. It's the first on my list today, and I want to get it out of the way so I can hopefully avoid Vandenburgh.

I'm just getting the vacuum out of the janitorial closet when I'm interrupted by an officious cough behind me.

"Miss Sayles," says the voice that always sets my teeth on edge.

Speak of the damn devil.

I turn and see Mr. Vandenburgh standing there, glaring at me with his perpetual scowl. "You're out of uniform," he growls. He looks up at me, puffing out his stomach. "Where's your name tag?"

I glance down at my blouse, cursing my luck. My name tag has been missing since yesterday, and I've been so engrossed in my thoughts with Gavin, I forgot all about it. "I'm sorry, Mr. Vandenburgh. I guess I lost it yesterday on shift. I'll put in for a replacement immediately."

"I see," Vandenburgh says disdainfully. "Well, you can fill out the paperwork for that at the same time you sign your write-up form. Follow me to my office." He begins to turn away.

"Write-up?" I ask, barely keeping my voice down, causing him to perform a dramatic spin about and fix a nasty scowl on his face. "You're writing me up over a name tag?"

"The employee conduct guide is very clear on this. Nobody is to be out of uniform when in a guest area," Vandenburgh says through gritted teeth. "Your name tag is an important part of your uniform."

Not as important as that uppity stick up your ass, I think angrily. I want so badly to tell him that he could go to hell with the high horse he rode in on, but I need this job.

When it's clear he's won, Vandenburgh turns with his nose raised high, and I follow him into his office. Inside, it's antiseptically clean, his cherry wood desk so polished it practically gleams. "Mr. Vandenburgh, I understand that I lost my name tag, but please . . ." I close my mouth when I see him arch his eyebrows. Well screw him. I'm not going to beg. It's actually what he wants to hear.

He pushes a sheet of paper across the table to me along with a pen. "If you'll fill this one out, Miss Sayles, for your new name tag. It'll be ready by your next shift, and you'll, of course, be docked the ten dollars for the cost of the tag. After that, you can sign your write-up form."

Anger burns my chest as I grip the pen and fill out the form. A write-up. For my name tag. How stupid.

It's just his way of getting one step closer to firing me, I think angrily. *He knows I already have one write-up, and now he only needs one more to get rid of me for good.*

The hotel runs a three-strike system. If you get three write-ups within a rolling twelve-month period, you're fired. It doesn't matter what they're for. This is my second strike, having been written up several months ago due to being late during a thunderstorm.

I finish the form, making sure my name is spelled correctly before I slide it over to Vandenburgh.

He smiles icily, taking the form, and I get up to leave, barely hiding the anger I feel.

"Oh, and Miss Sayles," he says, causing me to pause in the doorway.

"Yes?" I say cautiously.

"The marble floors in the lobby have been looking quite dull lately. I believe they could use a good coat of polish."

I almost lose my shit right then and there. Waxing floors? This has got to be a joke. Though I know it might cost me, I say through gritted teeth, "Mr. Vandenburgh, that's a job for Maintenance. They use the big motorized buffer."

"Yes, and the buffer is far too noisy and disruptive for me this time of day," Vandenburgh counters, clearly enjoying the frustration I'm displaying. "You'll need to do it by hand."

This man has got to be out of his mind. Never mind, I know he's out of his fucking mind. But as I look into his smiling face, I know he's just waiting for me to unleash. He gets off on this shit.

I swear to God, as soon as I get home, I'm gonna look online for another job. I don't have to put up with this.

I turn to leave again, but I'm stopped once more when Vandenburgh adds, "A hint, Miss Sayles. Go in small sections, or else you'll leave streaks and have to do it all over again." I swear he's about to burst into gales of maniacal laughter.

I don't know how I manage to leave his office without cussing him out to the moon and back, but I do it.

I even manage not to slam the door.

CHAPTER 6

GAVIN

Beep. Beep. Beep.

I groan as I wake up, the sound of an annoying alarm going off in my ears. Grabbing my pillow, I place it around my ears to muffle the sound. But after several moments, I toss the pillow to the side and mutter in annoyance, "Shut the fuck up," while grabbing my cell off the nightstand and silencing it.

I glance at the time. It's early still, 8:45. Rehearsals are supposed to start at 10:00. But I hardly got any practice in last night, my mind filled with thoughts of Brianna. No matter how hard I tried, I couldn't get her out of my head and focus on my lines for more than a minute.

As if summoned by thinking Brianna's name, my cock swells, straining against my boxers, stretching to its limits. *Fuck.*

Just another problem I have to deal with.

Groaning, I roll onto my back and stare up at the ceiling, my cock throbbing painfully, begging me to take care of it. I clench my jaw, trying to ignore the urge. I don't need this shit right now. I've got to be able to perform today.

It should be easy. I've always been good under pressure. I'm used to being the best at what I do. But I feel off my game.

It pisses me off. I've always been about control, dominating situations and those around me. But Bunny is resisting my charm, taunting me with her sweet pouty lips. She can't keep it up for long, though. She wants me. I can see it in her gorgeous eyes.

A soft groan escapes my lips as I slip my hand down my abs and under the elastic band of my boxers. With a surge of discipline, I stop myself before I grab my dick, and I scowl up at the ceiling.

Fuck that.

I'm not doing this. If anyone's going to make me blow a load, it's going to be *her*. She's playing hard to get, but it's only a matter of time. What's that saying, *good things come to those who wait?* I can hold out a little while longer. I grit my teeth, ignoring another pulsing throb. *Nope.* My hand just won't do.

I roll out of bed, ignoring the dull ache in my balls, and make my way to the shower stall inside the bathroom. I make sure the water is as cold as I can bear, shivering as the dual showerheads pound into my chest and water cascades down my washboard abs.

I stay in the cold stream until my erection finally subsides and then I jump out, quickly drying off.

Chime. My eyes are drawn to my cell when I step out of the bathroom. *Voicemail.* I hold in a groan, already knowing who it is. But I know I have to listen to it anyway.

Gavin, it's Miranda. Just a quick reminder, you'd better be on your game today. I saw the sheet for today, and there's a ton of work to be done. See you on set.

My excitement dims somewhat as I grab some black dress pants, pulling them on. I'm not looking forward to living up to Miranda's expectations when I know I haven't been giving my lines—or any of the script, for that matter—my undivided attention.

You've got to get yourself together, man, I tell myself as I slip into a white dress shirt and polished shoes. *You can't let this girl ruin your acting career before it even gets started. She's not worth it.*

I'm lying to myself. I know it as soon as it enters my mind.

The truth is, Brianna has awakened a fire that I haven't felt in a long time by running from me. More than that, there's something about her, something I can't put my finger on, that draws me to her like a moth to the flame.

Brianna's not like the other women I've been with. She doesn't seem to care that I'm a sports star with all the trappings money, fame, and good looks can buy. Or that I have a huge cock that would have her coming so hard she'd forget what her name was.

And that makes me want her all the more.

CHAPTER 7

BRIANNA

I'm grumbling to myself by the time I make it down to the maintenance room. Inside, I quickly change out of my uniform to a jumpsuit, grab some wax and scrubbing pads, and then head back up to the lobby.

Before I can get to work, I'm spotted by Mindy as she's walking out of the coffee shop. She rushes over to see what's going on.

"What the hell is this?" she demands quietly, eyeing my getup.

"My *punishment*," I reply out of the side of my mouth, my face a dark scowl. "For a missing name tag."

"That humpty dumpty ass sonofabitch," Mindy hisses, casting an angry glare toward Vandenburgh's office. I know she'd love nothing more than to let him have a piece of her mind, but she's coasting on two strikes herself, courtesy of yours truly. If she weren't so popular with the coffee shop patrons, Vandenburgh would've found a reason to fire her long ago. "What a fuck-face!"

"You're telling me," I mutter.

She shakes her head sadly before her frown morphs into a playful grin. Can't ever keep her down long. "Hey, guess what?"

"What?" I ask cautiously. She's giving me that snarky half-smirk so I know it's going to be silly.

Mindy giggles as she gestures at the coffee shop. "V-man decided the coffee shop needs some more decoration, so we've got ourselves a brand-new fish. Girl, you've got to see this thing! It's got lips so big, it looks like it's giving head." She starts bobbing her head forward, her mouth open wide.

Normally, I'd be laughing my ass off at her antics, but I can barely manage to crack a smile. I know Mindy's just trying to lift my mood though, bless her heart.

Mindy stops and rubs my shoulder when she sees her crack failed, her smile rapidly fading. "I'll have a sandwich ready for you on break," she promises, walking back to the coffee shop.

"Thanks," I say with a graciousness I don't feel. "See you then."

I get to work, getting on my hands and knees near the elevators. My plan is to do this area until Vandenburgh leaves for lunch. Then I'll just call Jimmy to take care of the entire lobby really fast with the buffer. I might need my job, but there's no way I'm going to subject myself to hours of torture. Screw Vandenburgh.

My hands are red from scrubbing and irritated by the solution by the time I'm on the last area, my back aching and sore. I don't even notice when the elevator in front of me opens and polished dress shoes stop in front of my face.

I freeze when I hear that deep voice.

"Well, well, look who we have here."

Oh, no. Not again.

I look up slowly and my breath stills in my lungs. Gavin is standing above me. The scent of his cologne, a heavy masculine fragrance, wafts down to my nose, causing my skin to prickle.

"Good morning," I say, blushing. I cringe. I must look and sound so weak, like a love-struck schoolgirl. Instead of being polite, I should be telling him off about yesterday, but I feel like now's not the time. Especially with Vandenburgh nearby.

"Good morning to you too," Gavin says, stepping off the elevator. He pauses, looking down at me and frowning. "Are you waxing the floor?" he asks, his deep voice suddenly on edge.

"I am," I reply, surprised by his intensity.

Gavin inquires, "Isn't your job to clean the rooms?"

I nod.

He glances toward the lobby, a scowl on his face. "Then why are you waxing the floor? Don't they have a janitor?"

Yeah, but that doesn't matter when you work for a creep like Vandenburgh.

The words are on my lips. I almost tell him about Vandenburgh being a major douche, but I don't.

Gavin can't help me. And I don't know why he cares anyway. He has a movie to shoot.

"Someone spilled something," I lie instead, looking away. "And I just have to clean it up."

"I know bullshit when I hear it," Gavin growls, looking around, practically fuming.

I'm at a loss for words. Why the hell does he care?

I'm about to tell Gavin he shouldn't worry about me and continue on his way when Vandenburgh appears from behind. "Miss Sayles, your job was to polish the marble, not gossip with hotel guests," he says. He stares down his nose at me in a condescending manner. "First you lose your name tag, and now this. If you're not going to take your job seriously—"

"She was doing her job just fine," Gavin interrupts, a note of anger entering his tone. "I was asking her for help. You said she's missing her name tag?"

Vandenburgh nods, suddenly very docile.

Gavin shakes his head and takes a small metal tag out of his pocket, handing it to me. "It's my fault, Brianna. I bumped into you in the hallway and it got caught on my sleeve. Sorry about that."

I reach out and take it, unsure of what to say. "Th–thank you."

"You see?" Gavin asks, looking at Mr. Vandenburgh. "All my fault."

Suddenly, Vandenburgh's trying hard to kiss Gavin's ass. "Of course it was just a misunderstanding, Mr. Adams. Miss Sayles has just proven to be a bit of a problem in the past."

"She's been very helpful. And my room is in perfect order," Gavin says, cutting off Vandenburgh and crossing his arms over his chest. "In fact, I'd like to speak with her. I need her help with something. Mind if I borrow Brianna here for an hour or so?"

I gape in disbelief. This isn't going how I expected it to.

Vandenburgh glances over at me. It's clear he doesn't want to let me out of his sight and wants me to continue scrubbing the floor.

But Gavin is a celebrity. Vandenburgh might despise me, but he can't afford to not kiss Gavin's ass.

Still, I know it irks him when he forces the next words from his lips. "Of course not, Mr. Adams. I'll just make some adjustments."

"Thank you," Gavin says with a smirk.

Vandenburgh looks like he's been bitch slapped when he rushes off, muttering to himself under his breath. I would laugh my ass off at him if I weren't so shocked and if I knew it wouldn't get my ass fired.

Gavin watches for a moment before he turns back, holding his hand out to me.

I stare at his hand for a moment before taking it. A spark of electricity shoots up my arm as he pulls me to my feet with ease, his grip strong and firm. I'm disappointed when he lets go, but I don't let it show.

"There," he says, flashing me a charming grin. "I just had to do something. You're too pretty to be scrubbing floors."

Warmth flows through my chest at his words and I almost forget that I'm supposed to be on guard.

He's only trying to be nice cause he wants something, a voice in the back of my head warns.

"Thank you," I tell him. "But you didn't have to do that for me."

Gavin waves me away. "Sure I did." He nods toward the coffee shop, glancing at his watch. "Come on, let's get some coffee and a bagel. I have a few minutes to kill before I head off to the set, and you look like you could use a break."

I glance with uncertainty toward Vandenburgh's office. While I appreciate Gavin's standing up for me, I don't know if I should be going *anywhere* with him. Especially when I know what he's *really* after.

Gavin doesn't give me a chance to say no. "Come on," he says, taking my hand in his and leading me toward the cafe. "My treat."

Dumbstruck, I let him lead me halfway to the door, my heart pounding every step of the way, before I stop and pull my hand out of his.

"Wait," I say, looking down at my jumpsuit. "I can't." I know we're not going anywhere special, but I look like shit. And I don't want to be seen with Gavin with this outfit on. Who knows if paparazzi are lurking around, waiting to take an embarrassing picture? "Vandenburgh will kill me. And I look awful," I add.

Gavin scowls. "Don't worry about shorty. I'll take care of him, trust me." He gives me a smoldering look that makes my heart do a backflip. "And you'd look beautiful even if you were wearing rags."

A furious blush comes to my cheeks and I lower my head as a warm, fuzzy feeling flows through my chest. I shouldn't be listening to anything he says. Knowing what I know about him, it should go in one ear and out the other. But I can't help but be flattered.

"Thank you," I say softly.

He winks at me, taking my hand in his again. I don't even bother objecting this time. And I allow him to lead me across the lobby, where he opens the cafe door for me.

Mindy's eyes practically pop out of her head when we walk in, like she can't believe what she's seeing. After she recovers, she walks over, looking as if she's going through great pains to keep a straight face, and hands Gavin a menu. "Nice to see you again, Mr. Adams. Is this the girl you've been looking for all this time?"

Careful, Mindy, I warn her with my eyes. Hers are sparkling with mischief, and I know she's just itching for a chance to say or do something silly that will embarrass me.

"The very one," Gavin says easily, leading me to a corner table. Mindy follows us over as he helps me slide into my seat before sinking into his.

Mindy smacks herself against her head, playing dumb. "Damn! I wish I would have known you were talking about Brianna when you came into the coffee shop. I would have gone and gotten her out of the back."

Amusement sparkles in Gavin's eyes as he waves away her faux concern. "It's not a big deal. I'm just glad I found her." His eyes turn on me, and I feel my cheeks heating all over again. "We have a lot to talk about."

Mindy tosses me a playful wink, her eyes screaming, *Girl, you'd better let him have his way with you. Or else!*

"That's so sweet," Mindy says, grinning. "It's not every day a big sports star comes waltzing into our hotel. On a date with one of my co-workers, no less. I must say, I'm a little jealous."

"We're not on a date," I say so quickly I almost don't understand myself. "We're just having coffee."

Gavin agrees. "Just having coffee." But his eyes, which are burning into mine with fire, seem to say otherwise.

"Oh, okay," Mindy says. "Well, excuse me. Didn't mean to rouse the *snake*."

I shoot her a murderous scowl, but Gavin only laughs.

Grinning, Mindy asks, "So what can I get the two of you?"

"Let's see." Gavin flips through the menu for a moment before looking up at Mindy. "Any suggestions?"

Mindy screws up her face, thinking. "We've got a pretty good patty melt if you're looking for something real to eat. If not, we've got some awesome pecan cinnamon rolls."

"I'll take two of those and two lattes," Gavin says before pausing to look at me. "Unless you want something different?"

Of course not. Mindy recommended my favorite. At least she did one good thing.

I shake my head, although a part of me thinks he's arrogant for ordering for me. But the other part of me likes it. "That's fine."

Mindy nods after scribbling on her notepad. "Okay, your order will be coming right up." Tossing me another playful grin, she walks over behind the counter and starts messing with the machine.

Gavin watches her for a moment and then turns his piercing gaze on me, a slight smile playing across his lips. "A friend of yours?"

I nod, trying to relax but failing. I'm trembling with anxiety. And I'm not sure if it's because Gavin is a celebrity or if it's because I know I shouldn't be here with him. Or both. "My bestie. Though she gets on my last nerve sometimes."

Gavin chuckles, a knowing look on his face. "I kind of figured that when I came in here to ask about you the other day."

It takes a moment for what he says to register. "You knew?" I accuse.

Gavin nods. "I didn't know if you were best friends, but I know she knew exactly where you were."

"She was just covering for me," I try to explain. "Didn't want me to get into trouble."

Gavin waves away my worry. "You don't have to explain anything to me. I understand. You were worried about your job after what happened. And I don't hold it against you. Now . . . you running away from me though . . ." His voice trails off as his eyes bore into me and I literally squirm in my seat.

I avert my gaze, my blush now furious.

Thankfully, Mindy rescues the awkward moment by coming back with our rolls and lattes, setting them down in front of us. "Do you guys need anything else?" she asks, looking back and forth between us, her eyes sparkling with mischief. "A *super-size* banana split for dessert, perhaps?"

I almost roll my eyes at her emphasis on super-size. "No, I think we're good," I say almost stonily, wanting to smack her upside her head.

Mindy nods, seeing my growing irritation. "Okie dokie. Holler if you need me. It's my absolute *pleasure* to serve." She walks away with a wink and a twirl of her skirt, her heels clicking across the floor.

Gavin chuckles when Mindy's gone, shaking his head at her antics. "She must be a trip to hang out with."

I roll my eyes. "Trust me, you'd get tired of her within five minutes. And that's only if she didn't talk for the first two."

Gavin laughs. "You crack me up."

I shrug, picking up a roll and taking a bite. The sweet cinnamon and icing melt in my mouth like butter and I'm forced to hold in a groan. At least Mindy can do one thing right. Her rolls are always slammin'. "Just kidding. I love her."

Gavin takes a sip of his latte. "So how long have you been working here?"

I freeze for a moment, suddenly wary. I'm finding it hard to believe that Gavin is really interested in my boring ass life. He's a huge sports star who can have any woman he wants, for God's sake.

This is why he's here, a voice in the back of my head says. *Because I ran from him and his ego can't handle it. He doesn't really care about getting to know me. He just wants to pretend to be nice so he can get my guard down along with my panties.*

I almost get up and leave, but when I see the way Gavin is staring at me with such intense interest, I stay in my seat.

Just answer, I reason. *What harm can it do anyway? It's not like he can do anything with the information. And maybe after he sees how boring I am, he'll leave me alone.*

"A couple of years part-time," I finally reply, washing some of my roll down with a sip of latte. "I'm hoping to quit soon, though. After I finish school."

With how crazy Vandenburgh gets, it can't happen soon enough.

Gavin toys with the rim of his cup, his gorgeous eyes never leaving my face. "I see." He slowly takes another sip. "You grow up in this area?"

"Born and raised," I reply proudly. "Always been a small-town girl."

Gavin chuckles. "Can't say that I'd love living in a place like this, but I admire your hometown spirit."

"What about you?" I ask. "How'd you get into football?"

Gavin sits back in his seat. "Well, I've had a knack for playing ball for as long as I can remember," he says, his eyes growing distant. "I remember I used to play so much when I was little I got blisters from throwing and catching the ball. Eventually, it paid off. I got drafted, left school pretty early . . . and the rest is history."

I take a sip of latte. "What position do you play?" I can't remember what I'd read about Gavin when I looked him up. The only thing that stuck in my mind was the size of his . . .

Gavin arches an eyebrow.

I blush yet again, shaking my head. "I honestly didn't know who you were until Mindy told me."

Gavin doesn't get angry at my admission like I expect him to. I figure he has an ego bigger than his dick and gets mad when people don't recognize him. "Well, I'm just a running back. Some say the best in the league."

His cockiness is not lost on me as I ask, "So why are you doing this movie, if you're so good?"

A slight smirk plays across Gavin's lips as he replies, "Miranda, my agent, thought it would be good for my image. With all the rumors about me going around . . ." his voice trails off and he clenches his jaw, suddenly irritated.

He doesn't have to say what those rumors are for me to catch his meaning.

Suddenly, a ringtone of *All I do is win* goes off at Gavin's hip.

Holding a finger up to me, he fishes his cell out of his pocket. "Speak of the devil," he mutters before answering.

"Yeah? I'm having coffee. What do you mean I have five minutes before you crack my nuts? Ok. Fine. On my way." He hangs up his cell, sticking it back in his pocket while shaking his head and muttering under his breath. "Terrible timing."

"Trouble?" I ask lightly.

"Yeah," he groans. "That was Miranda, threatening to bust my ass to get to rehearsals." He gets up from his seat. "Sorry, but I'm going to have to cut our little date short."

My breath catches in my throat. *Did he just call this a date?*

"But I'd like to continue this. What about tonight after filming?" he asks.

My lips open and close like a fish for a few moments before I can find my voice. "I-I-I don't know—"

Gavin cuts me off. "You know my room number. I'll see you there at eight." He walks off, leaving me speechless.

He's not even out the door well before Mindy comes scurrying over, nearly tripping and falling flat on her face in the process.

"Did I hear Gavin invite you to his room tonight?" she asks breathlessly, her eyes wide.

Why Mindy, you eavesdropping bitch!

I cross my arms over my chest, scowling at her. "You were spying on us," I accuse.

"What? No I wasn't," Mindy protests. She pauses and then adds, "I couldn't help but hear. You were talking so loud!"

I growl, "Get the fuck out of here!"

Mindy tries to keep a straight face. "You were."

I shake my head. "You're hopeless."

Mindy laughs. "You should know that by now." She stops to stare at me. "But you are going, right?"

CHAPTER 8

GAVIN

"*W*hat is it about your past that keeps coming between us?" I ask flatly, looking Leslie in the eyes. "Every time we start to get close, something gets in the way."

"CUT!" the director, Jim, yells, and I lean away from Leslie, holding back a groan of frustration. This is the tenth take on this mini-scene, and I'm getting pissed.

Jim is too. "What the fuck was that, Gavin?" he snarls, moving in front of the cameras as he stomps over. We're shooting in a borrowed house on the outskirts of town and I'm completely boning it. Two days in a row, I've been fucking up. "You delivered your lines with the emotion of a goddamned robot!"

I'd be able to deliver if I didn't have you shouting CUT! all the fucking time. I bite back the words that will earn me an even bigger headache. Instead, I scowl at him. "I'm trying my best, Jim. Do have any useful advice for me rather than blowing up every other take?"

"Yeah. I'd like you to say the lines like you actually cared about

Leslie, and not like some high school kid doing *Romeo & Juliet.* That'd be a good place to fucking start!" Jim snaps.

He's right, of course. I'm delivering my lines with the emotion of a cardboard box. But I can't help it. When I look at Leslie, there's no connection. She's pretty, but I just can't bring myself to say my words with the conviction the script demands.

Jim looks like he wants to continue his rant, but he stops and takes a deep breath, waving his hands at the crew. "Okay, okay, everyone . . . take ten." He turns to me and shakes his head, sighing. "I'm sorry for losing my temper, Gavin. I just didn't expect for us to still be stuck on this scene several hours later. Go get yourself a drink or something, get your head right, and then we can continue."

Giving Leslie an apology, I walk off the set, heading into the catering area and grabbing a bottle of Perrier. I down half of it in one swig, resisting the urge to throw the rest of it across the yard as I make my way to my trailer.

I fucking suck. Reading my lines shouldn't be this hard.

I know exactly what the problem is—Brianna. *I've been waiting long enough. It's going to end tonight.*

Seeing her this morning made things worse. My pulse speeds up as I remember walking in on her scrubbing the floors on her hands and knees, her ass sticking out behind her seductively. She's gotten under my skin like no girl has done in years. Without even trying. And now, I'm going to make things worse by having her in my bed.

I sit down in the chair, relaxing and undoing my belt and fly to relieve the pressure on my balls from the tight jeans they're having me wear when the door flies open.

"You just keep getting worse," Miranda says, storming into the room like a tornado, dressed in her red jumpsuit. Scowling, she stops right in front of me, slapping her hand down on the granite countertop and leaning on it. "I don't exactly expect Leonardo DiCaprio from you, but could you at least *try*? Or are you just hungover from drinking too much?"

"You know I don't drink like that," I growl, opening my eyes and leaving my fly open. "I'm just having a rough afternoon."

"It seems to be becoming a habit," Miranda says, jabbing a long, manicured fingernail at me. "Jim just told me that the shooting is behind schedule!"

I know I pay her to do this, but I'm fed up with her badgering. "I'm doing my best, Miranda. Maybe you should be her love interest if you think you could do better. They can start calling this shit Rug Munch Wars."

I shouldn't have said that. But shit, I'm not making myself look like a fool on purpose here. I *am* trying.

Miranda's lip quivers and I can see she wants to say more, but she also can see the look on my face. This isn't funny Gavin, or the Gavin who likes to flirt, or the Gavin who can get grumpy. She sees that I'm serious. Instead, she just shakes her head. "Well, try to get it together and nail your next scenes."

"I'll do that!" I yell after her, leaning back and letting my nuts relax again. I gotta talk to the wardrobe guys. This country boy wearing tight jeans stuff has to go. My character's supposed to be an auto mechanic. Maybe they can get me a set of dirty coveralls.

I sigh, looking at the ceiling. *Brianna. Just a few hours, and you'll be mine. And it can't come fast enough.*

I chuckle at the double meaning then frown as another thought goes through my head. She looked so innocent, and inside, I feel bad about maybe taking that innocence.

Just fucking her to clear my head would be like spray painting the Mona Lisa.

But I'm Gavin Adams, and there's no way I could be thinking of . . .

It's just a fling, something to get my head right.

Isn't it?

CHAPTER 9

BRIANNA

Oh, my God. I hardly recognize myself.

I gaze at my reflection in the mirror as I run my hands over the sleek red dress, turning myself to the side to see how it hugs my curves. The dress seems to bring out the best in my figure and I wouldn't have worn it had Mindy not talked me into it. Or talked me into going up to Gavin's room tonight.

I still can't believe I'm doing this.

Gavin invited me to his room as if he knew I would just come running to him because he's a celebrity.

It annoys me.

I'm not easy. I don't do hookups. And I don't do one-night stands.

So why did I let Mindy talk me into this again?

Deep down, I know why, even if I don't want to admit it. Since seeing him, I've felt this pull to him, and the size of his dick is just part of the issues at hand. The way he looks at me, even some subtle undertone to his voice pulls at me, and I can't get him off my mind.

One way or another, yes or no, I have to know.

The door to the break room opens and in strolls Mindy, her eyes widening in shock when she sees me. "Holy shit, baby got back! I do damn good work!"

"More like baby got fat," I mutter as I rub my hands over my hips and ass. I've been here for nearly thirty minutes, trying to work up the nerve to wear this thing. I've even added a gold necklace, sparkling fake diamond earrings, and a bracelet that Mindy brought me along with the dress for good measure. I'm nervous that it might be a bit too much, though. She had gotten it for me on break, gleefully getting my 'supplies' while I did the rest of my work. I hope she didn't go buy the dress. There's no way I could fit her clothes. I have to admit, though—she outdid herself, but I feel like I'm playing dress-up. I'm just not used to dressing like this. "You think I've overdone it?"

"Overdone what?" Mindy asks, coming closer to inspect my curves. She's still dressed in heels, white shirt, black apron and skirt, and she looks unusually fresh-faced for this time of day. She's loving this. "You look smokin', girl!"

I roll my eyes. "Please. This makes my ass look huge! I barely fit this!" I complain.

Mindy places her hands on her hips and gives me *the look* while saying, "Are you serious? Big is in! He's gonna love it."

I huff out a laugh, feeling butterflies in my stomach. "Yeah, love it right up until it starts jiggling like Jell-O."

"Just look at Kim Kardashian and what it's done for her," Mindy points out.

I groan. "Oh, Jesus, and that's supposed to make me feel better about myself?"

Mindy laughs, slapping me on the arm. "Oh, shut up. You know what I mean."

"It's the truth," I say.

Mindy waves away my anxiety. "Well, you need to stop worrying. If I were a guy, I'd bone you."

I laugh incredulously. Mindy seriously has no limits. "Will you stop?"

She chuckles evilly. "Seriously. I would." She shakes her head. "You look hot as hell, Bri."

I want to deny her compliment, but I have to admit I look better than I have in a long time. I don't normally get this made up, just a little for work. I don't have the time or the reason to.

The sound of footsteps in the hallway pulls my eyes away from the mirror and my stomach tightens with panic. Nobody should be down here. The evening shift went on at least an hour ago, and the afternoon shift's all gone home.

Mindy pokes her head out, and then she looks back at me with wide eyes. "Shit! It's Vandenburgh! Hide!"

"Where?" I ask, panicking. I really don't want to explain that I'm about to go up to a guest's room all dolled up, even if it is none of his damn business. I wouldn't even have time to catch my breath before I'd get my pink slip.

Thinking quickly, Mindy rushes over and opens the broom closet, motioning for me to jump in.

I arch an eyebrow, knowing it's dusty as hell in there, along with a few slimy surprises. And knowing the stuff I've seen swept up off the floors, I'm not anxious to get in there with this dress.

"Get your badonkadonk ass in there!" she growls, grabbing me by the arm, shoving me inside, and closing the door. It doesn't close all the way, leaving a small crack I can peek through.

A moment later, the break room door opens and I hear Vandenburgh's voice. "What are you still doing here, Miss Price? You should've been home by now."

"Forgot my phone here in the break room. Came back to pick it up," Mindy lies, patting her pocket. Through the crack in the door, I can see her trying very hard to maintain her neutral expression. "Luckily, it was still here!" she adds for good measure.

"Yeah, sure. I'd better not find out you were milking overtime like your lazy friend Brianna," Vandenburgh grumbles. "If either of you think that your student status means I'll continue to tolerate your attitudes or performance, you're sorely mistaken."

I can see the frustration play across Mindy's face. "Mr. Vandenburgh, Brianna is a good worker—"

He cuts her off, making me clench my teeth. He's such an officious prick. "Miss Sayles is holding onto her position purely by my goodwill. If you don't want to join her on the unemployment line soon, I suggest you stop talking and go home."

He turns and leaves, and a moment later, Mindy opens the door to the closet, her eyes sparkling in anger. "Can you believe that son of a hoe?"

"Whatever," I reply, touched that she tried to defend me but not wanting to get into a bitchfest about our jerk of a boss. If I started in about Vandenburgh and all his stupid bullshit, I'd be here all night. And right now, I have other things to worry about. "Mindy, I don't—"

I'm interrupted by a beep from my cell, and I glance at the clock. *Shit.* "It's eight o'clock."

Mindy makes a face, gesturing toward the doorway. She seems almost as anxious as I am, practically trembling with excitement. "Then why aren't you hauling ass for the elevator?"

Because I'm not sure I want to do this.

Anxiety twists my stomach. "I don't know if I can do this."

Mindy plants her hands firmly on my shoulders and starts pulling me toward the door. "Oh no, missy. You're not pulling this wishy-washy mess with me."

"Hey!" I protest. "I didn't even get to make sure that my breath smelled good!"

"It smells like roses!" Mindy says with a laugh before growing serious. "Seriously, just go. You need this, and who knows what might happen? You're selling yourself short if you don't learn to have fun every now and then. Live a little."

Before I can offer more protests, she shoves me out the door with an enigmatic smile, and I make my way slowly to the employee elevator. Inside, I push the button for the sixth floor, my heart pounding so hard I feel it in my neck.

I try to combat my anxiety by holding onto Mindy's words of

encouragement. *Everything is going to be okay,* I tell myself. *Mindy thought I looked good. There's no reason to worry.*

It does little to help.

Ding.

I step out on the top floor, feeling dizzy with anxiety. I almost stop and turn around, but I eventually make it to Gavin's door.

My breathing ragged, I raise my hand to knock and then freeze, looking down at my dress.

Jesus, look at me. Gavin's going to think I'm literally here just to sleep with him.

But aren't I? I mean, I might as well have written *Fuck me, Gavin* on my panties, I'm so dolled up. What sort of schoolgirl fantasy am I having to even think that Gavin could want me for more than a hard *schtupping* and that I'm here for the same reason.

Is this the sort of person I want to be?

"I can't do this," I mutter, feeling weak in the knees as my self-confidence plunges to near-zero.

I begin to turn away, but before I can take a step, the door to Gavin's suite swings open.

Fuck me.

My breath stills in my lungs at the sight of him. Hair slicked and parted to the side, he's got on black pants and a white dress shirt that's unbuttoned halfway down, his normal attire, it seems. I can see the smooth, hard skin of his chest and a hint of his rock-hard abs.

Desire courses through my stomach as the smell of his masculine cologne hits my nose and he grins at me. A cocky grin that says, *I knew you were coming*. I should slap him, tell him that he's an arrogant prick and I've changed my mind.

I should, but I don't.

I can't.

Still grinning, Gavin holds out a hand to me and says in a deep voice that makes me want to drop to my knees, "I've been expecting you."

CHAPTER 10

GAVIN

I'm having a hard time keeping myself under control as Brianna walks into the room ahead of me, her hips swaying with each seductive step. My eyes on her ass, my dick hardens in my pants to the point of being strangled as it screams to be let out. *Fuck.* I don't even think she knows what she does to me.

I bite my lower lip, lust gripping my loins.

Those legs.

That ass.

"Sorry about my outfit," Brianna says softly, pulling my gaze away from her voluptuous body. "I didn't know if you'd like it or not."

If I didn't know better, I'd swear she's lying. She has to know how much she turns me on in that thing. But her voice sounds sincere, and I remind myself Brianna's innocence is one of the things I love.

"I think I like it just as much as your maid uniform, and about a thousand times better than the jumpsuit," I say, trying to keep my voice steady.

Brianna blushes fiercely, causing my cock to strain against my pants even more. I swear it's going to bust out if this keeps up. "Thank you," she says sweetly. "Mindy is the one who forced me to wear it, actually."

Thank you, Mindy.

I lead her over to the white couch in the living area of the suite, sensing her nervousness that only serves to enhance my desire. She seems so sweet. So *innocent* in her mannerisms. But dressed up in that sexy red dress . . . there's nothing innocent about what it makes me want to do to her.

I struggle to put a lid on my desire as I help her settle onto the couch and she looks around the room, her lips parting in surprise.

"Wow," she breathes. She takes in the candles that I've lit around the room and the other little touches I've done, like the smooth classical music I have playing in the background. Nothing loud, just enough to ease the mood. "I've cleaned this room a hundred times. I don't think I've ever imagined it like this. Thank you."

"You're welcome," I tell her, grinning, pleased by her reaction. I've taken great pains to set things up perfectly, giving us a breathtaking view of the surrounding area.

"Wine?" I ask, gesturing to the two glasses and the red wine bottle I've set out, along with the thick white candles. "It's supposed to be the best in town."

At my offer, she bites her lower lip, her eyes wide and dark. I know what she's thinking. That she shouldn't be here. That I'm just some player who's going to fuck her raw and then leave. But it doesn't have to be that way. We both can have a good time, even if it's only for one night.

But what if it's not? A voice in my head asks.

For some reason, having Brianna for one night doesn't seem like it's going to be enough. Though it should. I'm only here for a week and then I'm gone. She knows that, and you can't have a meaningful relationship in that amount of time.

I push my troubled thoughts away, deciding the best thing I can do right now is make her comfortable.

"Come on," I urge. "Have a glass. You've earned it. You work hard and need to relax."

She nervously fidgets with her fingers for a moment before letting out a soft sigh. "Okay," she breathes. "You're right. I do deserve some relaxation with all the crap I have to put up with."

You'd deserve it just for how gorgeous you are.

I grin at her. "I promise, you'll enjoy this."

I pour the wine, the dark red nearly the same tone as her dress as it gurgles into the glasses before I pass it to her, raising a toast. "To relaxation and less *crap* to deal with."

She smiles, and I feel my desire and the troubling little other thing in my head both react to it. "To less crap."

We clink glasses, and I take a sip, savoring the rich tones and dark flavors. I'm going to have to get a few bottles of this for home. It's pretty damn good. But that's probably because of whom I'm sharing it with. Brianna looks enraptured as she sips her wine before sighing deeply. "Thank you. I didn't know if I would have the time to make it up here, so I'm glad I came now."

The two candles give her face a warm glow as she takes a sip, and I'm once again impressed with how incredibly beautiful she is.

"I'm glad you found the time too," I tell her with an easy smile, sitting next to her but giving her enough space where she doesn't feel crowded. I could tell she liked it when I pushed up on her before, but this is different. The couch is just right. There's enough space that we could touch, but we don't have to.

"And your dress . . . you're truly stunning," I add. I love that she made the effort to dress up for me. It shows that she cares about what I think, if nothing else.

A blush shading her cheeks, Brianna sets her glass down, fiddling with the bracelet on her wrist. "Are you just playing with me?"

I shake my head. "No, ma'am." *My cock most certainly doesn't think so.* "You're gorgeous."

She drops her head to hide her furious blushing, her eyelashes fluttering. Judging by her reaction, she obviously isn't aware of how gorgeous she is, which is a shame.

But when I'm done with her tonight, she's going to know that she's beautiful in every way.

"Thank you." She raises her eyes to gaze at me. "You look handsome, too."

I flash her a boyish grin. "I try."

An awkward silence settles over our conversation, as if she's embarrassed and can't think of anything to say until she asks, "So . . . um, how is the movie coming along?"

She won't think so, but I'm pleased by her question. A lot of women, after the glow of my celebrity fades away, only want to talk about how soon I'll fuck them and how much money I have in my bank account. I barely know her, but I just *know* Brianna isn't like that. She's quality. I search for the words. "It's a learning experience. I feel like I'm all over the place, forgetting my lines here and there."

Because of you, I want to say, but that's pushing it too fast. She's not relaxed yet.

Her eyes go wide at my admission. I don't think she expected me to be that honest. After all, she thinks I'm a cocky prick who thinks he's the best. My reputation on the internet certainly says I am. "Really?"

I nod, shrugging. "I've been having problems connecting to my character since I first set foot on the set. It's harder to pretend than it is to focus on the reality of some linebacker trying to tear my head off." I chuckle. "It's crazy, because when I first heard I'd be in the movie, I was like, I can do this shit. It's easy. But nope. First day, I nearly kicked a dude's teeth in."

Brianna's pouty lips part in horror. "Seriously?"

I nod, huffing out another laugh. "Yeah. Chipped his tooth. He's probably somewhere right now sticking needles into my balls with his voodoo doll."

Brianna lets out a laugh, a sweet sound that reminds me of honey. "That's terrible!"

I nod. "Yeah, it was. I almost gave my agent a stroke when it happened."

Brianna's smile slowly fades after a short pause. "You have a co-star, though, right? A woman?"

I hesitate for a moment, sensing her nervousness. "Yeah, I do. Her name's Leslie Hart. The studio wanted a blonde."

"Is she hot?" Brianna asks, then rolls her eyes a half-second later and snorts. "Stupid me, of course she is."

She doesn't even come close to you, darling.

Brianna has no idea how easily I've been replacing Leslie's face with hers during the lines I've actually been able to pull off. "She's not my type," I say to put her at ease while giving her a direct, intense look.

You are.

Brianna ducks her head to hide her embarrassment. But when she looks back up, she's chewing her lip thoughtfully. "Will there be love scenes?" she asks.

I freeze, taken off guard. Is my Brianna jealous? I'm not totally sure, but I think Miranda said there would be at least one. At the time I accepted the script, I didn't give a fuck. I didn't care one way or another.

"I haven't read that far in the script," I say. "But I don't think it will be anything that'd push the movie too far. Someone said they're aiming for PG-13 with this."

The corner of Brianna's lips draw down and I know she's disappointed. I don't want her to feel that way, so I decide to change the subject.

"So, how was your day?" I ask smoothly, as if she never asked the question. "Vandenburgh finally cut you some slack after I stepped in for you?"

Bri seems to relax. Maybe just talking about the daily grind is reassuring to her. "He didn't bother me much. But the rest of my day was awful. I had a guest walk in on me cleaning a room and claimed that he had a DND sign on the door when he didn't. He yelled at me to get out . . . kind of put a damper on my mood."

Anger clenches my stomach. I'm pissed. No one yells at my Bunny. "What a douche."

Brianna nods, scowling. "Just another irate asshole. He's not the first and he won't be the last."

I tightly clench my wine glass. "You catch his name?"

Brianna screws up her pretty face for a moment. "Lance something. I think he's part of your movie crew."

Lance. Funny how we were just talking about the shithead.

Okay, now I don't feel so bad about kicking you in the mouth.

I make a mental note to have a word with him and maybe reinforce it a little. "I'll check later and see if he's part of the crew," I assure her.

Brianna shakes her head vigorously. "Don't do that. It's okay. Worse things have happened, trust me."

I set my jaw, letting it drop for now. I pause, gesturing across the room to the small dinner table, which is set with candles, two plates, and covers to keep the contents warm. "Shall we?"

Brianna nods softly as I get up and help her out of her seat. I lead her over to the table, holding the chair out for her. When she's seated, I refill her wine glass before revealing the lamb chops. "A little coffee shop manager happened to mention you like these."

Brianna tries to scowl, but then she chuckles softly, shaking her head. "I swear, that girl…"

"If it helps, she didn't volunteer it. I asked," I tell her as I sit down.

We start eating, and while the lamb isn't Michelin Star quality, I've had a lot worse. "So tell me more about yourself," I ask her. "Where do you live? What do you like to do when you're not here at the hotel?"

Brianna chews slowly, thinking about how she wants to answer, and I can see she's got something she wants to hide. It's probably because she doesn't have much, but I don't care about any of that. "I've got an apartment close to the university," she finally says. "It's convenient, I guess. As for free time, I don't really have a lot of it. I'm either working here or in school. In the time I do have free, I'm either with Mindy or just trying to rest. You know, normal boring things."

"Boring?" I ask wistfully. "With all the paparazzi I have to deal with, I'd love boring every once in a while. It would be nice, just for once, to be able to go somewhere without someone bringing up that damn video."

"About that . . ." she says slowly. "How does it feel to know that everyone . . ." She pauses, struggling to find the words.

"Has seen my junk?" I finish for her.

She blushes, but she doesn't hide her face. "Yeah," she says.

I shrug. "I admit, it did bother me at first. But then I just said the hell with it. I have nothing to be ashamed of. I still hate that's all people talk about, though."

"Nothing at all," Brianna mutters under her breath, but I hear it anyway.

I bring the wine glass to my lips, hiding my smile and pretending like I didn't notice.

She asks a moment later, "I've been wondering. How long will you be in town? I think people will miss it when production shuts down."

"Just the rest of the week, maybe a day or two more if they need reshoots," I tell her. The disappointment that reflects in her eyes stings, though I don't know why. We both know I'm here for a short time and it's not like we really know each other. "I have to report to offseason workouts. It's part of my contract. If I don't show up to at least eighty percent of them, I get docked a million dollars."

I don't usually tell strangers about my financial details, but I feel at ease with Brianna.

She nods in understanding, and part of me starts doing the math on just how many days I could skip to have a few more boring days in this town, when she starts blushing furiously.

"What is it?"

"I've been thinking . . ." she says, her voice trailing off as she bites her lower lip. Her eyes are sparkling with a burning need that makes me want to groan and causes blood to rush into my cock.

I gesture at her, feeling like this is finally going somewhere. "Go on."

"It must be so awful!" she says quickly.

I arch an eyebrow. "What is?"

She gestures at me. "You know, being known for . . ." I think it's cute that she can't come right out and say it.

"For the size of my dick?" I ask. I have to hold back a grin. She can barely keep her mind off it, even as she's trying to be a good girl.

She nods, her face as red as her dress. "Sorry for bringing it up again. I just couldn't . . ."

Help yourself.

It's hard to hide my grin as I shake my head. It's refreshing that she's worried about how I feel rather than assume it's all fun and games being *Anaconda Adams*. It lets me know she's empathetic, which has always been an absent trait in the girls I've met.

I finish my bite, then set my fork down, my voice sounding surprisingly harsher than I'd like. "It's annoying as fuck. No one cares about my talent. Just about my looks and who I'm fucking and which side my dick is hanging in my pants. I've gotten used to it by now, but I still would like to be taken seriously and treated like a man, not some hypersexual manwhore that the media makes me out to be. They tend to exaggerate."

Her blush fades as she studies me, and there's a hint of a sadness in her eyes. "Sympathy must be difficult," she surmises softly. "Everyone must think you've got it all."

I nod. She's hit the nail right on the fucking head. "It was at first, but now I've adjusted. I have my own reasons for doing this film, but Miranda thinks doing a movie will get people's mind off it. I'm not so sure."

"So how long have you known Miranda?" Brianna asks. "You seem close."

I shrug. "Few years. She's been a help, but don't doubt it—she's in it for the money."

Silence falls over the table and Brianna becomes pensive. I let her get lost in thought, my eyes never leaving her pretty face. I could learn to like this, having dinner and spending the rest of the time here with Brianna.

She looks at me out of her reverie, her eyes inquisitive. "Can I ask you something?"

"Shoot."

"Is this all a game to you?" Brianna asks.

Her question makes me pause. I would be lying if I said there isn't a part of me that wants to take her just because I've had to work for it, to prove my dominance over her. But then there's the other little voice that's been bugging me, saying that she's different. And I want to find out more.

Finally, I sit back in my seat and reply, "I'm not gonna lie. I'm a bastard with a huge ego who doesn't like being denied anything." I pause, shaking my head. "But there's something about you."

She's almost breathless, her skin paling as she gazes at me, hanging onto my every word. "Like what?"

"I can't explain it . . . but I can tell you that you make me feel like I'm more than just a big dick and a bank account."

Brianna bites her lip again and fingers her butter knife. Her nail seems to run up and down the length of it, and when she speaks again, her voice is so soft that I barely hear it. "I have to admit." She flushes deeply. "I've spent the past few nights wondering what something like that would feel like."

At her words, my cock grows so hard I nearly wince. Seeing her sitting there, so vulnerable, her defenses lowering, turns me on more than I thought possible. I clench my fists at my sides as my cock stretches the material of my dress pants to the limit.

"It's been said that it's the best damn thing in the world," I reply.

Her breathing is ragged, and I'm surprised she's actually able to come back at me. "Is that by the same *media* that you say exaggerates?"

I grin. She's saucy when she wants to be. "Maybe. Only one way to find out. But some girls . . . just can't handle it."

She bites her lip again, her face scrunching in thought, her chest heaving. "I think I'm ready," she breathes suddenly.

"For what?" I ask. Though I know where this is going, I still want to hear it from those sweet lips of hers. It'll make it all the better.

She folds her hands in front of her on the table and looks me in the eye with more confidence than I thought she was capable of.

I nearly groan at her direct, challenging gaze, turned on by the hunger she's now displaying.

But her next words send me over the edge.

"For you to fuck me."

CHAPTER 11

BRIANNA

What the hell did I just do?

As soon as the words escape my lips, I suck in a sharp breath, my mind racing with panic, my heart pounding like a jackhammer. I didn't mean to say that. It was like my lips moved of their own volition and I had absolutely no control.

I'm frozen in my seat, unable to move. Where the hell did that confidence come from? It's like I channeled my inner Mindy. Gavin has melted me into a puddle on the floor every time I've been in his presence. I've sealed my fate with my words. And now it's time for reckoning.

He's out of his chair and over to my side in an instant, pulling me in for a kiss. His lips smash against mine, demanding and unrelenting. I moan into his mouth as he pulls me up out of my seat, wrapping me in a fierce embrace. My knees go weak as I melt into his arms, his tongue searching around in my mouth.

Below, his cock presses against my stomach, throbbing and pulsating as his hands move down to squeeze my ass, pressing me against his hard body. I kiss him back just as passionately, digging my nails into his back, rubbing my pussy up against the bulge in his pants.

I'm rewarded with a soft groan from Gavin, and he pulls away from our kiss, leaving me breathless, my chest heaving as I suck in ragged breaths.

"Gavin," I gasp, my pussy clenching with uncontrollable need. "Please—" My words are torn away as he abruptly picks me up and carries me into the bedroom. He crosses the room in three quick strides, setting me down on the bed gently, his eyes gleaming with desire.

He climbs on next to me, his hands immediately going to my dress, sliding the zipper down and peeling it to the side, exposing my breasts. My nipples pebble as the cool air hits them, and he smiles down at me, his eyes burning with desire.

He lowers his head, covering my throat with passionate kisses before sucking on my right nipple, making me tilt my head back and moan. His hungry tongue sends electricity jolting through me, a soft cry escaping my lips when he bites down softly.

"Gavin!" I moan, running my hands up and down his muscular back.

"Mmm," he groans, his breathing heavy with lust as he pulls away and rains kisses down my body. When he makes it to my hips, I lift up, and he eases off the rest of my dress and my panties, tossing them to the bedroom floor.

I groan, knowing what's to come. I grip the bedding in preparation, needing it. *Wanting it.*

His eyes burning with intensity, Gavin locks his gaze with mine, sliding two fingers inside me, making me cry out and grab at his shoulders. "Fuck!"

He starts pumping his fingers in and out of me. Each thrust stretches me wider, sending waves of pleasure through my body. Bucking wildly, I claw at the bedding, overwhelmed by the intense sensations.

"You're so wet for me," he says, a thirst in his eyes.

"Fuck yeah!" I moan, my hips taking on a life of their own to meet his thrusts, the bed rocking softly back and forth.

Grinning, his thumb finds my clit and begins to rub in a firm circular motion. I cry out, my limbs blasted by shockwaves of pleasure, a fire igniting in my core. Several thrusts later, I'm forced to let go, my stomach curling as I'm brought closer to the edge.

"Yes," Gavin hisses as he feels my pussy clenching tightly around his fingers, his eyes burning into my face.

His intense gaze sends me over the edge. I toss my head from side to side as his fingers curl inside me, driving me mad. "Gavin . . . I'm going . . ." my words split into a loud cry as a fiery explosion goes off inside my stomach, the room spinning around me like a merry-go-round.

"Not yet!" he commands, pulling me back from the edge. He lowers his head and his tongue replaces his thumb. My body shivers as he licks me.

Gavin is relentless, his mouth clamping down on my throbbing pussy while I'm rocked by wave after wave of pleasure. My back arches, my fingers grabbing the bedding as stars shoot across my vision.

"Oh, fuck!" I cry breathlessly as he pulls his fingers out and his tongue slithers inside me, stroking my pussy and slipping between my lips, nibbling and sucking me deeply. I lose all sense of time and my hips jerk and buck as Gavin holds me in place and devours me.

"Gavin . . ." I gasp when I can breathe again, lowering my back to the bed. I'm soaked in sweat, my body literally spasming from coming so hard.

My eyes are drawn to him as he slides off the bed, standing up to unbutton his shirt. Breathless, I watch as he pulls it off and tosses it to the side, exposing his ripped, chiseled torso. Then he drops his pants and my breath stills in my lungs as his enormous cock swings free.

It's so big, thick and full. Fuck. I want to taste it.

I watch as he picks up his pants and pulls a small packet out of the pocket. He rips it open and pulls out a condom, slipping it on. He moves back over to the bed, his cock swaying with each step.

Unconsciously, I start to reach for it, wanting to stroke him, but Gavin waves my hand away.

"No," he says gently, climbing back onto the bed. "I'm in control."

I want to protest, my mouth watering with need. But I can't refuse him.

"Okay," I breathe.

He positions himself between my legs, his huge cock swaying with each movement. Anxiety twists my stomach and I tense. I've never had anything that big inside me before. And I don't know what it's going to feel like.

Gavin places a comforting hand on my thigh. "Relax," he tells me softly. "I'll be gentle." I hear what's unsaid. *At first.*

The unspoken words excite and frighten me all at once.

I nod gently at him, trying to relax against the bedding, my thighs trembling from anxiety and excitement.

He lines his cock up with my entrance and then slowly, he pushes in. I let out a soft whimper as he penetrates me, several inches of him dipping inside and spreading me wide.

Gavin pauses for a moment when he sees my face tighten. He must know what he's doing to me.

"It's okay," I say, still wanting more of him. "Keep going."

Reassured, he starts with tiny thrusts, each one going a fraction of an inch deeper than the last. I reach up and place my hands on his back, digging my nails in deep to bear the sensation.

It's almost unbearable, the desire and the intensity, but I let him go as far as he can go until . . .

Gavin groans as I squeeze my pussy around his entire shaft. *Balls deep.* "Fuck," he breathes. "You feel so fucking good." He gently seesaws his cock along the length of my canal for several moments, letting me adjust to his size.

I quiver in submission as he pins my knees to the bed and starts thrusting, long, hard, deep thrusts that pound into me like a sledgehammer, his flesh smacking up against mine.

Smack. Smack. Smack.

I dig my nails deep into Gavin's back, holding on for dear life as he pounds me with unrestrained power. Fire blazes within my core as my cries come out in ragged gasps, my body feeling like it's being swept away by a tidal wave of ecstasy. I can hardly take it, overwhelmed by the incredible force plowing into me, screaming out as the headboard bounces against the wall in time to his thrusts.

"Oh, God!" I yell as his balls slap up against my ass.

"You're about to meet him," Gavin promises me, somehow speeding up. He lifts my hips off the bed, giving him total control. Our hips crash into each other over and over again as Gavin's breath quickens and the burning in my core becomes unbearable.

Smack.

Smack.

One. Two. Three. I can take no more.

Faintly, I hear Gavin cry out as I scream, stars shooting across my vision as he throws his head back. He pulls out, ripping his condom off and firing streams of seed on my chest and stomach, moaning and groaning with each squirt.

When it's over, I lie there breathless, my mind blown, my limbs still shuddering from my second intense orgasm. I don't think I'll ever be the same again.

With his breathing labored and covered in sweat, Gavin slides from the bed and grabs a towel, cleaning me up. Then he collapses next to me, drawing me into his arms.

I lie there in his grasp, recovering. A silence settles over the room, and for a time, the only sounds are our pounding heartbeats and deep breaths.

But I'm beginning to feel uneasy. The fact that he's not saying anything is starting to make me self-conscious, right when I'd let go of all that.

He looks down at me, droplets of sweat running down his face, and smiles.

It's all I needed. I let out a relieved sigh, resting my head on his chest. Nothing else matters right now.

CHAPTER 12

GAVIN

She's so fucking beautiful.

Brianna's soft snores fill the room as I hold her in my arms, a soft breast pressed against my side and her head on my chest. I've been up since dawn, unable to sleep, transfixed by the thing of beauty beside me.

I run my hand along her arm, enjoying the feel of her soft flesh as a ray of sunlight illuminates her features. She looks so sweet. So *innocent.* Innocent and vulnerable in a way that makes me want to protect her. I inhale deeply, taking in her feminine scent, and almost groan at the need that flows through me.

It's not what I expected the morning after, even though I did have that lingering feeling this wouldn't be the end. Now, I want her even *more.*

I need to get out of here, I tell myself. *Clear my head so I can process. I'm sure I'll be fine in a few hours.*

I glance at the bedside clock and feel dismayed. I've got about an hour before I need to be on set.

I gently slide out of bed, carefully tucking a pillow under Bri's head. She lets out a soft sigh as I let go, clenching the bedding and mumbling something softly. I freeze, waiting for her eyes to pop open, but they don't.

Being as quiet as possible, I go about getting ready, taking a quick shower and shaving before getting dressed. My mind is on the previous night as I fix my cufflinks, gazing at my reflection in the mirror.

I can still feel her nails digging into my back, her lips parted, moaning and crying out my name with need as I plowed into her body with an unrelenting force. She was coming so hard on my dick that I thought it was about to be crushed by the powerful clenches of her pussy. But it only made me come just as hard.

My cock hardens in my pants as I remember those powerful sensations. Every touch, every moment was electric for us both. I could see it in her eyes. It was perfect, the way her body reacted to me, taking me in, holding me. Caressing me. It was so intense that I wanted to try for round two, but I knew she wouldn't be able to handle it. Not after that onslaught.

When I'm done fixing my shirt, I wipe down my face and return to the bedroom.

I stand there for a moment, gazing at Brianna, watching her chest rise and fall with each breath. She's rolled onto her back, the blanket half-covering her stomach. Once again, I'm impressed by how beautiful she is under the morning sun. Like some angel crafted by divine hands.

She snorts once and I tense, but her peaceful snoring resumes and I relax.

If she hasn't woken up by now, she isn't going to. But that's a good thing. It makes it easier for me.

I walk over to the chair and gather my blazer and put it on with a smooth flourish. Then I make my way to the door, but I stop before I place my hand on the doorknob, turning back to gaze at her slumbering form.

I don't know why it's so fucking hard to just leave without waking her up and telling her where I'm going. I don't owe her anything. I'll be gone in a week. And there's no reason to pretend that this will be anything other than what it was. *A one-night stand.* That's all it will ever be. Two weeks from now, I'm going to be doing wind sprints and squats and downing protein shakes all day. By then, I'll just be a faded memory in her mind, although hopefully, a pleasurable one.

Besides, she deserves better than an asshole like me. She needs to find a good man, someone who'll be able to devote his life to her. Not a celebrity who will disrupt her way of living and cause her to live out her life in the public eye. It would be cruel to subject her to that kind of scrutiny.

But when I think about her being with another man, anger forms inside me.

I'm surprised at the possessiveness I feel. At how much I care about not leaving her without telling her where I'm going. I've never felt this way with anyone.

She's going to hate me when she wakes up, I think as I gaze at the gentle rise and fall of her breasts, wanting nothing more than to go over and slide back into bed with her.

What she'll think of me shouldn't bother me. We both knew what we were getting into. We both knew that this wouldn't last.

Instinctively, I grab a pen off the desk and scribble a note on a piece of paper.

> *Brianna,*
>
> *I'm sorry I had to leave. You were sleeping so peacefully and I didn't want to disturb you. I'll be shooting late today. Things are behind schedule, so I don't know if I'll be able to see you today before you go home.*
>
> *Last night was amazing. Let's get together again. This evening, meet me in the coffee shop around 7:30. Dress casual.*
>
> *I'll be in touch.*
>
> *-G*

I hold the paper in my hand when I'm done, debating on whether to bunch it up and throw it in the trash. There's a high chance this will make her hate me even more, assuming that she'd want to get together again.

But a part of me doesn't want things to end this way—her waking up to my phantom and hating my guts. Leaving the note at least lets her know that I'm open for more . . . if she's willing.

I hope I don't regret this.

Setting my jaw, I set the note down on the desk and walk out the door.

❄

"CUT!" THE DIRECTOR YELLS. A BELL RINGS, AND I STEP BACK, blinking as the lights flood the room. I turn to see Jim grinning at me while flashing a thumbs-up. "Damn, you did good, Anaconda. That's the first time this week that you delivered your lines like you meant them!"

In front of me, Leslie's smiling, biting her lip and pressing her hand to her chest. She's flushed a little. I can tell she was buying every word that was coming out of my mouth. "Wow, Gavin, I felt the passion in your words," she says, breathless, her chest heaving. "It almost felt like you really cared for me."

But you mean nothing to me, I think, shrugging. She stares at me as if expecting me to say something. But I don't know what to say.

What am I supposed to say? The whole time she was looking at me, I didn't see Leslie Hart, the beautiful model and actress, but an unknown brunette whom I'd left sleeping in my bed this morning.

"Thanks. I'm working on it," I finally offer, hoping she'll be satisfied with the simple response.

Jim claps his hands. "Good. We're done for the day."

I nod gratefully and head toward my trailer, ready to get my clothes off. As I pass Jim, he reaches out and grabs my arm. "Seriously, Gavin, that was good shit. I'm looking forward to tomorrow."

"What's tomorrow?" I ask, and Jim gives me an incredulous look. "No, really. What's tomorrow?"

"Tomorrow's the love scene," Jim says, grinning with excitement.

"Don't tell me you're not looking forward to it. Hell, I'm looking forward to it with the way you pulled today's scenes off."

Fuck.

I hold in a groan as the image of Brianna's angelic face sleeping peacefully flashes before my eyes. I know I signed a contract when I agreed to do this movie, but there's no way I'm performing a fucking love scene with Leslie.

My relationship with Brianna is just starting. I can't fuck it up already.

Relationship? What relationship? I've only known her for a couple of days, and I'm already making business decisions based on this girl. I need to get my head back on straight.

"There's going to be a double for that though, right?" I ask, suddenly annoyed.

"No . . . no stunt double," Jim says, shaking his head while giving me a raised eyebrow. "Why?"

I clench my jaw, tight-lipped. A feeling of dread grips my stomach. After a moment, I clear my throat and declare firmly, "You're going to need to get a double."

Jim laughs at me like a fool until he realizes that I'm actually serious, and his grin slowly fades into an angry scowl. "Are you kidding me? You've slept with more women than I could dream of, and now you want a double to push up on Leslie and show your ass? Please tell me you're joking."

I turn when I hear the sound of footsteps. Drawn by our heated exchange, Leslie's wandered over, hurt reflecting in her eyes. "Did I do something wrong, Gavin?" she asks softly, her brow drawn into a frown. "Is that why this is a problem?"

I gently shake my head, trying to hold back the irritation I feel. "Of course not, Leslie. You're great. It's just . . ." My voice trails off as I get lost in thought. How can I possibly explain to them what's really going on? That after being with Brianna, I can't even think about touching another woman, let alone dry humping her like a dog in heat? Hell, the only reason the last scene came off so well was because I was seeing her face on Leslie's body the whole time. "I need a stunt double." I turn to Jim and repeat.

Fuck explaining anything. I don't owe either of them. It's none of their business, as far as I'm concerned.

"A stunt double?" Jim repeats, shaking his head again. "And just where are we going to get one of those on short notice?"

"I don't know," I say, feeling frustrated. "Make one of the other stunt actors or get one of the extras to do it." I feel like an asshole. I mean, if I want a career in acting, I'm not going to always be able to rely on a double for this shit. But I'm not doing it right now.

Jim glares, looking like he wants to attack me with his bare hands. "Why? You signed a contract that stated it wasn't a problem."

"I just don't think I'll be able to give the passion that the scene needs!" I snap, not meaning to be so testy.

"What passion?" Jim growls, incredulous. "You don't need passion to dry hump her for a few minutes! I mean look at you, for crying out loud. Give the female fans a few frames of that famous ass of yours, so at least someone gets something out of this godforsaken movie! Heaven knows, they're not going to be getting much out of your acting ability."

I clench my jaw, fighting back the anger surging through me.

"Look," I say through gritted teeth. "Find a double or find someone to replace me."

I stalk off set to my trailer, slamming the door shut behind me. Miranda barges in a second later.

She gestures angrily, flicking a manicured fingernail at my face. "What the hell was that about?"

"He's a prick!" I growl as I clench my fists. I'm proud of myself for maintaining control and not cursing Jim out. He was testing me with that last bit. "None of these people know shit about me."

"Never mind that," Miranda says, lowering her voice a little. "Whatever it is that's making you act this way, it's not worth it."

Oh, but she is.

Miranda continues, "Keep a barrier between you if that will help you feel any better. They make special skin-colored thongs that she can wear."

"It's not about that," I say, turning away. "I don't care if they shove a giant tube sock on my dick. That's not what this is about."

Miranda tries to stare me down, scowling, but then softens after a moment. "I really don't get you right now, Gavin Adams. Are you really not doing this because you don't want people to see your ass? They've seen a lot more than that!"

My jaw clenches at the thought of that fucking video, and it takes extreme effort not to unleash on Miranda. "Look, just remember who you work for. Make sure there's a double tomorrow."

I can feel her eyes burning holes into my back, but I don't care. Finally, she speaks, her voice both confused and angry. "You know, you've been acting strange ever since we got here. This isn't like you at all."

I want to let her have it. She needs to realize I'm the boss here. But she's just doing her job. I hired her in the first place because she'd stand up to me. She's just looking out for my best interest. And hers, of course.

Instead of going off on her, I turn and shake my head. "Just been something on my mind."

She starts to come forward. "What—"

I cut her off, flatly saying, "It doesn't matter. Just get my back on this."

Miranda stares at me for a long moment before unleashing a sigh that I almost feel across the trailer. "Fine," she agrees. "I'll handle it. But you have got to get it together, Gavin. We can't afford to fuck up on your first movie. If this goes badly, you can expect some major repercussions . . . for the both of us."

No shit. I fuck this up, I won't be working in movies beyond doing cameos and maybe a run-in at WrestleMania. I don't say the words that are on my mind.

Instead, I watch Miranda walk over to the door and pause with her hand on the doorknob, turning back to study me with compassionate eyes.

"You've got charisma, Gavin. You've got talent. But it's like football, you gotta be willing to go the extra yard. Let that sit and marinate."

I nod. "I will."

Miranda shakes her head, probably thinking I'm a lost cause, and swings the door open. "You have an interview in a few hours. Be prepared." She walks out, closing the door behind her.

Outside, I hear her heels clicking across the pavement and then fading into the distance. I let out a groan a moment later, taking a seat at the table and placing my head in my hands.

I don't know why I'm letting this bother me so much. I'm so close to screwing up a great opportunity that could set me up for my life after football.

But all I can think about right now is about how I left Brianna all alone back in my room.

CHAPTER 13

BRIANNA

My body aches and my thighs are two bags of vanilla pudding as I totter into the back of the coffee shop, feeling like I've been through the CrossFit Games. Mindy's behind the counter, whistling to herself as she preps everything for opening. Dressed in her usual work uniform, her hair looking shiny and glossy, she turns when she hears me approach.

"You look good this morning . . ." Mindy pauses, a devious grin spreading across her face. "Besides walking like you have a stick up your ass." She squints at me as if recognizing an old acquaintance. "Ol' grand daddy one ball, is that you? You've really improved your walk since I last saw you."

"You need to be killed for what you did," I growl, trying to maintain my scowl and not chuckle at her stupid joke. Mindy knows damn well why I'm walking funny.

She laughs at my empty threat and pours me a cup of coffee, passing it to me as she watches me make my way to the counter.

"Don't," I say dangerously, seeing the joke that forms on her lips.

Since waking up, everything from my knees to my chest aches. Even my toes hurt. Even though I loved every moment of last night with Gavin, my body totally hates me right now.

"It couldn't have been that bad," Mindy says with another giggle. "You can still walk at least. Well . . . kind of."

"Bitch," I hiss. I've only got a few minutes before I need to get my ass downstairs, grab my cart, and get to work, but I needed the caffeine more than I needed to make sure my bleach supply is good. I just pray that Vandenburgh doesn't see me and give me some shit. "This is half your fault, Mindy. I'd have never gone up there if you hadn't made it sound like it would be the best time of my life!"

I really shouldn't be blaming Mindy. In the end, it was my decision to go up there. But I'm pissed at myself for doing it. It ended up just like I thought it would—heartache. Even now, my blood boils thinking about waking up in an empty bed with Gavin nowhere to be found.

I knew and it expected it. Still, I can't get over the fact that he couldn't be bothered to rouse me before he left. All because I couldn't resist his handsome face, gorgeous body, and enormous dick.

Ugh.

"Well it was, wasn't it?" Mindy asks, seeing me lost in thought. I don't readily have an answer. I'm feeling so many emotions right now.

Finally, I sip my coffee before ruefully smiling, trying to find the words.

"It was." I swallow. I hate admitting it because I feel like shit now.

But I've never experienced a night like that. And the worst part about it is . . . I'd do it all again tonight. "He shook me from my toes to my ears, but this morning, I woke up with him gone and the bed empty. All I had was the smell of him on the pillows and sheets and a twisted up blanket that at least covered my ass, if not my dignity."

Mindy stops, her smile disappearing as she sees how distressed I am. "Fuck Vandenburgh for a few minutes. The coffee shop can handle itself."

She leads me to the back, where she pulls me in for a hug. "Talk to me, babe."

I take a deep breath, wiping away a single tear that's escaped my eye. "I don't know what's wrong with me. I went up there knowing this would be all there was to it. It's just that . . . I feel cheap. And now that he's gotten what he wanted . . ." I shake my head.

Mindy lets out a soft sigh of empathy. "I'm so sorry, honey. I wouldn't have encouraged you to go up there if I knew you were going to end up feeling this way. I just wanted you to have a good time." She pauses, chewing on her lower lip in thought. "But I think you might be rushing to judgment, 'cause girl." She gives me a look, rolling her eyes to the ceiling. "I know a douchebag when I see one, and Gavin doesn't seem that bad at all. He seems down to earth for someone who has all that money and fame."

"That's probably part of his charm. I bet he's nice to all the girls," I growl, getting more pissed off as I think about it. I wasn't even that mad before I came in the coffee shop. But just talking about it is getting me worked up. "I guess it would have been nice to at least have gotten... something from him. I know he's got priorities, but maybe leaving me a text or a note or something would have made me feel better instead of waking up to an empty room."

Mindy gives me another hug, then she steps back, grinning mischievously. "I'm sorry if this seems insensitive right now, but I gotta know! How was it playing with the giant snake?"

I cross my arms, scowling. "Mindy!"

"Whaaa?" she asks, smirking. "Come on!"

"I just . . . can't with you," I say, shaking my head.

Mindy makes a face and sniffs. "You can't with me, but you can with that big ass monster dick? I see how it is."

I try to scowl, but I can't help but laugh. "Bitch! You're the one who wanted me to go swinging from it like Jane from Tarzan."

Mindy laughs, knowing she's getting through. "Bri, you know I'm just trying to cheer you up."

I let out a sigh. "I know. I've just never felt . . ."

So sexy. So vulnerable. So moved but so . . . cheap. I shake my head, trying to shake the feeling. "I just haven't done this kind of thing before. I feel like a whore."

"Girl, please," Mindy says dismissively. "Don't even start with that. You are both consenting adults. And I'm here to tell you, there's nothing wrong with getting your freak on once in awhile."

I laugh. "I know. It's just that—"

"With all the hard work you put in dealing with Vandenburgh, you deserve it," Mindy cuts in.

I know what she's saying. And I must've told myself the same thing a hundred times already.

Mindy continues, her voice laced with irritation, "And you know what? if Vandenburgh actually got laid himself every once in a while, maybe he wouldn't act like such an ass all the time."

The mere mention of Vandenburgh having sex makes my stomach lurch. "Next time, can you wait until after breakfast to bring up something like that?"

Mindy frowns and lifts her chin, her voice dropping into the same haughty tones Mr. Vandenburgh likes to use. "Miss Sayles, I have spent the past year making you my slave because I'm mad my man pussy isn't getting fucked. Last time I seen some action is when my finger slipped through the toilet paper."

I try to fight it, but I can't help it. I burst into gales of laughter, having to grab ahold of the counter to keep from falling over. Seeing me overcome, Mindy starts laughing too until we're both holding onto each other, chortling like a pair of schoolgirls.

We've almost recovered from our giggling fit when Vandenburgh walks into the coffee shop. Mindy goes still immediately, her mirth fleeing like a bank robber on the run. "Jesus, does he have a tracer on us or something?" she hisses angrily. "He always comes in at the wrong time."

Wiping the tears of laughter from my eyes and putting on a solemn face, I have to agree. This is getting old.

Vandenburgh walks around the counter and into the back room. "Miss Sayles," he says in almost an exact copy of Mindy's imitation from moments before, "the coffee storage room doesn't need your attention. I suggest you get off your backside and get to work."

I resist the urge to tell him exactly what he can shove up his backside and nod respectfully. Beside me, Mindy tenses. I think she's about to speak up for me, bless her heart. But she needn't bother.

Vandenburgh turns his nasty scowl on her as if sensing her words before she can speak. "Isn't there a coffee machine that needs cleaning?"

Mindy's lip curls, and for a moment, I fear she's going to go off the rails. But after several blinks, she slinks off. She stops once, behind Vandenburgh, flipping him off so that I see it. To hide my smile, I quickly scurry off, saying, "Have a nice afternoon, Mr. Vandenburgh."

I leave the coffee shop and go about starting my shift.

As I go from room to room, floor to floor, dusting, cleaning, wiping, and vacuuming, my mind wanders to my future. If I can stay on track, and that's a big if, I've got just under one year before I'm done with school and I can tell Vandenburgh exactly what I think of his wannabe British-accented ass. In some ways, it's the only thing that keeps me coming in every shift, wanting to outlast him and then having the privilege of being able to tell him to kiss my ass just once.

When I get up to the penthouses, I see the suite that's being used by the movie crew bustling with people coming in and out. And Leslie Hart still has the 'do not disturb' sign on her door. That leaves Gavin's suite.

I go over and let myself in. A part of me is anxious when I step inside, but I relax when I see he isn't there. I figured he'd be gone, but a part of me was worried that he'd show up out of the blue. With all the emotions churning inside me, I really don't want to face him right now.

As I go about cleaning up the room, I have the sudden urge to snoop. I do my best to keep the impulse at bay, stripping the bed of the sweaty sheets—sheets that held my sweat—and placing new ones on it. But by the time I'm done making the bed and vacuuming, I find myself unconsciously going over to his things.

I start looking through his wardrobe, but I stop myself.

What the hell am I doing?

It was a one-night stand. There's no reason for me to be looking through his things. I'm not his girlfriend. And even if I were, this isn't right.

I close the wardrobe and turn around, leaning against the closet and sucking in a deep breath. It's crazy how out of control I am after just one night. Maybe I should switch places with another maid so she can do this floor in my place. It'd probably be for the best if I didn't see Gavin for the rest of the time he's here.

But even thinking about not seeing him again makes me sick to my stomach.

I'm about to pack up and leave when my eyes fall on a single piece of paper on the desk near the TV console. I walk over and pick it up. There's a note scribbled on it. I frown, wondering how I hadn't seen it this morning before I left.

Probably because I was pissed like hell, I tell myself as I start reading.

Brianna,

I'm sorry I had to leave. You were sleeping so peacefully and I didn't want to disturb you. I'll be shooting late today. Things are behind schedule, so I don't know if I'll be able to see you today before you go home.

Last night was amazing. Let's get together again. This evening, meet me in the coffee shop around 7:30. Dress casual.

I'll be in touch.

-G

Underneath, he leaves his phone number.

I re-read it, then read it again. He wants to actually see me again. I shake my head as I stare at his words. I don't know what to feel about them. On one hand, I'm relieved that he wants to see me again. Me, a simple small-town girl. But on the other hand, I can't get over his tone that seems to say 'you're going whether you like it or not'.

I have the sudden urge to ball up the note and throw it in the trash. With all the emotions I'm feeling from just one night with this man, what's going to happen if we continue this and he just up and leaves in a week?

I suck in a deep breath, my skin pricking. I should just be done with Gavin Adams and his huge, throbbing, toe-curling . . . Jesus.

There's plenty of need left, a devilish voice whispers to me. *You've never felt anything like him before and will never feel anything like him again. You can't deny it.*

Shit. That evil fucking voice is right.

With my heart pounding furiously, I look around the desk and see the notepad and pen he used to write the note. With shaking hands, I pick up the pen and write my response.

Seven thirty tonight. Jeans, t-shirt, and regular shoes. I'll see you downstairs.

Damn me and my needs.

I'm going.

CHAPTER 14

GAVIN

"*So how is preparing for a movie like getting ready for football?" the reporter asks.*

"Uh, it's not," I mumble. "They both take prep work, but it's not really the same."

"Is there anything you can tell us about your character?" asks another reporter, a woman with blonde shoulder-length hair and an eager smirk. "Is he anything at all like you are in real life?"

I barely hear her words, my eyes unfocused.

"Mr. Adams?" the blonde woman says after several moments.

Watching the video of the press conference with Miranda at my side, I swear I look like an idiot, albeit a good-looking one. Part of it I blame on all the flashing cameras, but the other . . . I just look plain stupid.

I turn the TV off in disgust, resisting the urge to throw the remote control across the room. "I look like a moron!" I growl, unable to believe how embarrassing I'd acted.

Miranda, who's sitting across from me, looking sharp and crisp in her white business suit and heels, her hair pulled up into an elegant bun with dramatic makeup painted on her face, just shakes her head in pity.

She's probably wanting to kick my ass, but I'm already suffering as it is. The interview has spread like wildfire to several major news stations, even though it was filmed as a local piece. And I'm sure I'll be the butt of everyone's jokes come morning. I'll probably end up as water cooler talk among the production crew.

"I should've nailed it," I lament, "but I couldn't focus." And the sad thing is, I didn't even get asked about the video and I still couldn't get it together for more than a few moments.

Good God, what the fuck is wrong with me?

But deep down, I know exactly what's wrong.

I want *more*. More than one night. I want to be able to ask Brianna about her day. I want to be able to share boring ass meals with her in this podunk little town. I even want to know simple shit like what her favorite brand of shampoo is and if she has to use conditioner on a daily basis.

Jesus, Gavin, did you seriously just think that? A very real fear begins to creep up from the depths of my stomach along with a feeling of alarm. *I'm so fucked.*

Miranda waves her hands to get my attention. "Earth to Gavin."

My eyes refocus on her face and I clear my throat. "Yeah?"

She points a manicured fingernail at my head. "What was going on with you today? And why does it seem I have to keep asking you this same question lately?"

"I wasn't feeling the questions." I lie for about the tenth time. The lie is a lot easier to say than the truth. Miranda wouldn't understand anyway, especially if I told her Brianna and I have basically only shared one night.

But she's not buying it, an irritated scowl spreading across her face. "Are you serious? What's there to feel? Those had to be the easiest questions you've gotten in a long time."

Miranda stares at me expectantly, waiting for a response. But I have nothing to say. Quite frankly, I'm tired of my excuses. And I know she is too.

"Are you on drugs?" Miranda asks suddenly when I don't answer. "Is there something I don't know that you're not telling me?" she adds.

I huff out a disbelieving laugh. "What?"

Miranda glares at me. "Don't play stupid, Gavin, something's going on. It's like you're on another planet this week. And don't try to blame it on the nerves. You should be used to the spotlight by now." She leans forward, giving me a direct look. "So what are you on?"

Irritation flares in my chest. "I'm not *on* anything," I growl. "It disappoints me that you would even think that. You know I don't mess with that shit. The league would be on my ass in a second if I did."

"Well, something's going on!" Miranda hisses. "Because what I saw today" —she shakes her head, at a loss for words— "I've *never* seen one of my clients behave this way. If it's not drugs, I'm worried about your health."

"I'm fine," I answer tersely, fed up with this whole conversation.

I could tell her what's going on, but somehow, I know it will make things worse. Besides, I have a reputation I need to maintain, and admitting that I'm getting lovesick will make me look weak.

Miranda's scowl morphs into a compassionate frown. "Can I arrange to have a psychologist stop in and give you a checkup?"

I shake my head. "Miranda, I—"

She speaks over me. "We all have tough times in our lives, Gavin. It was before you and I met professionally, but I went through a divorce when I was thirty-five. I had some tough times then, too. Talking to a psychologist really helped."

The revelation from Miranda makes my anger dissipate like clouds on a wind gust and I relax in my seat. "I know you're worried about me, Miranda," I say gently but firmly. "But trust me, you don't need to bring in a shrink. I'm going to get my shit together. Promise."

For a moment, Miranda looks like she wants to keep pressing the issue. But then she rises to her feet. "I hope so, Gavin," she says as she makes her way over to the door. "I really do," she adds before she walks out, "Because I'm not sure how much more of this I can take."

When she's gone, I look out the window, putting my head against the cool glass and hoping that I'll stay true to my word.

❄

I STARE DOWN AT THE NOTE IN THE PALM OF MY HAND. IT'S strange. I've gotten plenty of fan letters in the course of my playing career, and more than a few of them have been from women who've offered me everything from their hearts to their bodies to . . . well, damn near everything.

But this sweet little note, scribbled by a woman I barely even know, is more valuable to me than any of those.

I grin as I read Brianna's neat handwriting several times.

Seven thirty tonight. Jeans, t-shirts, and regular shoes. I'll see you downstairs.

-B

I fold the note and stuff it in my pocket, heading down to the elevators and making my way to the coffee shop. I recognize Mindy behind the counter as soon as I open the door. She must be pulling a double shift. "Hello."

Mindy looks up and flashes me a smile, but my eyes are only looking for one thing.

I suck in a sharp breath when I see *her*. Seated at the end of the counter, she's dressed casually like we agreed, only she's wearing a sundress instead of jeans. But she could be wearing a potato sack and I'd still be smitten.

"Gavin." Brianna greets me shyly. Her hair looks glossy and is curled at the ends, and she has a hint of light makeup on. Fuck, she's so gorgeous. "It's nice to see you."

I flash her an easy smile. She looks so nervous sitting there, so vulnerable. "You look beautiful—" is all I get out before Mindy marches over and shoves a bag into my hands.

"You owe me twenty dollars," she declares, placing her hands on her hips.

"What's this?" I ask, reaching into my pocket and handing her a hundred by habit. I notice I don't get change, the little wiseass.

Mindy nods at the bag, her eyes sparkling. "It's cinnamon rolls, sandwiches, and a little blanket in the bottom. Oh, and don't forget your lattes. I heard about your little thing." She clamps a hand over her mouth. "Whoops? I meant to say I heard about your *big* thing."

Brianna rolls her eyes and snaps, "Mindy!"

Mindy laughs, drawing a chuckle from me. "I just wanted to make sure the two of you were prepared."

Brianna rises to her feet and comes around to my side. "Thank you."

"Okay!" Mindy says abruptly, suddenly shoving me and Brianna out the front door. "Y'all have fun now, ya hear?"

I chuckle as I walk Brianna outside the hotel, my hand splayed across her lower back. "She really is a trip," I remark, enjoying the feel of her soft body. It feels good to touch her, to pretend that she's mine. "But I'm surprised you haven't strangled her by now."

"She's my best friend. What am I supposed to do?" she asks.

I laugh. "With a friend like her? Not a damn thing."

Brianna sucks in a sharp breath when we reach my ride waiting for us at valet parking. "Wow," she breathes when she sees the red Lotus. It's not what I'm used to. The British styling is a bit too small for my frame, but it's the best that Miranda could get. "This yours?"

"Just for the week," I admit, walking over to open the door for her.

She hesitates for a moment, her soft lips parted in awe, before sitting down into the seat.

Grinning, I shut the door, go around to the driver's side, and get behind the wheel. Gripping the smooth leather, I toss her a wink while she's checking out the inside of the cabin.

"This is really nice," she says softly. "I've never been inside something so sporty or . . . luxurious before."

A part of me wants to promise her the world—luxury cars, expensive jewelry, and the best money can buy. She deserves it all. But when her eyes lock with mine, I'm nearly paralyzed by fear. Never have I been this out of control over my emotions. And it scares the shit out of me that I feel this way when I hardly know her.

Swallowing back a lump in my throat, I start the engine, not letting on to the inner turmoil roiling inside. "So where are we going?" I ask Brianna casually.

She looks at me like I'm crazy, and I grin.. "You said you were taking me to a park and you don't know where we're going?" she asks incredulously.

I shrug. "Nope. I just wanted to take you *somewhere*. You're the one who's lived here all your life. Tell me where we should go." I grin and add, "Preferably, somewhere we'll be alone."

Brianna bites her lower lip, a light blush shading her cheeks. She's probably thinking the same thing I am—secluded is private, and private means . . .

Finally, she looks at me through long eyelashes and smiles, snapping her fingers. "Oh, I know. Go to Bear Lake Park."

"Okay, and where's that?" I ask. I nod at the vehicle's console. "This thing doesn't have a GPS."

Brianna laughs. "You mean to tell me that superstar Gavin Adams doesn't know how to find his way around a little ol' town like this?"

I snort. "I'm a football player, not a Rand McNally Atlas." I chuckle. "I don't even know my way out of a paper bag except at home. I spend most of my time being chauffeured around."

Brianna chortles. "At least you're honest." She points off to the side. "But to answer your question, it's on the other side of town. Turn left out of the lot, and I'll get you there."

I pull out of the parking lot, impressed by the smooth ride. At the first stop sign, I drop the top, letting the wind ruffle through our hair.

"After a long day, that feels great." Brianna sighs with pleasure.

I grin at her. "I'm glad you like it." I look around, noticing the shops outlined in the fading glow of the sun and the lack of traffic on the roads. "You know, this place isn't too bad. It feels much less hectic here, unlike life in the city."

"It definitely has appeal," Brianna agrees softly, looking at me through lowered lashes.

"I never thought I'd say this," I say as the light turns green and I continue up the street, "but I feel like I could learn to love a place like this."

Brianna's lips part in surprise, a wind gust flowing through the cabin and blowing her hair around her seat as she laughs. "I'm shocked to hear you say that."

I shrug, turning left at a sign I see for Bear Lake Park. "Yeah, I didn't care for it when I got here, but like you said. It's got a certain charm."

Brianna purses her lips for a moment before saying, "That's good."

"What is?" I ask curiously.

Brianna smiles. "That even someone like you can change your mind on a place like this."

I go silent, lost in thought. Honestly, if someone would've told me before today that I'd be doing this, I'd have said they were out of their fucking minds.

But now . . .

"Over there." She points. "That's Shera's Bakery," Brianna says as I drive by a bright pink clapboard building.

"Who is Shera?" I ask, raising an eyebrow.

Brianna replies, her eyes on the building as we pass, "She's a nice old lady who loves to help people." She shakes her head, pushing her hair out of her eyes. "When I was eight, I crashed my bike and twisted my ankle near her shop. When Shera saw me sobbing in pain, she didn't bat an eye. She brought me inside, gave me a donut, and called her son to escort me home because my bike was busted up from my fall."

"That was nice of her," I remark. Brianna nods. "Yeah. She's just like that. She'd give you the clothes off her back if you asked her to."

"I'd like to meet her one day," I say without even thinking.

Shit, Gavin, what are you doing?

Brianna's eyes widen with surprise.

Can't go back now.

Brianna is touched, gently patting my leg. "She would love that! She's never met a celebrity before."

Before I can say anything, Brianna snaps her finger. She points as we come up to an intersection. "Turn right there."

I turn down a road lined with beautiful trees and sunlight filtering through the branches. It's beautiful, unlike any view you get in the city.

"There." Brianna points as we come up on a small sign just behind a tiny parking area.

"Bear Lake Park?" I ask, rolling the car to a slow stop.

Brianna smiles, a dreamy expression coming over her face. "Yeah. We're here."

CHAPTER 15

BRIANNA

The birds sing and the insects buzz as Gavin shuts off the engine of the sports car. Inside me, though, my engine is still running hot. I seem to be in overdrive anytime I'm in his presence.

"So, where should we eat?" Gavin asks. "After all, you know this park better than I do."

I'm not sure if he's meaning to do this, but it's powerful. My head is swirling in confusion after the fact that I just accepted a second date with him. But by giving me the choice of where we go on the date, I feel like I have more confidence, more *control* over what's happening. If I take him to one of the open spaces, there's no way we'll get into anything naughty.

But on the other hand . . . "There's a small clearing up ahead, along the trail," I say softly.

Gavin gets out of his side of the car and then helps me out. The low-slung sports car makes me have to stretch out my leg, and I notice the way he looks at my thighs as I get out of the seat, but I don't care. His wandering eyes make me feel hot. *Wanted*.

"Get the food," I order, "and I'll show you where to go."

Gavin chuckles at the audacity of my commanding tone, but his sexy smirk tells me that he'll play this game for a little while longer. "As you wish, gorgeous," he says in a deep voice, bowing his head.

A flush comes to my cheeks and my nipples tighten at his tone. Nothing has happened and my heart is already bouncing around in my chest.

Gavin comes around the car and holds his arm out to me in a gentlemanly fashion. I shake my head and reach out and take his hand. "Here, let me show you where," I say softly.

Gavin looks surprised that I took his hand, but then he smiles and shakes his head. "You know, it's funny. I can't remember the last time I let a girl lead me anywhere."

How many girls have you been with? I hate that it popped into my head, but I ignore it.

"Well, you won't have trouble remembering after this, will you?" I ask.

Gavin arches a mysterious eyebrow and replies in a low voice, "That depends."

I shiver at his words, a flush spreading across my cheeks.

Lowering my head to hide my embarrassment, I lead him through the park, turning at the spot where the trail leads away from the lake and deeper into the woods that surround the area. I'm grateful for the shade. It's hot as hell, one of those days where the humidity makes you feel like you're taking a shower even with your t-shirt on.

As we move through the trees, a cool breeze gusts through the area, kissing my skin and making me feel refreshed.

Finally, we reach the clearing I had in mind from the moment I decided to come here. It's not very big, only about fifteen feet across, and it's semi-famous in the town for its location as a make-out spot.

Gavin lets out a low whistle, surveying the area. "This looks like something out of a storybook."

I can see what he means. The grass in this area is a brighter green and softer than the normal bluegrass that dominates the surrounding land. On one side is a brook, a burbling little rivulet that adds a touch of coolness and pleasant background noise. "I'm glad you like it."

Gavin spreads out the blanket in the shaded area and then looks around. "This place seems so peaceful and serene."

"Yeah," I say, sinking down onto the blanket and taking off my sandals. "I used to come up here all the time with Mindy to play hide and seek when we were little. This was one of our secret play areas. Later, I started jogging, and I found this a great place to relax after a jog around the lake since it's always cool here. It's too bad. When I started school and working at the hotel, all that stopped."

"That sucks," Gavin says, relaxing with his hands on his splayed-out knees. I feel a need growing in me as I see the bulge of his cock inside his black jeans. *Fuck.* Is he hard for me?

I tear my eyes away from the mouth-watering image. "Yeah, but thank God cleaning all those rooms and going up and down the floors keeps me from gaining too much weight."

"I can see that," Gavin says as he looks at me with appreciation, causing my skin to prickle. I nearly squirm under the heat of his gaze, a flush shading my cheeks. He might be that hard, but I'm burning up and wet too. "Whatever it is that you're doing, keep doing it."

"Thank you," I say softly through lowered lashes, feeling more at ease. This feels different from before. Then, we both knew as soon as I stepped into the room that there was only one purpose for my being there—for him to fuck me senseless.

This time, Gavin is being a gentleman. And I'm not complaining. I love the idea of being courted. In fact, I don't think I've ever been treated this way before by a man. The last guys I dated were more or less local boys who would take me to the local theater and then try to take me to the back of their car or truck for some inelegant fumbling inside my shirt.

"So how was your day?" I ask, taking a bite of one of Mindy's cinnamon rolls. I can't help it. I have to close my eyes. It's so damn good. I have to thank her for these.

"I actually did a pretty good job, for the most part. At least the director thought so."

The good news makes me smile. "Really? That's wonderful!" I gush. "So I guess being an actor is something you can do after all."

For some reason, Gavin's expression remains neutral at my praise. He doesn't look happy, as if something is weighing on his mind. But before I can ask him what's wrong, the look is gone, replaced by a wide smile that doesn't seem altogether genuine.

"Yeah, I just need to keep it up," Gavin agrees, his voice lacking conviction.

I reach out, concerned, placing my hand on his forearm. "Are you all right?"

Gavin grins at me, still looking a little artificial. "Yeah, why?"

"It's just . . ." I stare at him. "You don't seem too happy. Is everything okay?"

Gavin doesn't reply right away, instead looking away. When he looks back at me, his grin has faded, but he looks more genuine too. "Just thinking about all the work I have left to do."

His words pierce the little fantasy that we've been weaving around ourselves in the grove, and I start to feel ill. I *know* he won't be here long, but I wish he could stay longer. I feel like I'm just getting to know him. "Gavin . . ."

"Was your day okay?" he asks, cutting me off with a smile. "I mean, you know . . ."

"It was fine," I say, smoothing over the rough parts. "I only had to see Vandenburgh once. That's always a good day."

Gavin grunts. "Once is more than enough for me. I can't imagine working for him."

"Ain't that the truth," I grumble, then laugh. "But never mind him. You don't need to listen to me bitch about my boss. I'm sure you've got a laundry list of your own complaints."

Gavin chuckles and nods. "Yeah, guess so." He peers at me with interest. "So what are you planning to do with your degree once you graduate?"

I pick at my half-eaten cinnamon roll before setting it down. "I'm going to see what's out there. I still don't know if I want to stay local or go to a big city."

Gavin nods. "What do your parents say?"

I bite my lower lip, feeling nervous. "Honestly, I don't talk to them much. After they got divorced, they both left town. It was a nasty time, and there were a lot of hurt feelings and torn up relationships on both sides. Mom wanted me to come live in St. Louis, while Dad moved west and wanted me to follow him to Pueblo, Colorado. In the end, I decided to stay here. I was already in high school and I'd already been accepted to the local college. It caused a lot of bad blood all around. So we hardly see each other."

"I see," Gavin says, looking uncomfortable that he asked. "Sorry."

"Nothing you could have known," I say, waving it off. I really don't want to talk about them right now. I'm having a half-decent time, and I don't need to spoil the moment by bringing up my past and current heartaches. "So what about you?"

Gavin shakes his head. "Mine are about as supportive as they can be. But then again, I bought them both new BMWs for Christmas last year." He huffs out a chuckle. "They really can't complain about that."

I nod my head. "Yeah, that's gotta be gratifying for them. They must love having a son who's achieved so much."

Gavin snorts. "I haven't achieved anything in my mom's eyes. She wants grandbabies like yesterday. It's the only thing on her mind every time we talk. She wants to know right away whether I've found somebody to have children with. And when I say I haven't, she's disappointed."

Babies. Hmm. Until now, the thought was alien to me. Mainly because I hadn't met a man I wanted to settle down and start a family with.

Maybe you could with him, a voice whispers in the back my head.

Get the fuck out of here, I tell the voice. *That'll never happen.*

"And you don't think you can give her what she wants?"

"I'm sure I'm capable," Gavin says, grinning. "I just don't expect it to happen as soon as she'd like."

His answer disappoints me, although it shouldn't. If he'd have said, 'have my babies, now!' it would have been awkward as hell. Still, his answer bothers me in a way I can't quite put my finger on.

"Thankfully, my parents don't bother me about that. Yet." I shake my head. "I really don't think I could handle any more pressure. Between school and working for a man like Vandenburgh, I'd go crazy and need to be put in a straitjacket if I had to take care of a baby too."

Gavin nods, giving me a mysterious little smile as he says in agreement, "You definitely don't need any more pressure."

I grab my cinnamon roll and take the last delicious morsel into my mouth.

Suddenly, Gavin surprises me, leaning in until his lips are just a fraction of an inch from my ear. His breath tickles my skin, and his hot body is so close that I can't help but react. "You don't need any more pressure," he growls throatily, "but what you definitely need is more pleasure."

He's so close, and his intense gaze is so hypnotic that it takes me a moment to register what he's saying.

"What?" I breathe.

Gavin reaches up with his right hand and strokes my hair, sending shivers down my spine. I've always loved when a man plays with my hair. "You need more pleasure. Something to release all the pressure that's inside you."

My skin pricks and my nipples are hard in my light bra as I look into Gavin's eyes, seeing him look at me with fiery desire. "Oh."

He closes the rest of the distance between our bodies, and his lips are warm and thrilling. The first feather-like kiss quickly deepens, and he's kissing my throat, sending waves of desire through my body. Burning fire builds in my chest, and I pull his head up, kissing him hard. His tongue explores my mouth as his hands roam over my body, stroking and massaging every inch until I'm moaning against his tongue.

I raise my arms over my head, and Gavin pulls my dress up and off before kissing down my body. His tongue traces around my right nipple before he sucks, nibbling and biting the stiff nub until my eyes aren't able to focus. It feels so damn good.

"Gavin," I moan, running my hands through his thick hair. How can a man have me on the verge of coming with only his lips on my breast?

But it's not just his lips. It's the way his hands are stroking my thighs, cupping and massaging my ass and making my pussy clench with need.

Gavin starts kissing down my body, his tongue tracing over my belly button to reach my panties. I lift my hips and he slides them off, chuckling softly. "What?"

"Your panties. They're so innocent. So . . . boring." I blush, but Gavin stops me with a kiss right at the panty line. "Right now, the sexiest word in the world to me is *boring*."

He lowers his mouth, and I clench at the blanket as he slides his tongue over my pussy, stroking and making me gasp as he licks me all the way from bottom to top, quickly kissing my clit before lowering his tongue and starting again. His tongue is a devilish snake, squirming and stroking, working its way inside me and never stopping. Pleasure jolts through my body as he tastes me, sucking and nibbling on my lips until I'm gasping, barely able to breathe.

"Gavin . . . fuck . . ." I groan as he takes his tongue from between my lips, but he doesn't give me a chance to even breathe before he's sucking my clit, his tongue flickering over the tip. I scream breathlessly as pure white pleasure assaults my body, my chest growing tight and my heart forgetting to beat as he assaults my clit with his tongue and lips.

My toes curl, and I can feel the inferno building, ready to unleash. I'm quivering, a violin string that's this close to breaking if he strokes me one more time. And then he does. I cry out, my body uncurling as I come hard, my pussy juice gushing into his hungry mouth as I thrash. His powerful hands hold me against him, his hands clamped on my ass and not letting me move as he takes every drop until I'm limp on the blanket.

When I can breathe again, Gavin's looking at me with gleaming eyes, his grinning face literally dripping with my juices. "So fucking sweet."

His words re-energize my body, and I squirm around to my belly, crawling toward him. "My turn. You didn't let me last time."

I cup his pants, feeling the thick bulge running down his right pants leg, and for a moment, I'm shocked at what I'm thinking of doing, but that same voice that told me I need him tells me that I need to do this now. Gavin looks at me with lust in his eyes as I undo his belt and unzip his jeans, pulling his underpants down enough to free his massive cock.

He's huge. Even the head looks like a mouthful, and I look up at Gavin. He smiles and reaches down, stroking my hair again and reassuring me. "Open wide."

I start slowly, licking just the velvety soft tip, and he moans. His moans continue as I lick and kiss his shaft, tonguing his balls before licking all the way up to the tip and opening my mouth, sliding his tip into my mouth and sucking it like a lollipop with quick, slurping sucks that have him moaning deeply. I let him in deeper, swallowing him until my jaw aches and I can barely breathe. Gavin's eyes go wide as I start bobbing my head up and down his shaft, licking and sucking him hungrily. His cock tastes so manly, and I'm drooling as I take him as deep as I can.

With each stroke of his cock into my mouth, I try to swallow just a little bit more. It's going to be difficult, but I'm determined to make sure Gavin Adams never forgets me or this town.

Gavin's hands don't force me, but he brushes my hair out of my face as I plunge my mouth down on his cock, feeling him push past my gag reflex and into my throat. I swallow him, massaging him until he groans deeply and black fireworks explode in front of my eyes. I pull back, sweet oxygen flooding my lungs as I look up at him in triumph.

Gavin nods, and his hands tighten around my head as he holds me still and starts fucking my face. He groans as he thrusts, his balls slapping up against my chin. He speeds up, and I'm starting to gag, but I force myself to relax more, feeling my throat and tongue massage his cock.

I reach around, my fingers digging into his ass cheeks as he thrusts into my mouth, and he groans. "Fuck, Bri . . . I'm going to come . . ."

The first blast of his release is so deep that I just feel it rocket down my throat. He starts to pull back, my mouth clamped around his shaft while he fills my mouth with his cream.

When he's done, I tuck his cock back into his underpants before looking up and swallowing the last of his come, wiping the last bit off my chin and sucking my finger clean for him.

He smiles at me as I finally manage to gulp it down, asking jokingly, "did you enjoy your snack?"

I nod, making a face at the aftertaste. Sweet and tangy. "I sure did."

CHAPTER 16

GAVIN

I plop down in my chair, sighing to myself as I look at the glass of brandy in my hand. I really shouldn't be drinking, but I can't help it. I feel like shit.

What the fuck are you doing? I think to myself as I brood over my date with Brianna. *You're leaving in just a few more days. You know that after this, you're going to be so exhausted for the next eight months that you'll barely be able to email, let alone come see her.*

But you're screwing her again.

Worse, the way you talked to her . . . you're only going to hurt her.

That's why I'm holding the brandy in my hand. It was after we'd had sex and she'd gotten dressed. I offered to take her back to her apartment, figuring that after what we've been through, she would like to have a shower and get her things from the hotel later.

Instead, she insisted that she had to get some things from her locker and that it would be more convenient for her if I just took her there. Normally, I wouldn't have batted an eye, but there was something in the way she said it, like she wasn't really telling me the truth.

The fact is, I've been more honest with Brianna than I have been with almost any woman. Nobody else has heard about the way my mother is pressuring me, and I know for damn sure that I've told no one else that I sometimes feel like a failure. There's something about her that makes me open like a book.

But for her to be holding back from me, it bothers me.

I sigh and take a sip. This needs to stop. I know it's going to hurt, but the longer I let this go, the more problems there are going to be. I need to tell her that this has to stop.

You can't do that. Admit it, you're starting to need her.

I take another swig, wincing as the fiery alcohol burns its way down my throat. Sadly, my inner voice might be right. Just thinking about telling her that I won't see her again feels like a knife in my gut. It's all my fault though. I'm the one who let it get this far. I should've stuck to my plan of just one night.

Instead, I let her get inside. I feel weak.

Thoughts of her soft body, the way she kissed me, and the way her juices tasted flood my mind, making my cock hard as a rock.

It's not something I can easily forget. Nor do I want to.

But she's hiding something from me. Frustrated, I throw back the rest of my glass and look at the bottle. It's half-full, but I shouldn't drink any more. I'm feeling tipsy as fuck, and now that I can't think straight, maybe I can finally get some sleep.

❄

THE BLARING OF THE ROOM PHONE STARTLES ME AWAKE, SUNLIGHT stabbing daggers into my eyes and making me wince. I groan, grabbing my pounding head, the blood vessels in my temple feeling like they're going to burst. Fuck, I feel like shit. Drinking normally isn't my forte, so it's my fault I have a brutal hangover. I knew I shouldn't have drunk that much, but I did it anyway.

I'm tempted to just knock the phone to the floor and tell whoever is on the other end to go to hell, but I don't. Instead, I pick up the handset, wishing I had about a two-pound aspirin to take care of this headache. "Hello?"

"Hey." It's Miranda.

"Yeah?" I ask, my voice sounding slurred and groggy.

"What's going on?" she asks, sounding alarmed. "You sound like shit."

I clear my throat and try not to sound like a frog. "I just woke up."

"Hmm," she says, obviously not convinced. "Well, I've got some good news, but it's gonna cost you. The love scene has been delayed, but that means that you have to be down here in front of the fire station in town in thirty minutes."

"Huh? What for?" I ask, gritting my teeth at the pounding in my temple.

"It's part of the deal," Miranda says. "We need to do some publicity for the movie. Jim said he needs a few frames for the trailer and some stuff for the movie poster."

I hold back a groan, trying to process what she's saying.

There's a long pause on the other end of the line. I bet Miranda is nervous as fuck right now. "Can I count on you, Gavin?"

I rub my eyes and glance at the clock. I don't want to go. But what other choice do I have? "Okay, I'll be there," I grudgingly tell her, hanging up the phone.

I get up, get a quick rinse in the shower, and get dressed, my head pounding the entire time. I grab a pair of sunglasses and head down to the center of town, driving as fast as the speed limit will allow. Nineteen minutes later, I pull in front of the fire station, dry chewing a couple of Excedrin.

As I head to the front of the fire station, I see Miranda standing there with a photographer and a couple of women.

"What's this?" I ask. "I thought you said he needed stuff for the trailer."

"Thank goodness you're here!" Miranda says. She's smiling, and I swear she's got a look in her eyes that's already beginning to worry me. "You couldn't have come at a better time. The camera man just finished setting up. Kay, come over here." She motions one of the chicks over to me, a pretty blonde with big tits.

"Wait, hold up," I say, backing up, barely sparing the girl a glance. "What am I doing?"

Miranda's scowl could kill. "What do you mean? I already told you over the phone. A photo op for the movie. You know, the movie you signed a contract to act in?"

I cross my arms over my chest. I hate it, but I just need to get it over with. "Okay," I say flatly. "What do you want me to do?"

Miranda looks at me like I'm an imbecile. "Take off your shirt and just stand there."

Holding back a terse reply, I do as she asks, my head pounding like a war drum. One of the cameramen scrambles over to get my shirt when I have it off.

"Take the glasses off, please," Miranda commands next.

Another sharp stab between my eyes. "Really?"

Miranda shrugs. "Just in case."

I sigh and take my glasses off, stuffing them in my back pocket. It's right then that my headache increases almost one hundred-fold, and I wince at the blistering sunlight.

"Good, now Kay, Alana, get on either side of him," she orders the two models.

For the next half hour, I'm forced to pose in various poses with the models. It's all professional, and I make sure to keep my eyes in safe places and to avoid intimate contact.

By the time it's over, my head feels like it's filled with shards of glass whirling around in my brain and I can hardly stand.

"Thank you so much, Gavin," Miranda says as I'm putting my shirt back on, patting me on the back. "I know you really didn't want to do this, so I appreciate it."

I open my mouth to say something smart, but then I realize this is one of the few times she's actually being nice. "You owe me," is all I say, nodding goodbye to the models and walking to my car.

"Can you believe this guy?" I hear Miranda complain behind me to one of the girls, "I get him a movie deal, he can't even say his lines right, and *I* owe *him*?"

I take that back. She wasn't being nice. More like she hadn't gotten to mean yet.

❄

FINALLY, AFTER THE DAY OF SHOOTING, MY MIND IS ONLY ON ONE thing as I return to the hotel. *Brianna.* I want to go see her. Do something. But I feel like she's only going to deepen my problems.

Back in my room, I lie on my bed, staring up at the ceiling. It doesn't feel right, lying here. Not when I want her beside me.

I roll out of bed and head to the kitchen area, where I see the half-full bottle of brandy that I had last night. I'm about to grab it and pour it out when I hear a knock at the door.

Brianna. Must be.

I put the bottle back down on the counter and walk over to the door.

"Hello . . ." I start to say as I swing the door open wide with a large grin on my face. But instead of my innocent little bunny, it's Leslie Hart standing there with an answering grin.

"Leslie, what are you doing here?" I ask. I don't want to be a dick, but I feel like slamming the door in her face. There's only one person I want to see right now, and it sure as fuck isn't Leslie Hart.

Instead of answering me, Leslie steps into my room, that smile that's lit up dozens of magazine covers still on her face.

"Hello, Gavin," she greets sweetly.

I try to keep a polite tone of voice since I've pissed off enough people lately. "I'm not really looking for visitors right now."

"Don't worry, I only came here for a minute," she says. "It's kind of important."

Keeping a lid on my frustration, I close the door and gesture at the couch. "Go ahead."

Leslie crosses the room and sits down. She's dressed more casually than I expect her to be, like a normal person and not a Hollywood starlet. I don't want her to get the wrong idea, so I sit across from her in the leather chair, leaning back, my legs splayed out wide as if I own the room. "So what's on your mind?"

She looks at me with eyes that are a lot more perceptive than what she uses on set. It's like she's studying me, trying to get me to reveal something. But I don't have the time or the patience right now to figure it out. "Well?"

Leslie's smile comes back, but it's more real and less forced. For a second, I wonder if I'm seeing the real Leslie Hart for the first time. "I'm worried about you," she admits finally.

You and everyone else.

"And I don't want whatever this is to continue. This problem you're having. It affects all of us," she says, her face morphing into a mask of concern.

"I don't have a *problem*." The lie sounds hollow on my lips even as it leaves my mouth.

Leslie purses her lips thoughtfully before asking, "You sure about that? Everyone's noticed, and everyone's talking about it." She leans forward in her chair, her eyes flashing. "Is it personal?"

"My personal life is just that," I say flatly. "I haven't asked about yours, and I expect the same courtesy."

Leslie slowly sits back in her seat and nods. "I accept that. But here's the thing. Whatever you've got going on in your personal life is affecting business." She fiddles nervously with her shirt before letting out a sigh. "What I'm trying to say is that I want this movie to succeed. And that can't happen with you being distracted like this. There's already a shitload of negative press about another cookie-cutter female lead action movie." Leslie rolls her eyes. "And I want to be able to prove them wrong. But with the way things are headed, we're looking at a path that's straight to the DVD bargain bin."

I open my lips to say a sharp retort, but then I close them. She does have a point. I'm fucking things up for her and everybody else. And as much as I want to be able to say otherwise, there's no denying it.

Finally, I give her a grudging nod. "Fine. I'll admit it. I've been having a personal issue. But I'm gonna deal with it. We're going to shoot this movie and it's going to do great," I say firmly, making sure she knows that this matter is settled.

Leslie's frown splits into a grin and she relaxes. "That's all I wanted to hear."

I put on a fraudulent grin and rise to my feet, signaling that our meeting is over. It's not that seeing this real Leslie isn't interesting, but my mind is on one person only.

"Point taken," she says as she rises to her feet. I lead her to the door.

"See you at filming," I say in parting, holding open the door for her.

She nods, but before I can close the door, she stops and turns. "Gavin?"

I arch an eyebrow. "Yeah?"

The mask of concern returns and Leslie asks, "Listen, are you sure that you're okay? Anything you need?"

I shake my head. "I'll be fine. It's one of those problems you sort of have to work out on your own."

Relief spreads across her face as she says in a soft, warm voice, "Thank you."

"For what?" I ask, surprised.

She gestures between us. "For being a gentleman. This conversation was a lot easier than I thought it would be. Honestly, I thought you'd be an asshole. Glad I'm not the only one who's misunderstood."

I shake my head, knowing what she means. Being a celebrity is one thing we share in common. "And thanks for being a sport and dealing with my bullshit. Don't worry. I'll get it sorted."

Leslie smiles and gives me a quick, friendly hug and a peck on the cheek before she turns and walks off down the corridor.

CHAPTER 17

BRIANNA

*I*t's late. Afternoon shift. One of the most tiring simply because of the time of day that I start work.

Sighing with relief, I clock out and head toward the elevators, glad that the day's over. My body is practically screaming with anticipation. I *need* to see him. I've been waiting anxiously all day.

I don't know if he's going to be there, with his shooting schedule so out of whack, but my heart is pounding like a drum. And I can barely stand still as I wait for the elevator doors to open.

I can't count how many times I resisted the urge to send him a flirty little text. The only thing that kept me from doing it was that I didn't want to interrupt him on set. And I don't want to be perceived as a nuisance.

It was hard, keeping a lid on my urges. The only thing I could think about was his big dick in my mouth and the powerful sensation of blood pumping through it. He enjoyed taking me to my limits. I could see it in his eyes. There's something about the whole experience, though, that felt like it was more than sex.

Ding. I enter the elevator and begin straightening my clothes when the door closes. I hope Gavin doesn't mind that I'm not in my uniform. I have on a raggedy outfit that I brought to change into after my shift.

Of course, he may not even be there, in which case I'll leave him a note. A naughty grin plays across my face. I think I might leave him a little surprise as well.

Well, fuck. He's turning me into a bad girl already.

I'm still wearing my grin when I step out of the elevator and turn right toward his room. But it quickly fades when I see what's up ahead in Gavin's doorway.

Long, sexy legs. Beautiful blonde tresses, *all over* Gavin, giving him a kiss on the cheek as if he just showed her a great time. My blood is boiling so hot, it takes a moment to recognize Leslie Hart. I'm so shocked I'm frozen like a statue. I'm not even sure I'm breathing.

But before Leslie can spot me, I dart around the corner, my heart pounding like a hammer.

I lean against the wall, my chest heaving as I suck in deep, ragged breaths.

I knew it! a voice screams in my head. It's a battle to keep the tears at bay. I clench my hands into fists and bite my lower lip hard enough to draw blood. *That asshole was just playing me from the beginning.*

The sting of his betrayal hurts worse than a thousand hornet stings. And to think, I was coming up here to be with him.

Dizzy, weak, and feeling sick to my stomach, I pull away from my hiding place when I'm sure Leslie is gone.

I feel crushed as I make my way down to the coffee shop. When the staff elevator opens up on the lobby level, I expect Vandenburgh to appear just because my day can't get any shittier.

Thank fuck he doesn't.

I make it across the lobby and head for the coffee shop. It's after closing time, but I see Mindy. She looks up when I walk through the doorway. She must sense that I'm upset because she comes flying around the counter running as soon as the door's closed.

"Bri!" Mindy gasps, peering at me in concern. "What's wrong?"

I'm not gonna cry, I tell myself, looking into Mindy's worried face. *I won't fucking do it.*

"Gavin was with another girl . . ." I almost get it out, but then I burst into tears.

Mindy places a hand over her mouth in horror, and she pulls me in for a hug. "Oh, Bri, I'm so sorry."

She holds me for a few seconds while I try to compose myself.

Finally, I'm able to get out, "I was just going up there to see him." I pull away from her embrace and sniff several times, wiping my cheeks with the back of my hand.

"What did you see, exactly?" she asks, searching my tear-stained face.

Anger grips my stomach thinking about it. "She was leaving his room and was all over him. I saw her plant a kiss on him. That's all I needed to see."

"Damn," Mindy says, not really knowing what else to say. "Bri . . ."

"He's probably been doing the same thing with her!" I half-cry. I don't know why I'm so upset. I should've expected this. The man is a player, and he's not going to stop just because he got a piece of small-town girl tail.

Mindy gives me another hug. "I'm so sorry, Bri. I feel like this is my fault." She pulls back and looks at me.

"Maybe you should put some distance between you two. Can you maybe swap floors with someone so you don't have to clean his room while he's here? That way, you don't have to see him anymore."

I grow quiet, thinking. Mindy's right. Our relationship, or whatever the word you call this thing between Gavin and me, is over. I'm putting in for someone else to clean his room. I won't even fucking say goodbye. Fuck him.

"You're right," I say, straightening up and heading toward the counter. I need a shot of something to help me deal with the stress I'm feeling. "Fuck Gavin 'Anaconda' Adams. Got anything strong back there?"

CHAPTER 18

GAVIN

The next morning, my hands tremble as I button my shirt. But they're not trembling because of nervousness. They're trembling because of what I'm about to do.

After Leslie left, I sat there, thinking about what to do. It was a struggle, debating with myself. My heart was on one side and my brain on the other.

In the end, my brain won.

I have to tell Brianna that we should stop now.

It'll be the hardest thing I've ever done. I like her. She's real. Genuine. The opposite of the fake gold diggers who usually throw themselves at me.

It's hard though. I'd rather tell her that I want to take her out to dinner tonight when this filming is over, that maybe it'd be possible for me to see her during the weekends or during some of my off time during the season.

But that's not fair to her. I'm just being selfish.

This is for the best.

I tell myself this over and over while I'm getting dressed. But I just feel horribly conflicted. My heart is refusing to give up without a fight.

I pull my pants on and buckle my belt. And then I make sure the knots on my shoes are perfect. I retie them twice before I realize what I'm doing. *Wasting time.* I'm trying to do everything but what I *need* to do. I scowl at myself in the mirror, clenching my fists. "You're a bastard," I growl at my reflection. *For what you're about to do.*

I quell the urge to slug the mirror with my fist. Instead, I slowly make my way to the coffee shop, dreading every moment and hoping that Brianna won't be there.

Opening the door to the coffee shop, my heart skips a beat when I see Brianna standing there with Mindy. A part of me wants to turn back now before it's too late. There is still time for me to just grab a coffee and walk out and pretend I'm here on a little social visit.

But that's not what I do.

"Hey," I say, getting their attention. I stop as soon as they both look up at me, their eyes burning with aggression and anger. Brianna's eyes, in particular, are as cold as ice.

"Hey," I repeat, forcing myself to take a step forward. "You look good today."

Brianna is tight-lipped, looking like she wants to choke the shit out of me.

I frown, not sure what's going on. The last time we were together, she was happy. "Brianna?" I ask. "What's wrong?"

When she doesn't answer, I look to Mindy, who's strangely quiet. Very unusual. She's standing behind the counter, cleaning a mug and avoiding my gaze. There's no smile. There's none of the normal wisecracks or smirking that are what I've come to associate with Mindy. She's not her usual self. Something is *definitely* up.

"Seriously. What's going on?" I repeat.

Brianna slams her coffee cup down so hard it almost breaks and causes me to take an involuntary step back. "Don't you have a movie to film?" she asks with venom in her voice.

She's so mad she's practically trembling. All of my thoughts of trying to end it with her flee. The only thing I care about now is finding out why she's so angry. "I was just stopping by for a coffee before I start filming," I lie. I can't tell her I was here to break it off now. "Can we talk?"

She scowls at me. For a moment, I'm not sure if she wants to say yes or take the fork on the countertop and stab me in my balls. "Just for a second. Please."

Brianna continues to scowl at me before finally letting out a defeated sigh. Mindy jerks her head toward the back, and I go around the counter, allowing Brianna to lead me into the storage room. It feels weird to be back here, but whatever's going on, I want it to be in private.

"Listen—" I begin to say, but Brianna cuts me off with a shot right in the middle of my chest.

"I saw you!" she hisses in rage. "I should've known better!"

"Huh?" I ask, confused now.

"I saw Leslie Hart leaving your room. I saw her kiss you. You know, your co-star you tried to act like you were nonplussed about. I saw . . ." Brianna says, punching me right in the chest again. Maybe it's a country girl thing or maybe she's that damn angry with me, but Brianna's got some pop to those punches. If she weren't so upset, I'd be turned on.

"Wait a minute," I protest, trying to defend myself without having to grab her. "It wasn't like that." I shake my head in confusion, trying to get my words right. Why the hell does she think I was getting it on with Leslie? The little peck on the cheek at the door? "Listen to me, Brianna, this is all just one big misunderstanding."

She ignores me, convinced in what she saw. "I don't want to ever see you again. I should've listened to myself. You're just one big player . . ."

Brianna turns away, but I can see her shoulders shaking and I know she's crying.

Seeing her cry tears at my heart. Even though I came down with the intention of breaking things off, I can't let it end like this.

"Brianna, don't," I say, placing a hand on her shoulder. I want to turn her around, to pull her into my arms and admit that I was stupid. That I'm scared. I'm scared that I'm starting to *need* her.

Brianna spins, slapping me across the face and making my head rock back. "Don't fucking touch me!"

Mindy barges into the room at the sound of the commotion. Seeing Brianna's frazzled state, she rushes to her side and pulls her into a fierce, protective hug. Brianna starts to sob as Mindy holds her and strokes her hair.

"I think it's best if you just leave," Mindy says, shaking her head.

"I just need a chance to explain," I say, still confused. "But I will . . . for now."

"Go away," cries Brianna, her voice muffled by Mindy's chest. "Go break somebody else's heart."

Setting my jaw, I walk out of the coffee shop feeling like shit. I don't have the time to wait till Brianna calms down. I've got to be on set in the next few minutes. I barely make it to my car before a small group of paparazzi runs up, their cameras flashing in my face.

"Anaconda, have you shown Leslie Hart the snake yet?" one of them asks, grinning like a perverted high school boy.

I'm enraged, and it's only by a small miracle that I don't punch him right in the face. Instead, I shove them out of the way and get in my rental, speeding off like a bat out of hell.

❄

My mood hasn't improved by the time I'm on set. And at this point, the entire production team is avoiding me like the plague, only talking to me if they have to. I don't blame them.

I'm royally pissed. Somewhat at Leslie, who just came to talk professionally, but given my reputation and what Brianna saw, I can see how she misinterpreted it. I'm trying not to take it out on Leslie, but it's hard not to.

I should have just told Brianna right then it wasn't what it looked like. Leslie wasn't in my room for a booty call. And the hug and kiss were nothing.

A part of me wonders if I should just let her hate my guts. After all, five seconds before I opened the coffee shop door, I was ready to break it off with Brianna. This should be for the best.

But I can't end it this way. For the first time in my life, if I'm going to end it, I want to end it with letting her understand that I don't want to. That I'm ending it because she deserves better, even if I'm not the douchebag the media makes me out to be. I won't end it with her thinking I treated her like she didn't matter.

"Cut!" Jim yells, throwing his pen across the room and against the wall. "What the hell is going on, Gavin? I thought you were getting the hang of this!"

"Ow!" Leslie yells, getting my attention. I look down, realizing that my fingers are digging into her arm so deeply that she might develop a bruise.

Shit. I might be pissed at her, but that's no reason to hurt her. I let go, watching as the marks on her arm go from pale white to an angry pink. "I'm sorry," I mumble. "My mind was somewhere else."

"You were supposed to be taking her hand to put the engagement ring on it, not ripping her arm off and chewing on it like this is a zombie movie!" Jim snarls.

I give him a look, but I turn to Leslie. I need her help. "I need a moment with Leslie," I tell him, looking her in the eyes and ignoring Jim. "Just a couple of minutes."

"But . . ." Jim starts to object, but I'm already moving Leslie off the set and toward my trailer.

I yell over my shoulder, "Five minutes!"

There's a general rumble, but nobody makes too much fuss as I lead Leslie inside my trailer. As soon as the door closes, I step away, giving her space. I need to talk to her, not scare the shit out of her after what I just did to her arm.

"Okay, Gavin, I didn't scream bloody murder," she says as soon as we're alone. "So what's this all about?"

"About last night," I say. "And your visit to my suite."

"What about it?" she asks, rubbing her arm. "It obviously did you no good. You absolutely suck today. I thought you said you were going to work out your problem?"

I suck in a calming breath. She has no idea what's going on, and I know she didn't mean to cause any trouble. "You caused someone to get upset with me with that little visit."

"What?" Leslie gawks at me for a moment, then laughs in disbelief. "What on earth are you talking about?"

"Someone I care about got the wrong idea," I explain. "She saw when you left my room and thought . . . well, do I need to spell it out?"

Leslie scoffs. "Seriously?" She makes a face and then does a little laugh. "Well, I can certainly see how she'd think that, considering your reputation."

I let out a groan. "Please don't start with that. I hear enough about it already."

Leslie coughs, still grinning. "Sorry."

I'm silent for a moment, thinking. "Leslie, have you ever felt like you cared about someone? I mean, really cared about someone . . . but you know that it's stupid? That it probably won't work out, but deep inside, you wanted to say fuck it all? That no matter how stupid it might be, you want to be with them anyway?"

Leslie looks at me in shocked silence. "Yeah . . ." she says softly after a moment, looking up at me with distant eyes that are sad and yearning for something beyond the trailer. "I have." Her eyes refocus on my face. "What's this all about, Gavin?"

I take a deep breath, knowing I'm about to break one of the cardinal rules for a single guy. Simply put, never, ever talk with another woman about a girl that I'm dating, or seeing, or whatever it is I want to think of Brianna as. "Well, there's this girl that I've been seeing since I got to town—"

Leslie snaps her fingers, her face immediately lighting up in a huge smile. "I knew it! The way you've been acting was like a lovesick puppy. I saw it in my brother, about three years ago. He was stupid for days." She shakes her head sadly. "Too bad, too. He was totally taken by that damn gold digger."

I half chuckle. "Yeah, I guess. But she's not like that."

Leslie's smile dims somewhat after a moment. "Does Miranda know?"

"Hell, no. And I'd like to keep it that way," I tell her. Miranda's always looking for an angle on how to turn something into a publicity stunt. I don't want Brianna's picture plastered all over the tabloids.

"Oh, boy," Leslie says, reading my face and sighing. "That's not good. Keeping things from your agent."

"I'll worry about Miranda later. In the meantime, I need you to help me smooth things over with Brianna."

Leslie gives me a look, and I can tell what she's thinking. She wants to stay out of it. "I don't know . . ."

I look down, my cheeks red. "I know it sounds like some high school drama shit, but I just want to put her mind at ease."

Leslie stares at me for a long time before finally letting out a resigned sigh. "Okay. But she's not gonna grow claws and rip my face off as I walk through the door with you, is she?"

I chuckle. "No."

"You sure? You're Gavin 'Anaconda' Adams, and this girl sounds like she jumps to conclusions. I'm sure you've had some psychos before."

I shake my head. Sure, I've had some creepy fans before, but Brianna's not creepy. In fact, I think I understand what she's feeling. "Nah. You'll be fine."

"Okay," Leslie says, shaking her head. "If something happens, I'm going to hold you for the damages. My career's done if I end up with three-inch-deep nail marks on my face."

I laugh at the sour look on her face and wave away her concern. "Totally won't be necessary. I promise, you'll like her. Once you get to know her, you'll see she's the sweetest girl in the world."

CHAPTER 19

BRIANNA

I groan, trying to stretch a little. Damn, my back is killing me. I try to ignore the pulsing pain as I walk into the coffee shop after my shift. I feel like hell, and I know I should change clothes out of my maid uniform, but right now . . . I just don't give a shit.

"Rough day?" Mindy asks when she sees me. She looks so pretty in her black skirt, tan apron, and light blue blouse, her hair so glossy and her makeup still looking flawless. Meanwhile, I feel like I'm a poster child for frumpy.

I'm envious that she gets the easy work. She gets to stay in one place and make coffee all day, chatting with customers, getting tips, and flirting with whoever she wants to flirt with while my ass has to break my back changing mystery-stained sheets and vacuuming up coochie hair balls out of the fucking carpets.

I take a deep breath, lean against the counter, and let go of my envy. It's not like Mindy lords her job over me. And I know she'd love it if I could work here too. "Rough? How about . . . I'm just so fucking sick of this shit!"

Mindy gasps a little. She's not used to my being so blunt in uniform, especially in the shop. "Babe . . ."

I shrug. In reality, today wasn't any worse than my typical day. What made it so hard was the invisible weight that I had dragging on my neck all day.

Gavin.

I nearly told him I hated him, and I would have if he'd stayed any longer.

It hurts, and I don't want to admit it.

Somehow, even though I told myself not to get worked up, I'm heartbroken over his betrayal. I was opening up to him. I really thought we could maybe work something out. How could I be so foolish to think I could be anything but some plaything?

To see him with that tall, gorgeous blonde . . .

"Are you okay?" Mindy asks, drawing my eyes to her. I look down and see that my knuckles are turning white from how hard I'm making a fist.

"Yeah," I lie. "I'm fine."

"I don't know about that," Mindy argues, biting her lower lip. "For a second there, you looked like you wanted to murder me!"

I want to murder someone, I think inwardly. But Mindy is my best friend, and I know she cares about me.

"I'm just tired, that's all."

Mindy leans in, her eyes soft and concerned. "It's Gavin, right?"

Just hearing his name is like a stab to the heart, but still, I shake my head, staring at my balled-up napkin. "No."

Mindy arches an eyebrow and lifts my chin with her finger. "We've been friends for years, Bri. Don't lie to me. You don't have the skills for it."

She scowls at me for a long time, and I try to scowl back, denying everything before I nod and sigh.

"Yes, he's been on my mind all day. But I'm trying to—"

"What the fuck," Mindy mutters, cutting me off as she stares straight past me. "The nerve of that son of a—"

I turn around, and my heart freezes in my chest as red pulses of rage start to fill my vision.

How dare he!

Gavin, looking as sexy as always, walks in with the same blonde bimbo at his side. She's dressed in a super-sexy, clingy red dress, black heels, and a black belt at her waist. Leslie Hart might as well have *You Know You Want This* written on her the way she's dressed.

I'm too shocked to move or do anything. He must be coming to torment me and make fun of me for being stupid. He's just here to flaunt his A-list whore in front of my eyes.

"Coffee shop's closed," Mindy tries to say, her voice dripping acid, before she adds under her breath, "especially to cheap dyed blondes."

"No, it's not," Gavin says. He has a determined look in his eyes, but when he looks at me, I'm not sure what's going on behind his baby blues. "It says open until eight."

"Well then, I'm on break," Mindy says, not backing down in front of the man who's twice her size. "Come back in an hour. Preferably when we're not here."

Gavin's voice is firm, unmoved by Mindy's frigid tone. "Good thing I'm not here to see you then."

Ignoring Mindy, Gavin turns to me. "Brianna—"

"Don't even try it," I tell him, poking him in the chest. "You have some nerve coming in here with her!"

"Listen, Leslie and I aren't together."

I scoff. "Please. Let me guess, you guys are just *friends?*"

"Gavin is telling the truth," Leslie cuts in, placing a hand on his arm. "We're not together. We're just professional acquaintances. That's it."

I glare at her hand on his arm, my nostrils flaring. Seeing my fury, Leslie jerks it away as if she's touching a hot stove.

Gavin and Leslie exchange glances, and she mutters something under her breath that I don't quite hear. I'm sure she's insulting me, and whatever she's saying, it makes me even madder.

I'm about to go off on her, but before I can reply, a gruff but falsely-accented voice comes from the back room. "What on earth is going on here?"

Vandenburgh. Great, just what I need right now. He waddles out, his face pinched and his glasses pushed halfway down his nose. "Miss Sayles, what are you doing in uniform? And why is it that you're spending all this time talking to guests anyway? You're a maid, not a concierge."

I really am not in the mood. In fact, Vandenburgh can kiss my ass. I turn to him, about to open my lips to tell him what he can go do with himself, when Leslie suddenly lets out a surprised gasp.

"Oh, my goodness, Montclaire, it's you!" Leslie suddenly exclaims with an overly dramatic, stuffy British accent. I think she might have gotten it from Masterpiece Theater or something. She stares at Vandenburgh with wide eyes, leaning over just enough to give him a glance at the valley between her huge tits.

"Huh?" Vandenburgh asks, thrown off guard. "Miss Hart, what are you . . ."

Leslie walks over to Vandenburgh, a huge smile on her face. "Oh, don't act like you don't know it's me, my dear. We've been trading correspondence for months. I just didn't realize I'd finally get to meet you. Why didn't you say something? We've been voice chatting for a long time now."

"We have?" Vandenburgh says with confusion, flushing bright pink as Leslie pushes her boobs up against his shoulder and rubs his cheek.

Leslie smacks her forehead, raising her eyes to the ceiling. "Yes, darling! Don't you remember?" She smiles sweetly and looks down at Vandenburgh's nether regions. "You said you needed a beard so that your peers wouldn't know your little secret."

Leslie's act is so smooth, I almost believe her. Behind me, Mindy giggles a little. If there's a man who deserves to be humiliated, it's Vandenburgh.

Vandenburgh still looks stunned. "I did . . .?" he says, before scowling. "No, I didn't! What are you on, Miss Hart?"

Leslie laughs, squeezing Vandenburgh's cheek. "Oh, Vandypoo! It's me, Morticia, my love. And yes, you did. I think you're just delirious and it's time to take the medicine you told me about."

She wraps her arm around Vandenburgh, turning him toward the front door of the coffee shop. "Now, let's go get you a bath and get you in a diaper, just like you like."

She leads Vandenburgh from the room while he sputters, still off guard.

"You're totally insane!"

Leslie leans over and kisses him on the top of his head, and I don't think I've ever seen a man turn that red that quickly in my life. "No, that's just you hallucinating, darling. Come along now, I have your powder and pacifier ready."

The two disappear from view, Vandenburgh still not sure what to do. The glass door closes, and Gavin grins at me while Mindy laughs so hard I think she'll crack a rib. "Now do you believe me?"

I cross my arms across my chest. "That doesn't mean anything," I say stubbornly, but my defenses are crumbling. I highly doubt Leslie would've done that if they were here to be spiteful. She just saved me from getting fired.

"I don't know, Bri," Mindy says, still gasping. "To get that close to Vandenburgh with that little act? She's *got* to be telling the truth."

Gavin mouths a *thank you* to Mindy as my expression softens. "Now will you listen to me?"

I stare at him long and hard. It's hard to just drop my anger in an instant. But finally, I nod my head. "Two minutes."

Gavin takes a deep breath, and what comes out is a bit of a rush of words, as if he's really being timed. "What you saw that night wasn't what you think. Leslie was just there to find out what was going on with me because I couldn't deliver my lines."

I stare at him, letting it process, seeing the sincerity in his eyes.

"It was because of you," he confesses.

I gape. "Me?"

Gavin nods and reaches for my hands, and I find myself holding his fingers as he looks at me, his eyes burning with intensity as he speaks. "I can't even think without you near. The only way I can seem to get a halfway convincing line out is to imagine I'm talking to you and not Leslie."

I'm breathless at the conviction in his words, my heart racing like a track horse. I would've never known.

"And lately," he says, swallowing, "I don't even think I can breathe without you." By now, sweat has formed on his forehead, and as prideful as he is, I know it's taken a lot for him to admit something like this. Especially in front of Mindy.

All the doubts I feel fall away like leaves in the wind as I stare into the sincerity in his eyes, my heart feeling like it's bathing in warmth.

"Well isn't that sweet," Mindy mutters in awe, shaking her head. "Bri's pussy must be slammin'."

I'm so enthralled with Gavin's gaze that I can't even rebuke Mindy for her crassness.

171

Gavin takes me in his arms, pulling me close and putting his hands around my waist. "Can you forgive me?"

This close up, I can feel the warmth radiating from his hard body. I know I should tell him that I need time to think this over. But we don't have time. He'll be gone in a few days. And I don't want to waste another second being mad at him.

If I only have a few days with Gavin, then I'm going to use every second of them.

I put my arms around his neck and stand on my tiptoes, pulling him down into a soft kiss that is electric, not because it's arousing, but because there's emotion behind it that I never thought I'd feel.

"There's nothing to forgive," I breathe softly, looking into his eyes. "Let me change clothes, and then I want you to come with me."

"Where?" he asks, smiling. His beautiful eyes seem to pierce right through to my heart.

"To see the rest of me," I reply softly.

CHAPTER 20

"*T*urn right," Brianna says.

I do as she says, turning the Lotus at a corner and glancing over at her, my heart pounding in my chest.

She's changed out of her hotel uniform, and while it's nowhere near as exposing as the simple sundress she wore on our park date, I'm still enthralled by the simple t-shirt and jeans that she's wearing. "Up there by the gas station."

After we made up in the coffee shop, I was a little surprised when Brianna explained what she meant by seeing the rest of her. I almost expected her to ask me to take her back up to my suite. I guess my mind was in the gutter.

Going to her apartment probably would've scared me twenty-four hours ago. But now I'm excited to see this side of her, the real woman behind the eyes. "Okay, now what?"

"It's the brown apartment building up there on the right," Brianna says, pointing. I take a look at the building, and my first thought—it's a dump. Even back in my college days when I would visit friends or teammates who had apartments off campus, none of them lived in a place like this. It looks like the sort of place where you carry a BB gun to shoot the rats on a daily basis.

I glance over at Brianna. "So this is where you live?"

Her cheeks burn, and I realize that I may have hurt her feelings a little even if I didn't mean to. "Sad, isn't it?" she says in a melancholy tone, looking down in her lap. "I'm sure it's totally beneath anything that you've lived in, and that's why I didn't want to have you drop me off here after our date."

I shake my head and reach over to put a comforting hand on her thigh. "I'm not going to judge. I'm glad that you feel comfortable enough to show me where you live."

"You know, Gavin, you can say all the nice things you want to try and make me feel better, but the fact is . . . this place is a dump. And I don't know if you'll understand."

I rub her knee, partly to reassure her and partly because it's one hell of a knee. "I might be spoiled, but I'm not irredeemable. I want to genuinely get to know you, every part of you."

She blushes, and I get out of the car before her nervousness makes her ask me to take her someplace else. I help her out, realizing that this apartment has probably never seen a red Lotus sports car in front. I make sure I lock it before I gesture toward the building. "Lead on, please."

It's hard for me to keep from staring at her ass as she walks up the stairs in front of me, but when she stops halfway up and glances back, she smiles. "See anything you like?"

I nod, flashing her a boyish grin, my cock twitching in my pants. "Maybe."

Brianna laughs, blushing a little. "You're good at giving a hell of an ego boost, that's for sure."

We make our way up the rest of the stairs, and she leads me down the concrete walkway which has lines of laundry strung up on one side all the way to the end of the building. Brianna looks back at me nervously as she takes out her keys and puts one of them in the lock. "Last chance. If you want, we can go back to the suite instead of putting you through a night of torture."

I shake my head and put my hand over hers on the key and door-knob. "No. I want to see you."

She stares at me long and hard, biting her lip nervously. Finally, she shakes her head and then turns the key in the lock. "All right. Just don't say I didn't warn you."

There's a muted click, but instead of opening, Brianna has to lower her shoulder, shoving her way into the apartment. I help a little, and after a small fight, the door springs free and we step inside.

The first thing that hits me when I walk in is the smell. It's wet, like the place hasn't been aired out in a while, and it's musty, almost dank. If I didn't know better, I'd almost say it smells moldy.

It's dark and I can hardly see. I hear footsteps cross the room, and a single lightbulb comes on, casting faint illumination around the place.

Brianna spreads her arms out wide to either side, a grimace on her face. "Welcome to my home."

I suck in a deep breath. *What a shit hole*. It kills me that she lives like this.

The paint is peeling off the walls in places and the drywall is water-spotted in others, saggy and soft looking. The carpet is ragged, so threadbare that I can see the base material in spots. The furniture is all secondhand, and her table is being held up by a chunk of scrap wood on one side. Her couch looks like it'll collapse if I sit on it, and in the corner . . . shit, I don't want to even know what that is.

"See?" Bri says, her voice shaky as she sees the shock on my face. "I told you. Better than the White House."

I grin. At least she's keeping her sense of humor. "I had no idea."

Anger courses through my stomach. Whoever runs this place is a true slumlord.

"This is why I spend so much time at the hotel," Bri admits. "I hate being here. And I'm ashamed to have anyone over. I think you've joined a group of five people I've actually let inside."

Her voice firms, and I see the strength that is deep inside her come out. "But it won't be for long. I'm determined to make my way out of here. I've already picked out a nice little apartment on the west side. One with two bedrooms. I'm just waiting until I graduate and get something more long-term than working for Vandenburgh."

I walk over and sit down on the couch, my fears of collapse forgotten, and gesture Bri over. She bites her lower lip as she comes and sits beside me. As soon as her ass settles into the seat, my nose is tickled by a plume of dust.

I try to hold it in, but I sneeze, twice, my head rocketing forward to spray hard as I try to hold it back. "Sorry."

"Bless you," she says softly. She grabs a box of tissues off her rickety coffee table and hands it to me. "I haven't been able to dust in a while. I'm only part time, but I've been picking up extra shifts where I can while school is on break. You would think being a maid, I would keep it cleaner, but it's hard. I swear, the dust just grows in this place."

I sniff as another sneeze threatens. I gain control, shaking my head. "God damn."

"Yeah," Bri says. "Exactly."

My eyes are watery, and I have to wipe them with a tissue before I can focus on her. "How long have you lived here?"

"Since my parents left. When they split and I chose not to go with either of them, I had to find a place to live since they sold our home. At the time, I had a little savings from the odd jobs I worked in high school, and my Dad, as a sign of his generosity, gave me a thousand bucks and said he'd cosign since I was under eighteen at the time."

"Why put yourself through that?" I ask, still not understanding. Sure, she has college, but she's smart enough to get into anywhere, I'm sure of it. "Why stay here when you could have gone with them and lived a better life?"

Brianna's given me quite a few looks in our short time together, but for the first time, she gives me a look that makes me feel dumb. "A better life? Ha, I could argue that point. Mom gets on my last nerve, Gavin. I was never good enough for her. Daddy wasn't either. It would only be a day at our new place before we'd be at each other's throats."

"What about your father? Why not move with him then?" I ask.

She shakes her head. "Bless his heart, he has tried his best. He's rebuilt his life a lot too. But I wouldn't be able to deal with having a stepmother younger than me. I don't blame him. I've Skyped with them both, and she does seem to love him, but still . . . no. It's just too weird for me."

I shake my head, shocked. "But it seems like you would have just gone there for a little while, gotten yourself together, and left when the opportunity presented itself. Why stay here away from them?"

Brianna sucks in a deep breath and looks around the shitty apartment. "I've thought about that, and I guess the truth is that I love this place. It's the only place I've ever known. And it's mine. It's shit, but it's shit that I've paid for with my own hard work. And the community is small and caring. I like being a part of it. Maybe someday, I can give back."

My heart tugs in my chest at her words and I stare at the earnest look on her face. She seems so pure. I hardly deserve someone like this. It makes it even worse that in a few days . . .

My throat is tight as I say, "That is admirable. I respect that. I really do."

A blush comes to her cheeks and she looks away. "Thanks."

"You could've easily just gone with one of your parents and had a better life. Softer, at least."

She shakes her head. "My goals and ambitions must be boring and stupid to you. I'm sure you're used to the big city life and have everything. The cars, the houses, any woman you want . . ."

Not everything, my inner voice says. *Not yet. She's not yours yet.*

I clear my throat and shake my head. "Speaking from experience, none of that stuff means much. You can have all the money in the world, but it definitely doesn't bring happiness. Brings a lot of leeches, but not happiness."

I sit back against the couch, fighting back another sneeze. "You know, when I came here, I never thought it, but a part of me thinks that I would be happier living in a place like this. Well, like this town, not like this apartment."

Brianna stares at me like I'm a two-headed dragon. "Really? That's hard to believe."

I nod. "Really. Maybe I've had my fill. I don't know. Sure, staying in the best hotels and having luxury homes and cars is nice, but there is a downside to it."

My voice drops, becoming grimmer than I'd like as I realize I'm fully exposing myself to Brianna, something I haven't done with anyone before. Not to mention, I probably sound like an asshole who takes things for granted. "When I signed my rookie contract, I gave up any chance of having a private life. Every detail about me, flaws and all, is out there for the public to scrutinize. You're dissected and judged, oftentimes before you even know what you've done wrong."

I shake my head. "And the paparazzi are relentless, always coming at you when you least expect them, trying to get another embarrassing shot to sell to the papers."

"That does sound like it sucks," Brianna says. "And it's partly why I'd never want to be a celebrity. I couldn't handle all that scrutiny."

I nod. "Good. You'd hate it. I have to admit, at first, I loved the fame and fortune. The money's nice for sure. I have a big ego."

"And a big . . ." Brianna says with a soft laugh, wiggling her eyebrows at me.

I laugh, glad to feel a bit of humor in all of this, and continue. "But after a while, it gets old. A part of me wants my old life back. Just plain old Gavin."

Brianna gives me an inquisitive look. "What's stopping you from giving it up then? Retire from football, do this movie, and walk away."

I scratch at the stubble on my jaw, the stubble that I'm supposed to keep for my role, and think. "I guess I just don't want to disappoint anyone. My teammates, my coach, my family—all of them, in some way or another, depend on me. And I don't want them to think of me as a quitter."

Brianna places a soft, gentle hand on my thigh and fixes me with a deep look. "I can understand that."

Warmth heats my stomach and my cock hardens in my pants. It doesn't care about the emotions I'm showing. It just loves the touch of her hand on me. "So yeah, when you mention the money and the fame . . . it doesn't mean much to me. It can't replace a real person or the emptiness inside."

"Are you?" she asks softly.

My breath is heavy, and I turn to her, feeling exposed but liking it. "Am I what?"

Brianna stares into my eyes and leans close, her natural perfume overcoming the smell of the apartment. "Are you empty inside?"

Her words hit me hard. I've been the way I have been because I've been looking for something for so long, and now I think I've . . .

I begin to shake my head. "I don't think so anymore—"

"AH-CHOO!" Brianna sneezes violently, spraying my face with a gentle mist. I rear back, surprised, and she covers her mouth and nose, shocked and embarrassed.

"Oh, my God!" She gasps in embarrassment, her face flaming red as she tries to lift her shirt to wipe at my face. "I'm so fucking sorry. It's just that this goddamn dusty ass old couch—"

I hook my hand beneath her chin, bringing her eyes to mine. "Don't worry about it. I want you, Brianna. Every bit of you. Snot and all."

"You're really weird!" Brianna gets out before she has to laugh, and after a second, I can't help it and join in. Somewhere in that laughter, I draw her to me and our lips smash together.

My hands move on their own, running over her lush curves, hungry to feel her as she groans into my mouth. The couch creaks as she falls back and I get on top of her, greedily kissing her, my lips all over her body. I'm starving, and I'm going to have my fill.

My hands find her breast. Her nipples are hard, and I pinch them lightly through her shirt, making her moan and push my head down. "Gavin, I need you."

I look up, my heart pounding in my chest as I admit the truth. "I need you, too."

Brianna strokes my hair and smiles, swallowing. "Then not on the couch . . . or my bed." She chuckles. She looks at me with lust. "The floor?"

I look at the suspect carpet, and she laughs, getting off the couch and pulling her t-shirt off. "I'll go get a sheet. Trust me, those I get from the hotel. Don't tell Vandenburgh."

I chuckle and shake my head, kissing her hungrily as we get to our feet and her hands roam over my back, lightly scratching me through my shirt. "Your secrets are safe with me."

Brianna walks down the dim hallway, tossing me a smoldering look over her shoulder as she disappears into the next room. "And you're wearing too many clothes!"

I laugh and start stripping, listening as I hear a closet open before a quiet minute passes. When Brianna comes out of what I guess is her bedroom, she's fully stripped, wearing the sheet around her body like a toga, and my cock surges, standing straight out from my body as she smiles.

I pull her close and kiss her deeply, the sheet between us adding to the whole feeling. I can feel her hard nipples against my chest and the warmth of her skin as my cock presses against her hip, my hand going down to cup her ass and squeezing.

She moans as I kiss down her neck to suck at her throat, half squatting. I sink to my knees as I kiss over the cotton, sucking at her nipples and making her gasp as I tug on the fold of the sheet, working my way inside. "What are you doing?"

"Keep the toga on and I'll give you a special treat," I say before kissing the soft skin of her hip. She moans, and her hand pushes on my head through the sheet. I know what she wants, and it's the only thing on my mind too.

I ease Brianna's thighs apart with soft butterfly kisses until I can see the pink wetness of her pussy, and I lick, relishing her tangy sweet essence. It's sexy and erotic. I can't even see her breasts with the way she's holding the sheet as I suck and nibble on her pussy lips before lapping at her clit.

"Gavin," she gasps breathlessly as I torture her clit with the tip of my tongue, circling it over and over before flicking it quickly. I slide a hand up the inside of her thigh, and slide two fingers inside, pumping them in and out in time to my tongue.

"Mmm," I moan into her pussy as she clenches at my fingers, her body wanting more. I slide in a third finger, knowing that if I'm going to have her, I still need to warm her up.

"Fuck!" Brianna says, half stumbling back. I hold her up with one hand on her ass as I suck her clit, my other hand pumping my three fingers in and out of her fast and deep. As I feel her rise up in the wave of her impending orgasm, my cock is hard and throbbing in front of me.

"Come for me," I say, pulling my head back just long enough to say it before I bury my mouth in her pussy again, sucking her clit hard before biting it lightly. Brianna screams in lust, and I feel her ass shake in my hand as she starts to come, the wetness soaking my chin before I can pull myself down and drink the rest of what she releases.

I stand up, kissing my way up her tummy as I pull the sheet away to kiss her breasts before reaching her lips, kissing them gently before my own passion rises up and my own needs take over.

"I didn't think I could keep standing," Brianna says breathlessly, laughing gently as she kisses me back. Her soft hand wraps around my cock as our tongues swirl, and she smiles as she pulls back. "You have no idea how good you are at that."

I laugh, stroking her hair. "Better than I am at acting, that's for sure."

Brianna laughs and kisses me again, kissing down to my chest. I suck in a deep breath as she runs her hands down my chest, sliding her fingers along the ridges of my abs before grabbing my ass and squeezing.

She sinks to get down on her knees, and she holds my cock in both hands, looking up at me with the innocent wanton look that makes me so fucking horny. She pumps me with both hands as she licks her lips. "And how good am I at this?"

I don't have a chance to reply before she opens her mouth and runs her tongue over the head of my cock, teasing around the flare before gently sucking my head.

"Fuck," I groan, throwing my head back. Her sweet little lips feel so good around my cock.

Brianna hums sweetly as she begins slurping and sucking my cock, reaching down to rub her pussy. She wants more, and I want to give her more.

She takes as much of my cock as she can in this position, stroking it and bobbing her head in tandem, slightly gagging on it, but I don't want to force her. She holds my shaft in one hand and slowly massages my balls with the other, pulling to control the fire in my cock and helping draw it out. I groan again as they tighten and become full in her grasp, and I know that I'm going to come if she keeps this up.

"Fuck," I gasp, pulling back carefully and watching as she slurps the last bit of my cock, a line of spit dripping from the tip as she looks at me with questioning eyes. "You keep that up, and this'll be over too fast."

My balls are aching. I want to come so badly, and Brianna gasps, her chest heaving as she catches her breath. But as good as her mouth is, I want more.

"Why?" she asks, looking disappointed, wiping her lips with the back of her hand. "I don't mind."

"Are you ready?" I ask her, ignoring her question to pull her to her feet and kiss her, stroking her back and cupping her ass again.

"For what?" she asks breathlessly, her thighs trembling slightly. She was probably close to getting off again. But she needn't worry. I'm about to blow her mind. If she lets me.

I hesitate. I don't know if she's into it or not, but I have this burning need. The only problem is, I don't know if she'll curse me and kick me out.

But looking at her, I have the feeling that if I don't take the opportunity to at least find out, I'll be sorry. You only live once.

Fuck it. Just say it.

"Anal," I reply.

CHAPTER 21

BRIANNA

*H*is words hang in the air, and the first thought that goes through my mind is *Holy. Fuck.*

My eyes widen in surprise, and I can't help but stare at that gigantic hard cock that's still slick with my saliva. He wants to put that big thing in my ass? My thighs tremble, either from anxiety or anticipation.

"I . . . I've never done that before," I whisper, afraid. My heart is pounding like a war drum. I've never given much thought to anal beyond a few casual thoughts and loving the feel of Gavin's hands kneading my ass. But if I was sore before . . .

"I'll be gentle," Gavin says, sensing my thoughts.

I place a hand to my throat, sucking in a deep breath. A part of me wants to tell him no, but another is turned on by the idea. I didn't think I could take him in my pussy, and he blew my mind. I for damn sure didn't think I could deep throat him, but when I did . . .

"There's some lube in the cabinet, above the right counter," I hear myself say.

Oh, my God, what am I doing?

Gavin arches an eyebrow. "Done this before?"

I chuckle. "No. There are other uses for it, you know."

He laughs and turns, his ass flexing and making my thighs quiver as he walks away. I shiver again as I see his cock ready for me, and with each step, my eyes are glued to it as he walks over and comes back with the small bottle.

"Are you sure you want to do this?" he asks, setting it down on the raggedy end table. "I'm not gonna lie, I want to. But I don't want you to do something you're uncomfortable with."

I swallow thickly and nod. I'm scared but excited. "Yes," I whisper, spreading out my sheet on the carpet. "I trust you."

He sighs in relief, then he looks at me, a little nervous. "So, how do you wanna do this? Missionary or doggy? I suppose it doesn't matter."

I think about it for a minute, thinking how I want it. Finally, I know what I want. I want to see him. "Missionary."

"Missionary it is," he says, grinning and pulling me close. "I was hoping you'd say that."

Putting my hands on my hips, I step back and sink to the sheet, looking up at him nervously.

Gavin grins, and I lie back, spreading my legs and pulling my knees up. He walks over to the couch, getting my cleanest cushion, lifting my hips a little, and tucking it under me. I can feel the difference immediately—my ass is more exposed to him, and I feel open, vulnerable, but thrilled at the same time.

"Pull your knees up a little more," he says, his voice soft and commanding. "And relax. I'm going to rub it in."

My heart begins to pound and race as I do as he says. Oh, my God, I can't believe I'm doing this. "Like this?"

"Fucking beautiful," I hear him mutter. "Perfect."

I shiver, my limbs coursing with anxiety and excitement. I watch him coat his finger in the lube before he blinks and looks at me. "Rub yourself slowly. It's supposed to help."

The cool sensation of the substance causes me to let out a little gasp, and I groan, my right hand going to my pussy to rub as he massages my virgin asshole. My eyes roll back, and I gasp in a little bit of pain as he slips inside, my ass immediately feeling filled as he rubs his finger inside me. "Fuuuu . . ."

"Easy, easy," Gavin says. "Don't start tensing up on me already. The key is to relax. If anything, push out."

I try as he says, and I feel him work into me, my fear easing as he slides his finger in and out of my asshole, opening me up slowly until he adds a second finger, and I feel sexy. Filled. Vulnerable. His. He pulls out and wipes his fingers on the sheet before taking a condom out of his wallet and rolling it on before applying a fresh layer of lube on his cock. He gets up, rising above me and starting to bend down.

I look at him with excitement and also some hesitation. "Gavin?"

"Yes, Bri?" he asks, his eyes filled with concern and tenderness as he presses the big head of his cock against my asshole, pausing.

He's worried that I'm going to change my mind, but that's the last thing on my mind.

"I trust you," I repeat to him again.

He smiles and starts to push. There's a moment of pain at first as my already stretched asshole is stretched even further, and I hiss, nodding when Gavin gives me a look. "Do it."

The pain grows to agony for a second, but then he slips inside, my ass tightening around his cock, and I feel him slide into my deepest, most taboo place. He's huge, but he takes his time, slowly opening me up. It's strange, but my body seems to want to keep pushing him back out, and once he starts in past where his fingers reached, the pain starts again, but the look in his eyes as he mounts me drives me to keep going.

He groans as he slips in and out. "You okay?"

"Give it to me," I gasp, the need to feel him take me overcoming the pain. Also, my ass is loosening. He's taking me, and it's starting to feel good as he starts to rub against my ass, my fingers rubbing my pussy and adding to it all.

Gavin goes in slow strokes so that I'm slowly opened up, the pain and pleasure mixing into a heady mixture that's addictive. Gavin takes my hand off my pussy and replaces it with his own as he gets all the way in, stroking slowly and matching it with his thumb, making me feel a fire in my core that slowly spreads all over my body as he speeds up, his thick cock driving me wilder than ever.

His balls slap against my ass cheeks as he starts to fuck me harder. The sound of our flesh bounces off the walls, making me grunt with him. I reach down, grabbing my knees and hissing.

It hits me hard, different, like a lightning bolt with almost no warning. I'm screaming, coming as I feel him cry out, coming deep in my ass, the condom catching it. Part of me wishes it wasn't there. I want to feel his come inside me.

I collapse, Gavin beside me as he holds me, his cock still in my ass as he rolls me, pulling me on top as we both breathe deeply, trying to recover. Finally, I smile, putting my head on his shoulder. "That was amazing."

He grins, stroking my hair. "I'm glad you enjoyed it. I was worried you'd throw me out when I asked."

I laugh and turn to kiss his lips gently. "No, I don't think I have any limits with you. Everything you do, you wake me up. You make me feel sexier and hotter than I've ever felt before."

Gavin smiles and kisses my nose. "Thank you."

I frown and purse my lips as I feel him slip out of my ass. "But I'm pretty sure I'm not walking straight for at least a week."

Gavin laughs. "You definitely earned it. Just think how Mindy's gonna react when you waddle into the coffee shop tomorrow."

I punch him in the side, laughing. "Hey, how would you like if I put a damn log up your ass right before a game and then joked about it?"

Gavin winces a little from my punch but still laughs. "Not very much, but you've gotta admit it felt good."

"It did," I say, my fingers trembling as I trace his lips. "Thank you."

"No," he says, pulling me into his arms. "Thank you."

CHAPTER 22

*M*y eyes flutter open at a knocking sound. Beside me, Brianna is snoring softly, her head on my chest. It's dark in the room, and the smell of dust hits my nostrils. I wiggle my toes, which are halfway hanging off her twin-sized bed. We'd come here after using her tiny little shower to clean up, both of us so exhausted. I can barely fit on this thing with her, even with her using me as her body pillow. The mattress sucks too. My back would be fucked up for days if I had to sleep on this thing all the time.

Bump.

What the fuck was that? I'm immediately on edge, my heart racing. It's just my fucking luck if someone is trying to break in the first night that I have her this way. But I guess that's a good thing. She won't be taken advantage of. I can protect her. I look around for an object I can use as a weapon, anything, when I see it.

Moonlight is shining through the window and onto the wall, right on the ugly creature's face. It stares back at me with beady little eyes, defiant. This is his house, he's saying. The humans are just sort of bringing in the food. When he sees me move, he scurries off into a tiny hole in the wall and I hear bumping noises and squealing.

There must be a whole family of those fuckers in there. Sounds like there are more rats than people in this building, and Brianna's apartment is their Grand Central Station.

Now that I know there's no intruder, I relax, but I can't help but feel anger tightening my stomach. Brianna shouldn't be in a place like this. Here I am, living in the best of places. Everything is handed to me on a silver platter. And she's living here in this hell hole with a family of rats.

And to think when I came into the town, I hated it because it was just a place that didn't have a busy nightlife and luxury homes. To think that Brianna would sacrifice herself to stay in a place like this so she could one day help contribute to the community she loves.

The whole time, though, she doesn't have anything for herself. A shitty apartment that probably isn't up to building code, a job where the hotel manager is a fucking tinpot Napoleon with a fake British accent, and a single friend.

Actually, she does have that going for her.

Mindy's pretty fucking awesome as a bestie.

I don't have any idea how she does it. I look at her sleeping on my chest, and my eyes feel hot and heavy. She's like an angel, and she's in my arms . . . even if I don't deserve it.

My whole adult life, I've been obsessed with my image and my career. I've taken. I took contracts, I took money, and I took gifts. I took, and other than handing out a few toe-curling orgasms, what have I actually given?

Not a damn thing.

What good have I done with my money besides spend it on myself and pamper my spoiled parents? I give the bare minimum in time and money to charity to keep the team off my ass, and that's it.

I've been so self-centered, I think to myself.

I look down at Brianna, snoring softly against my chest. I feel a tightness in my stomach, a sort of heavy ball that's slowly building. Being with her makes me want to be a better person, a better man. The only thing is, I'm not sure if I could give it all up to be that way. I'm not sure, but I worry that the money and the fame have started to claim me too. I might be addicted to the fame. And she's better than that trap.

"Oh, my little Bunny," I softly whisper, squeezing her arm and placing my chin on her head. "What am I gonna do with you?"

❄

I WAKE UP TO THE SOUND OF RUNNING WATER. I LET OUT A GROAN, early morning sunlight streaming through the window. Yeah, now I know for sure that I'd have back problems in two seconds sleeping on this shitty bed. I look around groggily, hearing a faint hum from the tiny bathroom. Brianna must be in the shower, and I'm tempted to join her.

I yawn and stretch, scratching my stomach as I look down at my cock, which is more than happy at the idea of a morning shower with her. I'm about to get up and give Brianna a surprise when my cell goes off on the nightstand. I have the urge to ignore it, but I know better.

"Yeah?" I say when I pick up, not caring who's on the other end.

"Gavin, where are you?" Miranda growls. Well, good fucking morning to you too, Miranda.

"I'm right where I want to be," I say before I can stop myself. At least I don't tell her who I'm with.

"What the hell is wrong with you? Jim is going nuts over here!" In the background, I can hear yelling, and someone else goes running by, obviously trying to do something in the middle of the chaos to calm Jim down. "You knew this was the last day of filming! Today's the big scene!"

Oh, shit. I just remembered. They might have delayed it, but I'm supposed to film my bedroom scene with Leslie today, and there's another action scene.

"Fuck, forgot. I'm sorry."

"I need you here. Like, ten minutes ago!"

The line goes dead, and I stare at my phone for a second. "Damn."

She hung up on me. That's never happened to me before. Running my hand through my hair, I set my phone aside and get out of bed. I can hear Brianna humming cheerfully in the bathroom, some little pop tune that's been popular recently. Today was supposed to be her day off. We could've spent a lot of time together. We'd even said something about it when we went out to get some drive-through burgers. She's gonna be pissed. I completely forgot about everything else.

I hurry and get dressed. I'm gonna go there smelling like dust in day-old clothes that are slightly wrinkled, but it can't be helped.

I go over to the bathroom door to tell Brianna I'm going, but it's locked. I don't get why she locked it, but maybe it was out of habit.

I look around and find a pen on her nightstand, and inside the pocket of my pants is a piece of paper. I smooth it out and scribble down a note.

Brianna,

Thanks for the night of fun. I haven't had that much fun in a long time. I've gotta run. I completely forgot that it's my last day of filming. Miranda's up my ass and Jim's apparently going nuts over there.

I've left a little surprise for you so you can enjoy your day off. Have some fun. You deserve it.

-G

I reach into my pocket and pull out a clip of cash I keep with me and place it on top of the note. I don't know how much it is. I don't even count it, but I want to spoil her.

After I put the money under the note, I go over to the bathroom. Brianna's still humming softly to herself, barely audible over the shower, and I kiss my hand, putting it on the rickety wood before I quietly walk out.

CHAPTER 23

BRIANNA

The warm water rolls over me as I hum gently in the shower. This is my second shower since last night. I took one right after we had sex to help clean up, but I need another one now.

I can't stop thinking about last night.

I'm aching all over, but it's a good kind of hurt. A hurt that makes me want more. Even now, sitting in the shower with the water running over me, I wonder if he'll come in and take me again in the shower. Any hole he wants. Even now, my body is heating up and my nipples tighten as I think of the way the water would look running over his chiseled body.

My pussy pulses at the image as I turn and let the water hit me. I lower my head, panting, trying to resist the urge to reach down and rub myself.

Simply put, Gavin was amazing. He was everything that I could have ever imagined. He made this shitty apartment feel like a palace, and I was a princess with a naughty streak that he brings out. He was gentle, but then when I was ready, rough enough to make me feel wanton, ridden . . . taken and claimed.

I use up all of my hot water, rinsing myself before I step out. I dry myself off using another one of the luxuries I got from the hotel, a room towel that's been frayed on one corner and was ready for the garbage bin before I saved it, rubbing my skin until I'm pink and dry. Humming softly, my heart starts racing in anticipation. I imagine Gavin is awake now, waiting for me in my bed with a dreamy smile on his face. And maybe he has a way to help me with my still aching body and the voracious need that seems to be inside me when he's around.

I have a glow about myself when I step out into my bedroom, my towel wrapped around my chest loosely to see if I can entice him into one more round.

"Good morning, Mr. Movie Star . . ."

I freeze. The bed is empty. Gavin is gone.

My heart skips a beat and I take a breath. It's not like I have to search. I can turn around and see the entire bedroom. "Gavin?" I call, making sure he hasn't gotten up and gone to the kitchen. "Gavin, are you here?"

There's no response, and a crushing weight settles on my chest. If he were here, he'd answer me. My apartment is tiny as fuck. You can probably throw a paper airplane from one side to the other.

"Why the hell didn't he tell me he was leaving?" I mutter. He was asleep when I got in the shower, or at least he appeared to be. If he had to get up, why not knock on the door and tell me he was leaving?

The thought unsettles me. We'd talked about spending the day together, and now he's gone. Again. I'm not going to make the same mistake, so I look around for a note, confused when I see a stack of money sitting on a piece of paper on my nightstand.

I walk over and pick up the stack of bills. It must be a thousand dollars here. My heart racing, I pick up the note and read it. Anger twists my stomach as I read it. Enjoy my day off? "What the fuck?"

Leaving money with a woman after a night of sex is what men do with prostitutes. And while I feel like Gavin may have tapped into my inner slut, there's a world of difference between being a slut and being a whore. I wrap my arm across my chest, squeezing myself tight. Is that what Gavin thought this was? That by taking my ass cherry, he owed me something? To assuage his guilty conscience, he thinks giving me money will make things better?

I don't want his pity or his sympathy. I've stood on my own long before I even knew who Gavin Adams was. And yeah, I slept with him, but that doesn't mean he owes me anything. A part of me feels like he's just paying this because he knows that he'll be leaving tomorrow and this is his peace offering money.

I sink down onto the bed, barely able to breathe. Seeing the note and the money clip has jolted me out of my trance. I feel like I've deluded myself. He's going to be gone tomorrow. Can I really try to have a long-distance thing with a man who's going to have women throw themselves at him like Gavin Adams? And if I can't, why make my heartache that much worse?

Still, it angers me that he snuck out this morning and cheapened our experience by leaving money.

The more I think about everything, the more upset I get, regardless of his attempt at a nice note.

Eventually, I can take no more. I get up and start getting dressed. My second-best pants, a decent blouse, and just a touch of makeup. Although Vandenburgh is the last fucking person I want to have a chance to run into on my day off, I'm going in to work.

I need someone to talk to. And I know just the girl.

CHAPTER 24

"You're not taking her anywhere," I growl to the man, Kevin, in black leather holding Kara's arm. "If you try it, I'll fucking kill you, you fucking fuck face."

Someone was paid to write this? How many times can I say fuck in a sentence?

"Jack!" Kara cries weakly. She's bruised, bleeding from a cut on her cheek where Kevin's already smacked her around, and she knows what I'm doing is stupid. "Please don't do this. Go and save yourself!"

"No, Kara. I'm not letting him take you anywhere. He doesn't own you. Not anymore." I scowl angrily, stepping forward. My eyes dart around, but Kevin's alone. He looks like he's in decent shape, but I also know that he intends to hurt the woman I love, and come hell or high water, I'm not going to let her get taken away from me again.

Kevin laughs. "Would you listen to this shit? Kara, this prick doesn't even know you more than a few days, and now he thinks he can tell me that your puss isn't mine." He scowls at me. "Fuck off, dipshit. Kara's coming with me."

"Not if I have anything to say about it," I say, balling my fists. A few days? I've known her for years, almost since we were kids, and I've loved her nearly as long. Now that I finally have her, he's not going to take her from me. "Run, Kara, run!"

I rush forward, a roar of anger tearing from my chest while Kara lets out a scream. She tries to pull away from Kevin as I lower my shoulder and hit him in the stomach, lifting him high into the air to try and tear him away from her. When I feel his grip loosen, I turn, slamming him into the floor as we get into an epic struggle.

I began pounding away at him, letting loose with all of the rage that's been building inside me ever since Kara told me the truth about her past. But all of my strength and anger aren't helpful as my fist hits nothing but the wooden floorboards as Kevin deflects my punch. "Asshole!"

Kevin lets out a growl of rage and with a giant heave, throws me off him. I land on my back and scramble to my feet, barely avoiding the boot that goes slamming into the space my head had been seconds before. "You think you can just waltz up in here and take my shit?" Kevin growls, reaching for me. "You're a fucking dead man."

I slam my fist into the side of his face. I've had a few throw downs in my time, and all of the strength and muscle I've built in the auto shop are put behind it. He staggers, whining like a whipped dog as he grabs his face, and I smile. I grab him by his arm and pull him into me, wrapping my hands around him, ready to see if I can dribble his head like a basketball.

"I think you got that wrong, buddy," I growl in his ear. "I just proposed to 'your girl' right before you showed up, and after I'm done whipping the shit out of you, I'm going to take her back to my house and we're going to fuck all night long."

I begin choking Kevin as he struggles against me, raining blows against my abdomen, but I barely feel them. I've taken worse before. His struggles go weaker and weaker, and I think I have him. Suddenly, his knee comes up, hitting me in the balls, and my arms relax, letting him slam his head into my nose hard. Shocked and in pain, I lose my balance and fall backward, hitting my head on the pavement.

All sound goes fuzzy as if I'm underwater, and my vision immediately blurs. Somewhere in the background, I hear several startled screams and the director screaming, "CUT!" as I fade off into the darkness.

Shit.

I guess I fucked up again.

※

OH, MY FUCKING HEAD. I GROAN, BRINGING MY HAND TO MY forehead. I feel like my head's splitting in two. I open my eyes, immediately regretting it as I can feel the light pulse with my heartbeat. My vision is blurred. Not much is really that sharp, but I see a figure in white standing over me.

"Mr. Adams, I'm so glad you're awake," says a male voice. I'm trying hard to focus on his face but it's still blurry. "I'm Doctor Harmon."

"What happened?" I moan, having trouble remembering what went on. I remember starting the fight sequence for the final scene and everything going smoothly. I'd slammed the bad guy, we'd done the point where I was starting to choke him . . . and then just blackness.

"You had a little accident. Fell and hit your head on set," Dr. Harmon says. "Split your head open pretty badly, but nothing that a few stitches couldn't take care of."

No wonder it feels like it's about to explode.

"Am I all right? Any major bleeding?" I ask. Fear clutches me for a moment. The league is super strict on the concussion protocol nowadays, and if I've gotten a bad concussion, I could be sitting on the sidelines doing nothing but holding a clipboard and picking my nose for quite a while.

"You're fine," Dr. Harmon assures me. His face comes in clearer now. He's a short, bald man with patrician features and wide goggle-like glasses. He's looking at me with a faint smile on his face. "The bleeding was just on the surface. The stitches can come out in a week. The rest is just a small concussion. Grade one."

"Fuck," I mutter. A grade one concussion isn't the worst. At least I can feel my damn toes, but it'll still put me on the league's concussion protocol. The team's not going to like that, and there may be a chance I can't get cleared to do the workouts. I'll probably get docked pay. Fuck.

Dr. Harmon chuckles. "It'll be fine, Mr. Adams. I'm sure you'll be on the mend in no time. Just get a lot of rest and take your medication to treat the residual swelling, and I'm sure you'll be able to play. I read your medical history. You don't have a history of them."

"I fucking hope so," I mutter. I know I should be more graceful, but I feel like shit. Still, I try to make a joke. "At least the cut's on my bad side."

Dr. Harmon laughs again. "If you can sign this for me, I'd really appreciate it."

He grabs something from the inside of his white coat. It's a small, folded up girl's t-shirt with my jersey number on it.

I stare at him like he's a two-headed dragon. Is he fucking kidding me? I have stitches in my head, I'm now, for sure, on a concussion protocol, and this guy wants an autograph? "Are you serious?"

He cringes but doesn't relent, holding out a pen to me. "My daughter is a huge fan of yours. And she'd kill me if I didn't at least try. Please?"

I'm about to refuse, but then suddenly, the image of Brianna comes to me. She'd say that pink doughnut lady would do it without a problem. Hell, if he were a guest in the hotel asking for extra towels, Bri would do it with a smile on her face, even if she didn't want to on the inside. The man patched me together. I shouldn't be rude. "Sure. You're right, Doc. Who do I make it out to?"

"Tiffy," Harmon says, and I nod. Before I can scribble a word, he adds, "Could you sign it *Anaconda*?"

I stop for a second, about ready to change my mind. He's violating the laws of his job, and for some reason, I doubt 'Tiffy' is his daughter, but I'm able to stay calm and quickly scribble my signature. "Here. Hope she likes it."

"Thanks so much," Harmon says when I'm done, taking the pen and shirt back from me. "By the way, there's someone waiting outside to see you. I'm going to let her in and then start working on your discharge papers."

"I can go back today?" I ask, surprised but happy.

"You sure can. But like I said, you'll have to take it easy. My nurse, Missy, will be in here to explain the protocol you're supposed to follow before you're released. Just lie back, and we'll have you out of here ASAP."

He extends a hand to me. "It's a pleasure, Mr. Adams. It's not everyday we get someone like you in here."

I shake it. It's a habit, and while the t-shirt was bullshit, I try to be at least a little grateful. "Thank you."

When Harmon walks out, my heart thuds in my chest. He said a woman was waiting to see me. Having heard the news, it's got to be Brianna, right? I try to sit up straighter and look stronger. I don't want her worried about me. When the door opens, in walks . . .

Miranda. Of course, it would be her. I don't know what I was thinking as my heart sinks anyway. "Oh, thank God! You're all right!"

"Hey, Miranda," I say, trying to keep the disappointment out of my voice. I'm happy to see her, but I would prefer Bri here instead. I know news had to have gotten back to the hotel by now, and Mindy would have called her. She has to know.

But she's not here.

The breath tightens in my throat.

Miranda rushes over to my side, trying to peer back behind my head. "You're okay, right? The doctor said you were fine, but they lie all the time. You haven't suffered brain damage, have you—"

"I'm fine, Miranda," I say mildly. "Just a small concussion is all. The doc said that I should be fine, and I'll talk with the team, I guess. Can't hide it, but I think I'll be cleared by the time first practices start."

She breathes, and I'm touched to see the concern on her face. "Thank God . . ." she gets out before she pauses and frowns. "Although one could say you've suffered some kind of brain damage this trip. Maybe a smack in the head will get you back to normal."

"Very funny," I say, laughing. "I know it's been a hard week, but this time it wasn't me!"

Miranda chuckles and finds my stitches, tugging at my hair but not poking them directly. "Seriously, Gavin, I'm so glad you are all right. When I saw you hit your head, I thought for sure it would be something terrible. The sound of your head hitting the ground . . . well, once, I saw a watermelon fall out of a container in a semi truck and hit the pavement. It was kinda like that."

Mmm . . . watermelon. Sounds good right about now. I shake my head. "I'll be fine. Have I gotten any calls?"

"Oh, hell yeah, so many that I had to turn my phone off," Miranda says. "TMZ, ESPN, oh, and the team called too. There was Coach . . ."

I wave them all off. I don't care about them right now. "No one else? Brianna?"

Miranda arches her eyebrow. "No, no Brianna. Who's that?"

I should tell her. It would explain so many things about why I've been acting the way I have been, and the words are on my lips. But why bother? Tomorrow, I'll be gone, and obviously, she doesn't care that I'm injured. She knows as well as I do that she's wasting her time and doesn't want to be hurt.

"Nobody," I say quietly. "I guess."

Miranda peers at me suspiciously. She's known me too long. "You sure?"

"Yes," I say. I let out a groan as a spike of pain pulses through my head. "So I'm going to have to re-shoot that whole scene, I take it? That sucks. I was looking forward to being done with this shit."

Miranda lights up like a light bulb. "Actually, no."

"Huh?"

"Jim decided he would use the footage of you falling and hitting your head and made it so that 'Kara' picks up a gun and shoots that dude, killing him. He said the fight was very realistic."

"What the hell? That will make her look like the hero and me like a pussy. I thought that wasn't supposed to happen until I die."

Miranda shrugs her hands out to the side. "Just roll with it. We're constrained with time and he wasn't sure if you were going to be out for weeks. It would have cost a fortune to extend the filming license. The town jacked up the price when they found out that you were injured—some bullshit line about insurance—so they have to get everything done in just a few hours. There are secondary crews out right now, rushing around town trying to get the rest of the backing shots."

"Damn it," I grumble, but it's halfhearted. A part of me is elated, and another is upset about how I'm going to be portrayed. While I knew I wasn't going to be the star, I was supposed to be pretty badass.

You should be used to it by now, a cruel voice says in my head. *All image, no substance.*

Miranda nods, not knowing my inner dialogue. "Yep. I think he said something like, 'I can't bear another day of Gavin's wooden, cardboard acting, so this is the best thing that could happen to me.'"

Instead of getting mad, I can't help but laugh. The truth hurts, but not in this case. I know my performance has been hindered by a certain someone. The thought of Brianna brings me back down again and my smile quickly fades to a slight frown. "You know what? Fuck that guy."

"But look on the bright side," Miranda says, mistaking my frown as hurt over Jim's insult. "He also decided to go with your idea. They're cancelling the bedroom shoot and using a body double back in Hollywood. And at least this will make all the feminist fans happy with Leslie turning out to be the hero from minute one and you being her boy toy."

I give her a look, one that she reads loud and clear. I'm nobody's boy toy.

"Hey, I'm just trying to put a positive spin on this. You know me. You can now act like you're pro-women's movement in the interviews and be a spokesperson for women's rights!"

I groan, rolling my eyes. Miranda is out of her fucking mind.

"And the best thing of all, kiddo," Miranda says, gently slapping me on the arm. "We can get the fuck out of here by tomorrow evening. Already got the private plane booked for us."

The words should send me into a euphoric state. I can finally be done with all the stress and bullshit I've had to deal with since arriving. But it only causes a feeling of dread to settle onto my chest. Is that all I've got left?

"Gavin," Miranda asks, seeing my expression, a worried look on her face. "Are you all right? Is it your head?"

The dark feelings that I feel threaten to overwhelm me. I know that I'm anything but. I'm in fucking pain. One in my head. One in my heart. And I know which one hurts the most. With massive effort, I'm able to shove down my feelings and put on a fake smile. "I'm fine."

CHAPTER 25

I arrive at the hotel feeling shitty and down. Gavin leaving me with that clip of money shouldn't have made me feel this way. His note did seem sincere, but it bothers me. I don't like handouts, never have. Add in sex the night before, and I can't shake this feeling.

"Bri!" Mindy cries when she sees me walking into the coffee shop, a surprised look on her face. She's helping what looks like a disgruntled middle-aged woman who is put together quite well. She's wearing some nice slacks and a good blouse to go with the stuck-up look on her face.

I'd like to talk with Mindy immediately, but she has a long line of customers. "I'll be right with you in a minute."

I nod my head to her and take a seat in one of the booths, figuring it'll be ten minutes or more before she can get to me. I place my head on the table feeling like crap, waiting to talk to Mindy. As I sit there, I start smelling the cleaner that's used to scrub the tables and nausea begins to creep up from my stomach and through the rest of me. It seems half my life is soaked in this shit, and the other half . . .

I get up from my seat after a few minutes and begin to walk out. One of the reasons I came here is to talk to Mindy, but I'll be a skeleton by the time she gets through serving the slew of people streaming through the doors. I picked a wrong time. The lunch hour is coming in, and she's going to be slammed for a while.

"Bri, wait!" I hear her call behind me. "I have something to tell—"

Her voice is lost as I move through the doors and out into the lobby. There's a crowd here as well, people talking in a babble of voices that roll over each other, impossible to keep track of. It looks like most of the production crew for Gavin's movie. As I pass by, I hear people speaking his name, but I tune them out, intent on doing only one thing.

Near the elevators, I see Vandenburgh standing with a crew of camera people, smiling his face off while somebody interviews him for what I guess is a behind the scenes clip for the DVD home version of the movie. He's got his best suit on, and his chest is so puffed up today that he's nearly straining the buttons as he blathers on to the camera crew.

I stop in my tracks. He seems busy, but I'm not about to walk by him just in case. If he says anything to me, I'm going to be out of a job with the emotions whirling inside me.

That leaves only one option, and I let out a groan at the thought. *The stairs.*

I make it to the stairwell, pausing to look up at the six flights of hell in front of me before I laboriously begin my climb. Each step is a flex of muscles that don't want to be flexed right now. I could take the elevator at the next floor, but I'm actually relishing the pain right now. It gives me something else to focus on.

By the time I reach the sixth floor and Gavin's room, my ass and side are on fire. I'm completely out of breath too, a sheen of sweat on my skin.

I take my pass card out, looking at it in the dim light, and then I pause, thinking. I can get in trouble for this. I'm not on duty. Forget a write-up. Knowing Vandenburgh, he'd probably call the police.

But I have to do this. Gavin is leaving tomorrow. And this will be my last message to him.

I stick the card in the door and hear the click, glancing up and down the hallway once before pushing the door open, making as little sound as possible. The room is still unmade, and the faint aroma of his cologne hits me, making me slightly dizzy. It's so . . . *Gavin*.

Walking in further, I see things that bring back memories of my first night with him. There, on the kitchen counter, are two wine glasses. I see the candles, still in their holders on the table. I sway, nearly overcome with emotion.

I walk over and sit on the bed, thinking about how things could be. What could be. What, in the idle moments afterward, I daydreamed about.

But I know the truth. And I've known it since the moment I met him. My daydreams are just that. Nothing more. The foolish musings of a girl who should have known the difference between a relationship and just getting a good deep dicking.

Mindy's right. I did need it. Not for the orgasms, but to learn that hard lesson.

Taking a deep breath, I walk over to the desk and sit down. I grab the pen and paper and begin writing, but after a moment, I see water drip onto the paper and I wipe at my eyes.

"No," I whisper, tearing the sheet off and balling it up. "No. I'm the one in control. I'm the one in charge."

I start over, and it takes me two more tries to get the words just right and to make sure my hand doesn't shake as I write it. The tears are back as I write the last words. There is really no point in stringing this along further.

A single tear escapes my cheek and rolls down onto the piece of paper. I go to crumple it up and re-write it for a fourth time, but I need to get out of here. I just don't want him to think I was crying.

Sighing, I get up from my seat and leave the room—and my heart —behind me.

CHAPTER 26

GAVIN

"We have a few more press junkets to do tomorrow, you know," Miranda says as she pulls her rented Escalade in front of the Grand Waterways Hotel, "and then you can be free of this place."

I've been discharged after a few hours. In fact, the sun is still up even though it's late afternoon. I feel kind of like a mummy with the white bandage wrapped tightly around my forehead, a present from an over-enthusiastic nurse who wanted to make sure I didn't bleed any more. They gave me a few pills, some of them green and a couple that are pink, and told me everything would be all right and to have the stitches taken out at home in ten days.

I look out the window, a wistful feeling coming over me as I look around the town. "I don't know," I say. "I think I'm starting to like it here. It's been quite charming."

Miranda gapes in shock. "Gavin Adams, you sure that head wound isn't worse than they say? You were practically seething in rage when we first arrived here. I never would've imagined you enjoying a place like this. What's next, ready to go horseback riding?"

Because I've been pampered and spoiled my whole life, I think to myself, *I didn't see the real beauty of such a simple place.*

"You're being overly dramatic," I say, trying to remain calm. Maybe they gave me a shot or something, but I'm not too bad, actually. "You know, the people around here are nice. They care about one another."

Miranda's looking at me like I'm crazy. "Gavin, you're the one who practically took my head off for coming here!"

"Feelings change," I tell her.

Miranda shakes her head. "I guess I should be used to this by now. You've been acting strange ever since we got here, and now with that head wound, you'll be speaking another language soon. You'll be calling me ma'am and using y'all before you know it." She mutters the last bit under her breath.

I chuckle. "You might be onto something . . . ma'am."

Miranda gives me a startled look, then she sees me grinning and laughs slightly. "Okay, I deserve that one. I'll see you in the morning, kiddo."

"See ya, Miranda."

I get out of the car, stretching a little. I'm in pretty good shape, overall, and the paparazzi actually gives me a little bit of space. The worst is just a slight pounding when I finish standing up, but I've had worse from football and not even come out of the game.

Excitement courses through me as I walk through the doors. I was upset about Bri not calling or showing up at the hospital, but after giving it some thought, I figure maybe she hasn't heard the news. She did have the day off, and maybe she got mad and just sat in her apartment, fuming. In some ways, it's kind of cute, the image putting a little pep in my step as I wave to the doorman.

My plan is simple. I'll go upstairs and take a long, hot shower to clean up. I smell like dust, sweat, iodine, and ass. I'll drive over to her place and offer her a fitting apology for having to leave. And then I'll take her out for a date. Anywhere she wants to go.

On my way through the front door, I'm accosted by several crew members on their way out, their bags in their hands. For the most part, people are glad to see I'm okay, but I know some of their enthusiasm is from being relieved they won't have to work with me again. I don't blame them. I totally screwed up.

I'm passing the coffee shop when I see Mindy waving goodbye to a customer, and I feel like I could get information out of her. Maybe she's swapped a few texts or calls with Brianna, and I can get a gauge on how to apologize better.

I walk in, giving her a wave. "Hey."

"Hey!" Mindy says, perking up. She comes around, reaching for my bandage, and I chuckle, letting her touch it. "I heard about what happened on set. Are you all right?"

"I'm fine. It looks a lot worse than it is," I say, reassuring her. I gesture around, seeing the shop. "How's things going here?"

"It's been hectic. Camera people in and out. The whole crew seems to have stopped in at some point today."

"Yeah, a lot of them are leaving. They had flights scheduled out after the last scenes, and I heard they cancelled my bedroom scene, thank God."

"So the movie is done? Even with you having the accident?" Mindy asks, and I nod.

"Yeah. Apparently, Leslie Hart is one big bad ass." I tell Mindy all about the change of plans with the director, and she smirks.

"Seriously?" Mindy laughs, playfully punching me in the chest. "That's crazy. Gonna make you look like . . . well . . ."

"Tell me about it," I say, chuckling. I can't be down with Mindy. Her smile says she knows it's bullshit too. "Hey," I say after a moment. "Have you seen Brianna, by any chance?"

Mindy's face darkens. "I did, actually. She came in here looking sullen and out of it. I told her I'd be right with her in a minute, but she seemed to get fed up and walked out. I tried to tell her to wait but I was slammed, four customers on my docket."

"Do you think she heard about what happened?" I ask, concerned. Did I really piss her off that much?

Mindy purses her lips. "Everyone here was talking about it. You know, you're kinda famous, and the hotel was buzzing with the news."

Her words feel like a lance in my chest. She had to have known and she didn't call to check in. "Okay."

"You all right?" Mindy says, concerned.

"Just a little pounding from my headache." I wave it off. "Look, I'm going to . . ."

Mindy sucks in a breath, biting her lip and changing the subject. "So, you're really leaving tomorrow?"

It's hard to say the words, but I'm beginning to feel this was inevitable. "Yeah. Kinda have to."

Mindy's eyes are sad as she crosses her arms over her breasts and sighs. "Bri is going to hate that. Absolutely hate it."

Coulda fooled me.

"She'll get over it," I say. "We both will."

Mindy shakes her head sadly, giving me a look that says she knows I'm full of shit. "Well, you still owe me an autograph before you leave. If things are gonna fall to pieces, I'll be damned if I don't get at least a piece of the pie."

I chuckle. Bri's right—it's almost impossible to get mad at Mindy. "I'll make sure to bring it in personally tomorrow morning before I leave. I think I have something I can sign better than just a piece of paper for you."

Mindy beams. "Thanks."

I give her a quick handshake of thanks. "You take care, you hear?"

I'm trying to be funny, but it just feels slightly sad. I'm going to miss her. She firmly shakes back. "I will."

"And . . ." I stop, swallowing the lump in my throat. "Take care of Bri for me, will ya?"

Mindy nods, trying to smile, but I can see the glitter in her eyes. "Sure thing. I've been taking care of that rascal since before she could walk."

I smile back. It's better than the other option. "Aren't you two the same age?"

Mindy laughs and wipes at her eye. "Yeah, and?"

"You're impossible," I finally say with a laugh.

Mindy beams, smiling even as the first tear falls. "I wouldn't have it any other way."

I leave the coffee shop, my heart heavy. In the lobby, I'm swarmed by camera men, some crew, and fans. I do my best to engage them all, but I get fed up quickly, pushing my way through at the limits of my patience. When I see Vandenburgh, though, talking animatedly to a crowd, I have to pull him to the side.

"Yes, Mr. Adams?" Vandenburgh says in his uppity faux accent. "I heard about your accident. I'm glad you're all right."

"About Brianna," I say, ignoring his bullshit concern. "When I leave here, I want you to start treating your employees with respect. Brianna especially. No more making her get on her knees and clean floors, insulting her, and threatening her job. You got it?"

The pompous little prick sputters, knocked on his heels momentarily. "Mr. Adams, there are things that—"

"I know an asshole when I see one," I hiss in his ear. "And I am tired of assholes. So, I want you to promise me not to fire her until she quits on you. You got it?"

Anger spreads across his face. But I use my height to my advantage, staring him down. I don't even know what I'm doing or why he would listen to me, but I can't help myself.

"Yes, Mr. Adams," he says finally. "I'll leave Miss Sayles alone."

"Good. Because I don't want to have to start making phone calls." My words sound stupid to my ears, but I need to do something. If I have to end up leaving without talking to Brianna, I want to have at least done something meaningful for her.

I leave Vandenburgh before he can reply and go up to my room on the sixth floor. As I step off, I see Leslie directing a bellhop with her luggage. "Hey, I'm glad you're okay," she says. "I thought for sure that you were really injured."

"Yeah, just a little bump. I'll be fine, and you can see me on Sunday TV."

"It's crazy how things turned out with the movie," she says. "I hope you're not mad about it."

I shrug. I really don't care anymore. "Nah, it's okay. I'm glad you get the chance to shine. My acting was shit anyway."

"Yeah, but I understand." She leans in. "You really should see what you can do about that. I know you really care for her."

"I don't know. We come from two different worlds."

"And that's where the most explosive things happen, when two different worlds collide."

I chuckle at the aptness of her remark. "Like football and Hollywood?"

Leslie shakes her head. "Just . . . don't be like me and lose something you'll regret for the rest of your life."

Her words are heavy on me. I don't know what to say.

"Listen, handsome," Leslie says as she sees me lost in thought, chucking me on the arm. "I'll catch you later at the press promotions for the movies. And I'll make sure not to stay on your arm just in case. And maybe if you have a good story for me, I'll have a good story for you."

She winks and I give her a wave. "Thanks. See you around."

My mind is running when I step into the room. I'm conflicted, not sure what to do. I can get cleaned up and go over to Bri's apartment, but then what? Tell her, 'Yeah, I don't want to leave you, but now I have to.' Talk about an asshole move.

I sigh and shrug off my blazer. I head through the room toward the bathroom when I notice a stack of money on the desk. Arching an eyebrow, I walk over to see that it's my money clip sitting on top of a note. My heart pounds in my chest as I pick it up to read it.

Dear Gavin,

Leaving me with the money this morning did not sit well with me. I didn't sleep with you so I could get paid. And when I showed you my place, it wasn't for you to have sympathy for me.

I know you're a big star with everything in the world and I should be falling all over myself with gratitude.

But the truth is, I know this thing we have can never be. You're leaving. You get to go back to your big fancy house and your cars and return to being the cocky sports star and celebrity you're known for, with a slew of women on your arm.

And if this was your way for apologizing for all of that—I don't want it. I don't need your sympathy or your money.

So I'm leaving this here for you to give to someone else, perhaps someone who needs it more than me. And I wish you all the best with your sports and movie career.

Lastly, please don't try to contact me. There's no point and it's not worth the heartache. I don't want to ever see you again.

Bri

I stand there reading the words over and over, my head feeling like it's going to explode. It hurts reading this. And what hurts most of all is that it's true. I can't stay, and starting a long-distance relationship with a football star would be hell on her.

The only way I can have something meaningful with Bri is if I stay or she comes with me. And she's made it clear that she loves this place. It would be selfish of me to expect her to pack her bags and enter my crazy world of flashing cameras and salacious headlines after knowing me for just a week.

But now that she hates me, I guess the decision has been made for me.

I'm leaving.

CHAPTER 27

"I'm sorry, Miss Sayles," says the interviewer over the phone. I didn't want to take the call, but I had to. "While your qualifications are excellent, we've decided on another candidate at this time. We'll keep your application on file if there is another opening."

"Okay, thank you for your time," I whisper, trying to be polite as I hang up the phone.

I was hoping to get that job at Petersen and Associates so I could just quit and tell Vandenburgh to go fuck himself. I thought I had it in the bag. I knew the manager I'd be working for. I took a class with him. But now, that's no good.

Jesus. I don't know if I can deal with this anymore.

What does it matter anyway? I only have so much time before school is over and I'm gone.

At least Gavin is gone tomorrow so I don't have to worry about running into his ass again. Still, just thinking his name makes me clutch my hand to my chest. It hurts. I hate to admit it, but I don't want him to go. Deep down in my gut, I want him to stay.

But there is no other way. The man couldn't give up his entire career for me. That was a fool's dream anyway. I don't know why I ever deluded myself into thinking that. This is real life, not some Disney movie where the knight and the princess end up in a Happily Ever After with a talking cat.

The dark cloud on my chest has me wanting to talk to someone. Anyone. I know Mindy is out of the question right now. She's still at work. So I dial the only person I think I might be able to trust with my problems.

"Hello?" asks the familiar, high-pitched voice on the other end of the line. It's been months, but the voice hasn't changed at all. It still sounds like a woman who's on the edge of freaking out.

"Mom," I breathe. My mother, Cindy Sayles, is a woman who has aged well, and I'm surprised she hasn't remarried. She's a serial dater since the divorce. I guess most men aren't willing to put up with her nagging personality once they get past the still tight 48-year-old body.

"Bri! Where have you been, girl? It's been months since you last called me!"

"I know," I say. "I've been very busy."

"Doing what? Tipping cows? We all know that little town is boring as all get out."

I stiffen. This is why I don't like talking to my mother. She has about as much empathy as a brick, and it's obvious she thinks she's better now than the place she grew up in, and that bothers me.

"Tipping cows is a lot more fun than being stuck in traffic," I say, trying to keep a lid on my temper.

"Oh, Bri, you always have to be so passive-aggressive. I was just worried about you," Mom says. "I miss you, sweetheart."

"I know," I say softly, my anger evaporating. "How are things out there in the city?"

"I'm loving it. I still wish you'd come and be here with me. Was it really worth staying there?"

Before, I would have answered yes in a heartbeat. But now . . . now, I don't know what to think about my decision to stay here with the heartache that I feel. "I think so."

"You don't sound like you believe what you're saying," Mom says. There's a long pause where I think she wants me to reply before she continues. "Everything all right over there? Do you need me to have your father send you money?"

I suck in a breath. My mom is forever thinking problems can be solved by money. Preferably, someone else's money. Sure, money is nice, but I'm too prideful to take handouts. I would've accepted Gavin's money if I wasn't, even if it hurts that I gave it back. There was so much I could've done with that money.

"No, I'm fine," I finally reply. "Plus, I wouldn't want you to worry Dad on my behalf."

Mom sighs in relief. "Heaven knows I didn't want to, trust me. If he can ever stop long enough to dig his little winky out of his little homewrecking whore—"

"Mom, please don't!" I interrupt, knowing she's about to go into a rant about my dad and his mistress. I can't right now.

"You know, sometimes, I feel like you take your daddy's side over me. Even after all he did to us."

Ugh. I hate how she always twists things. "Mom, you know how I feel about what happened. And you know I don't like how things turned out between you guys. I just . . ."

"You just what?"

"I just can't deal with any of this right now."

"And you're sure you're okay?" Mom asks.

Of course I'm not good, I think to myself. *That's why I called.* But I'm not gonna get any help from this quarter. "As good as I'll ever be."

"Huh? What's that supposed to mean?" Mom asks, confused.

I don't have the energy to explain now. At least I got to hear a familiar voice. "I'm gonna go, Mom. I'll make sure to keep in touch. Love you."

"Bri, wait!"

I hang up the phone and let out a deep breath. I knew I shouldn't have called her. I always end up feeling bad. I just feel so vulnerable and in need of . . .

Gavin.

But Gavin is leaving tomorrow. I'll never see him again. That letter I wrote to him made sure of that. The thought hurts, but I need to get used to it.

My phone rings, and I almost hit the hang up button to ignore Mom when my finger freezes. It's Mindy. Talk about an angel.

"Hey," I answer.

"Hey, chica, why'd you run off like that today?" Mindy asks, her voice concerned. "I was almost free."

Please, girl, that line was as long as Gavin's dick, I think inwardly.

"I got tired of waiting," I lie through my teeth. "Plus, Vandenburgh was around tooting his horn. I didn't want to see him."

"Well, I'm on break now so I have time to talk. What was on your mind?"

I'm tight-lipped. "Nothing."

"Yes, there was," Mindy says, her lie detector at full strength even though it's the phone. *Damn.* "You looked all sad and sullen."

I sigh. "I've just been filling out these damn applications. I'm tired and stressed, that's all."

There's a pause on the other end of the line. "I know it's something more than that. Come on, Bri."

I can't bring myself to reply. It hurts too much.

"Gavin came lookin' for you," Mindy says suddenly.

The mention of his name catches my breath. "And?" I'm sitting on pins and needles waiting for her response.

"He was all banged up," Mindy says, "and seemed pretty worried about you."

My heart skips a beat. "All banged up? What's that mean?"

I can almost hear her nod through the phone. "Yeah. He had a bandage wrapped around his head. Told me he fell and hit his head on set, but I already knew that before he told me. I was trying to tell you about it before you ran out on me."

Pain pierces my chest. Now I feel terrible for not stopping and listening to Mindy. At the time, I was too wrapped up in my emotions and annoyed by all the people.

Gavin must feel terrible that I didn't check on him. I know I would.

"But he seemed all right though?" I ask worriedly.

Mindy laughs. "Yeah, girl. I can tell you're freaking out over it, but he's fine." Mindy pauses. "He was more concerned with seeing you, actually."

A feeling of relief washes over me. At least it was nothing serious. I'm not sure what I would've done if it were. "Worried about me?"

I wonder if he found the note I left him before or after he talked to Mindy.

"Yeah," Mindy replies. "I can tell he was really hurt. Probably because you hadn't called to see how he was doing." She pauses for a moment and I hear her suck in a deep breath. "Don't bite my head off, but will you please tell me what happened between you two? You both have been acting like lost puppies. Is it just because he's leaving tomorrow?"

That's a major part of it.

I part my lips to reply but pause, a heavy feeling weighing down my chest. I want to tell her everything, but it's hard because of the feelings it brings up.

Taking a deep breath, I tell her everything—about the sex, the dates, all of it.

Mindy pauses, processing it all. "I really think you should talk to him, Bri," Mindy says. "I don't think he meant anything by leaving you that money. And if he's leaving, don't let him go like this. You'll both regret it."

"What's there to say?" I ask. "It's just going to make everything harder. This was all a waste of time."

"I don't think it was," Mindy argues. "You both had an experience and enjoyed each other. That counts for something."

"Maybe he would come visit from time to time?" Mindy offers when I don't reply. "Or maybe even stay?"

I snort in disbelief. "I won't be some small-town booty call that he can stop in for. And he can't stay. He has obligations."

"Well, with how he was acting the other day and the way he looked today when he came in to ask about you . . . I wouldn't be so quick to judge."

I huff out a mirthless chuckle. "You're more delusional than I was when I first started having feelings for him."

"You don't have to believe it," Mindy tells me. "I just know what I saw."

I go silent, biting my lower lip in thought.

"I just want you to be happy, Bri," Mindy continues, her voice filled with concern.

That's gonna be really fucking hard with Gavin gone.

I sigh. "I know, and I thank you, Mindy. But I need to go. I'm emotionally exhausted."

Mindy's voice is aching with emotion. "Okay. Please, just take care of yourself. I know you really liked Gavin, but you can't let this wind up ruining your life."

I hang up the phone feeling even worse than I felt getting off the phone with Mom.

CHAPTER 28

GAVIN

"Mr. Adams, what would you say about your first filming experience?" asks the reporter. He's a tall, balding man dressed in a grey suit with a slight lisp. After five nonstop questions from him, it's becoming irritating.

I put on a tight smile, doing my best to stay cool as repeated flashes go off in my face, the room filled with sounds of *clicking* cameras. "It was amazing," I say with a cheer I don't feel. "It was a great experience."

"We heard about your injury," says another reporter, a chubby man in jeans and a t-shirt, his Cowboys hat on backward. "Are you okay?"

A stab of pain lances between my eyes, and it's an effort to maintain my smile. "I'm fine," I reply, wiggling my eyebrows. "Just a little bump. Nothing a little Tylenol won't fix."

"Mr. Adams," the first reporter says, "there are rumors that you started up an off-screen romance with your co-star, Leslie Hart. Is there anything you want to say to that?"

Now I have no problem faking my smile. The rumor is so absurd that I wonder what sort of Internet troll even tried to come up with it. "There's nothing to say," I say easily. "Leslie and I are co-workers, and she has always been professional with me. Whoever started that rumor is wrong."

"Mr. Adams," the same reporter asks, his voice causing me to grit my teeth. "Do you think doing this movie will make people forget about the Anaconda video?"

Always, always, always. Everything always comes back to that damn video. This time, though, I don't get angry. I don't feel capable. I just feel . . . dead inside.

"I certainly hope so," I say finally, flashing a wink and nodding my head at the crowd of reporters. "Thank you, but I've gotta get to offseason workouts."

"Okay, that will be all," Miranda says at my side as I rise to my feet. "Gavin is done taking questions now. He'll be signing a few autographs in the lobby for a few minutes and then we have to catch our flight. Thank you."

The crowd rushes forward, taking pictures, each flashbulb stinging my eyes and making my head throb a little bit more. I keep the smile on my face, ignoring the flashes even though I feel like shit. Security holds back most of the crowd as we make it into the hallway of the press venue.

"I think that's the best I've seen you do while we've been here," Miranda says out of the side of her mouth. "What's changed?"

I did my best at faking it, I think to myself. Truth be told, I'm in a nasty fucking mood. Nothing they said mattered. It was just a couple of minutes and it all seems like a blur to me. I don't even know what I said.

"Just glad to be done with all of this," I finally say. "Football time."

"I'm glad too," Miranda says as we reach the lobby where a small crowd waits. "I'm not sure I could've taken much more of airhead Gavin."

Before I can reply, I'm swarmed by a wall of clamoring fans. It's hard to keep the smile on my face, but I do it, signing a few t-shirts, books, and posters. I politely answer questions and pose for pictures, wanting it to end as fast as possible. The line of people seems endless, and after a while, I begin to get dizzy from all the stimuli surrounding me.

Suddenly, I'm caught off guard when one girl presses herself against my side, causing a hiss of warning from Miranda.

"Is your anaconda as big as they say it is?" she asks. Obviously a bimbo groupie, she has big tits and a low skirt. Her t-shirt is hand-cut in a V to show even more of her surgically enhanced cleavage.

I grit my teeth. I hate when fans invade my personal space and then ask me rude questions. "It's about as big as those fake tits of yours—"

"Sorry, folks, we're going to be moving along now," Miranda cuts in, doing quick damage control and shoving the girl and others out of the way. "Got a flight to catch!"

I press the opening, shouldering my way through the crowd as Miranda scrambles to catch up. "You just couldn't make it to the end without screwing up, could you?"

"Are you fucking serious?" I demand.

"You know better than that," Miranda says reproachfully. "It's not worth letting someone get under your skin."

She's right. But I'm not perfect and I'm tired of being expected to be. I turn to her as we walk out of the building and come up on our waiting limo.

"You know what, Miranda? I'm sorry I can't be a fucking robot twenty-four seven. Go here, say this, let this person grope you, never mind that everyone only wants to talk about my fucking cock! I'm sorry that I've got feelings and that I'm not always able to control them. You know, instead of ranting at me about it, how about from time to time, you actually remember that I'm a human being?"

Miranda grows silent, her face going stony.

Our driver gets out and opens the door for us, and I climb inside, taking a seat near the window. Miranda is in moments later, sitting as far away from me as she can. As we pull off, the cabin is plunged into tense silence.

I ignore it and stare out the window, my stomach in my throat. It's hard seeing the shops as we pass by, all the ones I've gotten used to seeing. I would've liked to visit them, but there's no time. I'm leaving this all behind. Leaving *her*.

I quell the sudden urge to command the driver to stop. What would I do anyway? I can't stay here. I have a contract with the league.

But man, it fucking *hurts*.

When we reach the airport, I literally feel like I'm short of breath.

"Are you all right?" Miranda asks. They're her first words since our little spat, and they're delivered in a tone that says she doesn't really give a shit. "You look kind of pale."

"Yeah," I lie, keeping my tone even. "Just ready to get back home."

Miranda grunts her agreement as the car rolls to a stop in front of our departure terminal. "Boy, I'm telling you, so am I."

Hustled by terminal security, we quickly get out and unload our luggage. Even though I'm pissed, I carry my and Miranda's luggage to the baggage area and get it checked in within ten minutes. Next, we get through the checkpoints with ease, and by the time we're boarding the plane, I'm convinced I'll need something to relax me to get through the flight.

"You sure do look pale," Miranda remarks again as we settle into our seats. It's a charter flight. The team wants my ass back in town ASAP, and they sent the owner's private jet to take care of it.

I wave away her concern. "Just feeling a little sick, that's all."

She peers at me. "You sure? I don't want to get up to thirty-five thousand feet in the air and we wind up with an emergency on our hands."

I set my jaw. "I'm good." *No, I'm not.*

Miranda continues to study me for a moment but then gives up and relaxes back in her seat.

The pre-flights are done within the next half hour, and the whole time, I stare out the windows, wishing that I could change things. When the plane jolts, signifying that it's moving, I grip the armrest as it begins to taxi.

Just as the plane turns onto the runway, I'm hit by a surge of adrenaline, my entire trip flashing before my eyes. Image after image coalesces before me, all of my special moments with Brianna. Her smile. Her touch. Her sweet, innocent laughter.

And in that moment, Leslie's words come back to haunt me.

Don't be like me and miss out on the best thing in your life.

Suddenly, my career as a sports star doesn't seem as important anymore.

"Stop the plane!" I yell, drawing the attention of the flight attendant.

"What the fuck?" Miranda cries in alarm as I rise out of my seat. "Gavin?"

I ignore her and yell again. "Turn the plane around. I have to get off!"

"Stop it!" Miranda commands, trying to grab at me. I swat her hand away.

"Sir," the flight attendant says, coming up to me. "We're about to take off. We can't just stop the plane on a whim."

"You can," I growl. "This is an emergency!"

The attendant frowns at me, disturbed by my frantic state. "What kind of emergency?"

I grab my carry-on and begin moving toward the exit. I don't give a fuck what this flight attendant, Miranda, the pilot, or what anyone else says. I don't even give a damn if I have to parachute out of this motherfucker. I'm getting off this fucking plane one way or the other.

"Love," I throw over my shoulder.

CHAPTER 29

BRIANNA

I draw a line of lip gloss on as I look at myself in the mirror, but I don't really care that much. Once again, it's time to go to fucking work. I really wanted to take the day off, but at least it'll keep my body and my mind busy.

My heart skips a beat as a pain lances my chest. It hurts to think about it.

Gavin's gone. *Forever*.

A deep sigh escapes my lips as I stare at my reflection. My eyes are puffy and bloodshot from crying all night. I suspect I'll go through many more days like this until I'm all cried out. But right now, I need to be strong and go to work.

I get my things, leave my apartment, and get in my car. As I start the engine, the radio comes on, but I quickly turn it off. I know the news will just be gossiping about Gavin and his departure. And I don't want to hear that right now.

As I traverse block after block, I find it difficult to concentrate, tears threatening to spill from my eyes. I told myself I wouldn't do this this morning. But it's damn near impossible. I grip the steering wheel tightly, trying to focus on the road, taking deep, calming breaths.

Don't cry, don't cry, don't cry, I chant.

I get a couple of blocks from the hotel when my car begins making a *chugging* noise, stuttering violently before finally dying and rolling to a stop in the middle of the street. "The hell?"

Trying to remain calm, I put my foot hard on the gas and turn the key. I get the motor to turn over, but it keeps sputtering, and I'm only barely able to pull over to the side of the road.

I hear someone honk their horn several times, and a lady yells out her window as she passes by, "Learn how to drive!"

I ignore the bitch and the surge of anger that goes through my chest, giving the gas everything I have with violent kicks.

Click. Click. Click.

Only dead silence now.

I shake my head, panic gripping me as I glance at the time. I only have ten minutes to clock in or I'm going to be late. Grabbing my cell, I dial the office but then stop. I can't exactly call in sick at this point. No matter what I say, Vandenburgh isn't going to care.

I imagine he has my slip written up already.

"God damn it!" I yell, hitting the steering wheel with my fists, blaring the horn. The sound causes a lady stepping out in front of my car to jump in alarm and look my way. When she sees me, she averts her gaze and scurries off. Yes, I know I must look like a mad, pissed off bitch. Because I am. I'm hurt and fucking fed up.

I get out of the car and take in my surroundings, not sure what I should do. There are several shops nearby, but I know no one is gonna be able to help me get my car up and running in time.

A heavy feeling settles on my chest as I consider my dwindling options. I can either call for help or just not go into work. For help, Mindy immediately pops in mind, but I quickly discard the idea. There's no way I'm making her leave her shift on my behalf. It will only end up getting us both in trouble.

And if I don't go into work, I'm as good as fired.

Shading my eyes, I peer down the street. I can see the hotel in the distance, just maybe a mile away. In my car, it would have taken me fewer than two minutes. But now . . .

I sigh, my body already aching as I realize there's only one thing left to do.

Run.

❄

MY RIBS ACHE, MY LUNGS BURN, AND MY ASS FEELS LIKE IT WAS dipped in gasoline and set on fire when I stagger through the front door of the Waterway twelve minutes later, covered in sweat. My heart pounding, I'm praying that my watch is slow, but when I clock in, I see that I'm two minutes late. Thankfully, there's no sign of Vandenburgh and I hope he doesn't take notice.

I'm walking through the lobby, still catching my breath, when I hear Mindy cry out, "Bri!"

She's standing in the doorway of the coffee shop, staring at me with wide eyes, waving me over. She looks cute as a button in her usual outfit, her hair pinned up with wispy bangs, a pale splash of rouge on her cheeks and shiny gloss on her lips.

"What's going on?" she asks me when I walk over, ushering me into the back room of the coffee shop.

"My car broke down," I rasp, trying to fill my lungs with air. I know I must look like hell, my hair in disarray and sweat dotting my forehead, but I don't care. I made it, and that's all that matters. "I had to half-jog, half-run all the way here."

"Oh, my God, why didn't you just call me?" Mindy demands, helping me into the back room and grabbing me a stool that I lean on gratefully.

I suck in gulps of oxygen, wanting to lean on Mindy for support, but I fight the urge, remaining against the stool. I need to stand on my own two feet. "I didn't want you to leave your shift. It was my fault."

Mindy scowls at me, placing her hands on her hips. "No, it wasn't. You could have called me. It's not a big deal."

I wave her away, coughing and shaking my head. "Well, it's okay now. I just need to get to work."

Mindy gives me a hug. And then she pulls back and appraises me with concern in her eyes. "Are you okay?"

I know what she's asking about, but I really don't wanna talk about it. "I'll live," I admit. "I've been through worse."

She shakes her head, sorrow reflecting in her eyes. "I'm so sorry. His plane left this morning, they said. They got into the limo just as I was opening up."

Tears sting my eyes. *Ugh.* I feel like shit. Lost the man I'd developed feelings for. Car broke down. And now I'm about to possibly lose my job.

How much more can a girl possibly take?

A huge lump forms in my throat and I clench my fists. I refuse to be brought to my knees by all of this. I was fine before Gavin came along, and I'll be fine again.

"Have you seen Vandenburgh?" I ask thickly. I don't bother replying to her statement. I don't want to talk about Gavin. "I didn't see him when I signed in, thank God."

Mindy shakes her head. "No, I haven't seen his uppity ass." She pauses and taps her cheek. "Haven't seen him since yesterday, in fact."

Relief flows through me. Maybe he took the day off and I won't have to worry about him today. "Good," I say. "That's the best news I've heard all morning."

"Damn sure is." Mindy hugs me again and then gives me a perceptive look. "I can see that you're trying to avoid talking about Gavin, but if there is anything—anything—I can do for you, please don't hesitate to ask."

"I will." I begin to turn away but then stop, my side aching from my run. "Tylenol?"

Mindy nods at me, quick to scurry off. "Let me go check!"

She runs back behind the counter and digs in her purse. "I don't have Tylenol, but will Midol help?"

"It'll have to do," I say. "At this point, I'm willing to take anything."

She pours me a cup of water, which I use to take a double dose of the pills.

"Thanks, Mindy," I say when I'm done. "You're a lifesaver."

"Anything for you, Miss Sayles," Mindy says, perfectly imitating Vandenburgh's accent.

We both share a laugh. I know the darkness isn't gonna recede soon, but Mindy will at least be the sunshine that helps push it away.

"Okay," I say, dreading having to work but knowing I have to. "Let me get to my shift."

"See you at break." I give Mindy a quick hug and start on my way.

I'm almost out the door when Mindy calls out, "Bri!"

I stop and turn around. "Yeah?"

She flashes an optimistic smile. "Everything's going to be all right. You'll see."

My aching heart says otherwise, but I manage to answer softly, "I hope so."

I leave the coffee shop, collect my cart and cleaning supplies, and then start my shift.

I spend the next few hours doing everything I can to focus on my job, trying to keep my mind off Gavin. He's gone. Abracadabra. Poof. Not coming back. I need to let that sink in.

And in a few weeks' time, I won't even remember his name, I tell myself as I drive on like a plow horse.

By the time I reach the sixth floor, I'm beyond exhausted. With all the movie production guests checking out on the same day, all the rooms were messy as fuck. It was a fucking nightmare. The little relief Midol had given has worn off, and I need a break. But I don't take one. I just want to get through this day without breaking down.

When I'm finally done vacuuming, scrubbing, and changing beds, my feet are killing me and my sides and head are pounding with a vengeance.

But I still have one room left. A room I've saved for last and have been avoiding. Room 603.

Gavin's.

I walk over to it, groaning with each step, and pause at the door.

A part of me wants to just walk off and leave because I don't want to be reminded of our time together. But I can't take the chance that it isn't messy inside, not when all the other rooms were that way. I must go in and do my job.

Sucking in a deep breath, I put the key in the door and turn it. *Click.* With a gentle tap of my foot, the door swings open.

My breath catches in my throat when I walk in. The room is spotless. Everything is in order, totally immaculate. It's the only room today that I've walked in on in this condition. Gavin had to have cleaned it or gotten someone to do it. His last gift to me.

"Oh," I whisper.

I bring a hand to my chest, choked by the simple sight of a clean room, as tears burn in my eyes. It's too late now, but I wish I hadn't been so prideful and stubborn. I should've just talked to him before he left.

Would it have been so bad to get a last goodbye from him?

I suck in another breath, inhaling deeply. The leftover scent of Gavin's cologne is on the air, causing my skin to prick. I sit down on the sofa, wrapping my arms around my chest as a torrent of emotions build inside. I wish my arms were his, holding me, hugging me, enveloping me in his warmth.

Tears roll down my cheeks as I get up and make my way over to the bed and lie down on it. Broken, I press my face softly to the covers. I can smell his scent stronger here, the pillowcases heavy with him. I sigh, wishing that he were lying here with me. Making love to me. "Gavin," I moan.

I jump with surprise when suddenly, the door bangs open. I'm on my feet in an instant, wiping the tears from my eyes. But it's too late.

Vandenburgh waddles into the room, a look of glee on his face.

"There you are, Miss Sayles," he says, out of breath. "I've been looking all over for you. But something told me I'd find you here."

"I'm sorry, sir," I say, flashing an easy, fake smile. "I was just finishing cleaning—"

Vandenburgh laughs, silencing me with a sharp gesture. "Save your lies, Miss Sayles. I saw you clocked in late this morning." His malicious grin is so wide I swear it's about to split his face.

I'm quick to defend myself. "I'm sorry about that. My car broke down and I had to run—"

Vandenburgh cuts in again. "That was your third strike. And do you know what that means, Miss Sayles?" He pauses, waiting for me to say something, and when I part my lips to reply, he snarls over me, "You're fired!"

Of course I am. And I bet this asshole has been salivating this entire time, waiting for me to clean all of my rooms before he fired me. Now the last thing I was clinging to is gone. But there is one thing I have left. My dignity. And since now I have nothing to lose, I'm not gonna take Vandenburgh's shit anymore.

Vandenburgh looks surprised when instead of slouching off, I get right in his face, towering over him even in his stacked-heel dress shoes.

"Well, you know what, you humpty dumpty ass son of a bitch?" I snarl, stealing Mindy's favorite insult she uses behind Vandenburgh's back. "I'm glad to be fired! I was so fucking sick of hearing your fake ass voice and seeing you sit on your ass while I busted mine anyway."

Vandenburgh is shocked by my reaction, his mouth dropping open.

My hands on my hips, I smile sweetly at him. I'm sure he thought I was gonna get down on my knees and beg him for my job. But as Mindy once said after one of her write-ups, fuck this, fuck that, fuck him, and fuck this place. I'll get through this somehow. I always have. With my parents being gone, I learned the best person to depend on is myself.

Vandenburgh finally seems to recover from his shock, snarling with spittle flying from his mouth. "How dare you, you trollop!"

I raise my head to the ceiling and let out a mocking laugh. "Trollop? This is the twenty-first century! How about getting with the times instead of sitting on your ass all day reading Playgirl magazine?"

Vandenburgh turns deep red, his anger overcoming his shock. I have a feeling he wishes he could choke the life out of me right now. Maybe I should keep pushing him to see if he'll do it. "Why, you little . . . if you are not off the premises within five minutes, I'm going to have security escort you out!"

I part my lips to deliver another biting insult when . . .

"That won't be necessary," says a deep voice behind us.

I spin around and my heart nearly stops. Gavin is standing in the doorway, glaring at Vandenburgh, his eyes burning with wrath.

"M–Mr. Adams," Vandenburgh stutters, his face turning as white as a sheet. "I thought you were gone on your flight."

"Change of plans. I forgot something very important here," Gavin replies, walking up to Vandenburgh. He looks at me, his eyes full of burning intensity.

I blink several times, wanting to pinch myself. Is this real? It can't be.

"I thought we had an agreement," Gavin growls, turning his gaze back to Vandenburgh. "I asked you to cut Brianna some slack."

"I–I . . ." Vandenburgh goes silent, then puffs out his chest. "I'm the general manager of this establishment. And while you might be famous, you don't have any say over how I do my job. Miss Sayles is fired because she's a horrible employee. And if you don't take your little pet and be gone from here, I'm going to have you *both* escorted out in handcuffs."

Gavin laughs. "I'm afraid you don't have that power anymore."

"You will get out *now*—" Vandenburgh stops, confused. "What do you mean?"

Gavin's grin is just as malicious as Vandenburgh's was a few minutes ago. "I made a few phone calls. Spoke with a few shareholders. Did you know that one of them happens to be a very big Gavin Adams fan? So he did me a little favor." Gavin smiles. "You're fired. The hotel's looking for a new general manager as we speak."

Vandenburgh's mouth opens and closes, and I swear he looks like Mindy's fish down in the coffee shop. "What? Impossible! You're lying!"

Gavin shakes his head. "Call Mr. Layman himself." Gavin raises his nose and speaks in his best Vandenburgh impression, "You are hereby relieved of duties . . . forthwith."

"You're a liar!" Vandenburgh howls. He digs his phone out of his pocket and dials, his face sweating as he talks to the person on the other end of the line. "Yes, Mr. Layman . . . yes. But sir, I . . . yes. Yes . . . sir! Sir, please! Yes–yes sir."

Vandenburgh turns off the phone, face white as a sheet, and he turns his rage-filled eyes on me. "You," he snarls, stabbing a pudgy finger at my face. "It was all because of *you* that this happened!"

Vandenburgh starts to step toward me, but in a swift move, Gavin steps in front of me and Vandenburgh suddenly changes his mind. Huffing angrily, he turns and storms from the room, yelling, "You haven't heard the last from me!"

"Indeed." Gavin chuckles, tossing him a little wave as he goes and slamming the door on his way out. When he's gone, Gavin turns to me, smiling a little and jamming his hands in his pockets. "Well."

I'm shaking, I'm so anxious and shocked. "Well what?"

Gavin laughs, rubbing his head and wincing as he hits his stitches. "Is that how you greet a man who just turned around a private plane and pissed off his team's owner so he could come back to you?"

I gape in astonishment.

Gavin moves in close, placing his arms around my waist. What he said hits me, and I start to tremble. In a heartbeat, everything I've been holding against him—the money, him being an egotistical lady slayer, the cockiness—it all slips away. "You said you came back for something very important," I breathe, biting my lip. "Did you find it?"

"Yes," Gavin says. "I did. The love of my life."

His words are like a freight train, nearly knocking me off my feet. I can't believe this. Tears form in my eyes as I look up at him. "You can't mean that. You've only known me for a week."

"I do," he says, pulling me closer. "Sometimes, you just know."

I can no longer hold them back. The droplets start rolling down my cheeks. "But what about the team? Your workouts, all the—"

"Shh," he murmurs, putting a finger to my lips. "I'll get it worked out. None of those things matters to me right now."

"But . . ." I protest weakly, my heart pounding so hard my vision blurs.

"I love you, Brianna Sayles, and I think I've loved you from the moment I set eyes on you," Gavin declares.

The breath stills in my lungs, the weight of his words pressing down on me. There is nothing but sincerity in his eyes. He truly *means* it. He's going to do whatever it takes to make it work. *Oh, my God.*

"I love you too," I reply, barely able to get the words out as I cup his face, my chest swirling with a maelstrom of emotion. "But I need your help with something," I plead.

"What?" he asks, and I smile, standing on my tiptoes to softly kiss him on the lips.

"Take me," I whisper, my body burning with need, my legs trembling with anticipation. "Now."

Gavin picks me up, carrying me over to the bed. "You don't have to tell me twice."

CHAPTER 30

GAVIN

*I*t must be a medical miracle.

At the first touch of her lips on mine and when she says she loves me, all the pain in my head disappears and fresh strength fills my body. She's like a feather as I pick her up in my arms and carry her over to the bed, laying her down like she's the most precious diamond on earth.

I lie down next to her, kissing her lips softly again, wanting this time to be different from any other time we've been together. We've fucked. We've had sex. Now, it's time for something special.

"Brianna," I whisper in her ear, kissing along the pink shell curve and nibbling. She responds with a breathy moan and her fingers dig into my neck, scratching lightly.

"Gavin," she moans, her other hand trying to get the buttons on my shirt undone. "Gavin, I want to feel you inside me."

"You will," I reassure her, kissing down her neck to the collar of her polyester maid uniform. I chuckle, thinking how sexy Brianna is that she can make this cheap rag look seductive. I find the zipper and pull it down, kissing lower as her creamy pale skin is exposed to my lips. "You will."

"No," she says, her voice desperate with a need that makes me lift my head from the hollow between her breasts, wondering. Brianna strokes my hair, biting her lower lip before she makes her decision. "No condom this time."

I nod, my heart swelling as we both know the trust involved. I lower my head again, kissing and sucking on her breasts until I reach the edge of her bra before I sit up, easing the uniform off her shoulders. Brianna sits up, helping me shrug the one-piece outfit off before she takes off her bra and panties, stretching out beautifully nude again for me, her nipples already hard and her cheeks flushed with desire.

"You are the most beautiful woman in the world," I say, stepping off the bed only long enough to take off my clothes before I join her, laughing when my shin bumps against something hard and cool. "You forgot your shoes."

Brianna looks down and laughs lightly. "Sort of distracted."

"Let me," I answer, kissing her fingertips before covering her body in soft kisses, working my way down to her feet and unknotting the black sneakers and taking them off.

I caress her foot, kissing my way up the inside of her thigh, spreading her legs as I work my way toward the pink petals of her wet, glistening pussy. "My sweet little Bunny."

Brianna chuckles at my nickname, blushing deeper. "If you mean I want to go at you like a rabbit, you're right."

"Well, let's find out," I reply, reaching out with my tongue to trace the soft lips of her pussy. She's tangy and sweet, that amazing Brianna flavor that I love, and as I nibble and suck on her pussy, her soft moans and cries of pleasure guide my tongue. I stroke her inner folds with the tip of my tongue, gathering her honey before I suck harder. I greedily drink her juices as her back arches and she grabs my head, grinding her pussy against my eager tongue and lips.

"Gavin, yes," Brianna moans as I find the hard clit and flick my tongue over it, stroking it in just the way that she likes best. Circling, I find her special spot and start sucking while with my right hand, I slide a finger inside her to rub at her inner button.

"Mmm," I moan against her clit as her pussy grips my finger and I start to rub, my finger and tongue stroking in tandem to bring her higher and higher. Her body starts to shake, and she pulls my hair harder, causing a little bit of pain from my stitches, but I don't care.

"Gavin . . . Gavin, I'm . . . oh," she groans before her hips lift, her thighs squeezing my head tightly as she comes, her voice rising into a breathless cry of ecstasy. I stay still, not wanting to torture her as she rides it out, my finger clamped deep inside her.

When she comes down, she's gasping, trembling, but the look in her eyes tells me that she wants more. "Better?"

I kiss my way up her body, sucking her left nipple and biting down a little. She hums happily as she strokes my shoulders and back, cooing. "Gavin, you can do that to me any time you want."

"I plan on it," I answer, working my way back up to her lips and tasting them. She sucks on my tongue, my passion rising when she wraps her legs around my waist and I can feel the warm wetness of her pussy sliding against the base of my cock. "Brianna . . ."

"You were soft and tender, and I thank you," she says, stroking my face before grinning. "But now . . . give it to me. All of it."

I line up with Brianna's entrance and push in, watching her face for the first sign of pain. I'm shocked as I sink deeper and deeper, half my cock, three quarters . . . all of my cock in one smooth, tight stroke that leaves us both trembling again.

She's still tight, her body gripping my cock perfectly as I push her knees up, opening her up more before I pull back, stroking in and out slowly, taking my time. My body is on fire as my cock is caressed and squeezed in a way that it's never felt before.

"Brianna," I growl, my eyes opening wide when she grabs my arms and digs her fingers in, a sliver of pain driving me to my animal point. "Get ready."

She doesn't say anything, but the sexy, feral grin on her face as I thrust my cock in hard tells me that she loves it too, and in seconds, the only sounds in the room are our harsh breathing and the sexy smack of our hips as I pound Brianna's body.

"Yes . . . yes . . . yes!" She grunts each time my balls slap against her ass, and I hear a creak as the headboard of the bed starts to hit the wall. My cock throbs, feeling fuller and harder than ever before in my life as I speed up, grinding my hips against her clit with each hammering thrust, driving into her with everything I have.

Brianna brings her hands up to my shoulders, clinging tightly as I speed up more and more, giving her everything I have, and she takes it, returning it to me with passion and desire. Sweat trickles down my face as I look into her beautiful eyes and she looks into mine, soulmates who have finally found each other, and in her eyes, I see a future. Not one of failure, but of love and acceptance, of success.

"Harder," she gasps, and somehow, I find the strength to up my efforts even more, pounding her so hard it sounds like she's getting spanked each time and my hips start to ache from the pounding action. I groan, my cock swelling inside her, and Brianna's fingers dig harder into my shoulders, her eyes going wide. "Yes . . . come in me . . . yes!"

My balls grow tight and hard against my body, and I shudder on the edge when Brianna's fingernails pierce my skin and I'm pushed over. I cry out, throwing my head back to scream my ecstasy as I fill her, fill my angel with what she wants, my cock seeming to be a never-ending stream of come and passion.

Brianna moans, her own cries joining mine as she comes again, her pussy squeezing my cock and sending me on another wave of intense feeling, my arms trembling and my heart skipping beats in my chest so often that I think I'm going to pass out.

When the moment passes, I look into her eyes, resting my forehead against hers, sharing her breath. "I love you."

"I love you too," Brianna says, gently stroking my neck.

We stay there for a long time until I slip out and lie next to her, letting her pillow her head on my chest. We both hum with the glow of what we just did, and Brianna smiles after a moment, running her fingers over the ridges of my abs.

"I don't need to ask anymore," she says with a chuckle before sighing happily. "I know you liked it."

I laugh softly, stroking her hair and kissing her head. "You have no idea how perfect you are for me."

Brianna nuzzles my chest, humming happily. "I think I fell in love with it the first time I saw it."

"It?" I ask, and Brianna nods, reaching down to wrap her fingers around my half-soft cock and stroking it.

"The Anaconda."

"Oh, Jesus," I groan, rolling my eyes as her soft hand strokes me, my cock certainly liking the attention again.

"It was a joke," she says with a laugh, kissing my chin as her hand keeps pumping my cock. Fresh tingles of desire course through me, and I moan softly even as I laugh.

"Between you and me, I'll be fine if I don't hear another cock joke for another hundred years."

Brianna smiles, shifting her body to look up at me. "But you love me."

I nod, my cock growing hard again from her attentions, and I know we're both thinking the same thing. "Of course, I love you now and forever."

Brianna smiles and swings her leg up and over my now fully hard cock, sinking down onto it and moaning deeply as I fill her again, my hands resting on her hips before she leans forward and kisses me. "And I love you, Gavin Adams."

The plane is the same one as last time, although the team is making me pay for the flight time myself as punishment for the mess that happened two days ago, but I don't care. What's important is the person sitting next to me as I reach across the small divider and take Brianna's hand. "First plane ride?"

She shakes her head, turning her head away from the rapidly shrinking town below us to look in my eyes. "I once flew to Pueblo to see my Dad, but I ended up driving back when the visit went weird and I cut it short. It's actually where I bought my car."

I laugh, leaning back as we rise to our cruising altitude and the flight attendant comes around with the beverage cart. "I guess it's something I've gotten used to. I probably have enough frequent flier miles to fly around the world."

Bri leans her seat back and sips her drink. "So, what now?"

I shrug, glad that Miranda decided to take a commercial flight back. I like the privacy with Brianna. "I've got offseason workouts starting tomorrow, but that's only a couple of hours in the morn-ings mostly. Summer camp starts next month, but you'll be going back to school then."

"On a much heavier schedule," she mentions, and I look over questioningly. "I decided, Gavin, that if you want to help me, I'm going to talk to the university. If I bust my ass, I can finish up my Master's for a January graduation."

"Do it," I reassure her. "You've got the brains and the talent to be whatever you want."

Brianna smiles, looking at me carefully. "Gavin, I love you, but I have to ask . . . can you do the long-distance relationship thing? I mean—"

"I promise you, Brianna. I'm going to commit to this."

She smiles at me and says, "That's all I wanted to hear."

❄

January

THE PLANE RIDE IS SHORT, JUST NINETY MINUTES FROM TAKEOFF TO landing, and the car's waiting for me as I drive through town to the university, walking up to the gates to see Mindy waiting for me, just like she said she would, bundled up but still looking Mindy-cute in a skirt with thick leggings. "You made good time."

I give her a hug—after all, she's Brianna's best friend—squeezing tightly. "Sorry about the attire. Jumped on the plane directly after the game."

"Bah, you're more comfortable than I am," she says with her normal sarcasm. "Sorry about the season."

"This is more important," I reply as we head through the gates and stand on the edge of the field. The graduates are seated by degree, and I watch as the Dean speaks again.

"Brianna Sayles, Business Management."

Mindy and I both explode in cheers, Mindy's piercing whistle shrilling across the entire stadium, making Brianna turn from the stage a hundred yards away, waving. We quiet down as the others are announced and Bri goes back to her seat, talking quietly.

"So, how's the coffee shop?"

Mindy chuckles. "You asking as my bestie's man, or as part-owner of the place?"

After getting Vandenburgh fired, I made an investment, purchasing the hotel coffee shop and making Mindy the manager. She's doing a good job. The place is turning a tidy profit, a bit more than before, and I think it's money well-spent. Best of all, Bri's been able to work on a part-time schedule when she wants. "Both."

"We're doing fine. Having Gavin Adams stuff on the walls has certainly helped with the tourist trade. Although I still get more tips."

"Oh, why's that?"

Mindy laughs. "On jersey days, I pull mine tighter to show more cleavage. Bri wears hers with a total 'my boyfriend's hot as hell' vibe."

When the ceremony finishes and the hats are tossed, I find

Brianna right in the middle of the field like we'd planned, sweeping her into a hug and kissing her deeply. "I'm so proud of you, babe!"

"Thanks," Brianna says, giggling as I spin her around. "Hey, I saw it on my phone—sorry about the playoffs."

I shrug, setting her down. "Four touchdowns though, a hell of a game to go out on."

"What do you mean, go out on?" she asks, and I grin, springing my first surprise.

"I decided—I told the team I'm not coming back next year. They weren't too upset. They'll save a ton on salary cap. I'm retiring from football, babe. It's been coming for a long time now. I'm done with being a celebrity and living in the limelight."

Brianna looks stunned, smiling. "So you mean . . .?"

"I'm coming to live here permanently," I agree, kissing her again. She pulls me close, but I step back, shocking her when I go to my knee. "And I was thinking, I want to start my new life right here. Brianna, will you marry me?"

I pull out the engagement ring from the pocket of my warmups, opening it to show her the Cartier diamond, nervous for only an instant before Brianna nods, tears in her eyes. "Yes!"

"Damn, I thought Bri's pussy was slammin' before, but if Gavin Adams is putting a ring on it, it must be out of this world!" Mindy jokes from beside us, but I ignore her as Brianna wraps her arms around my neck and kisses me again deeply, my cock stirring in my pants even though I'm beaten up and exhausted. "Congratulations, Bri!"

"I'm glad you asked," Brianna whispers in my ear, ignoring Mindy too after I put the ring on her finger. "I have some news for you, too. Remember when you came and visited at Thanksgiving?"

"How could I forget?" I ask, grinning. A win on Thanksgiving Day followed by three days of wonderful bliss with Brianna at her new apartment? I don't know which was sorer, my body from the game or my body from the number of times we made love that weekend.

"Well, I can't be sure . . . but I'd say that was the weekend that you left me with a little surprise," she says with a smile.

The news nearly brings me to my knees, a surge of elation washing over me. "You're fucking with me!"

Brianna shakes her head, her eyes filled with tears and pride. "Congratulations, Gavin Adams. You're going to be a father."

Tears come to my eyes as I pull Brianna close, kissing her again, my heart exploding with absolute joy.

Meanwhile, Mindy grins as she looks on, wiping tears from her eyes. Apparently, she's been in on it the whole time. "Guess the Anaconda is gonna be busy tonight!" she cracks, her voice filled with emotion.

I grin, a chuckle escaping my lips as I pull my sweet Bunny in for another kiss, growling, "You're damn right it will."

Irresistible Bachelor **Series (Interconnecting standalones):**
Anaconda || Mr. Fiance || Heartstopper
Stud Muffin || Mr. Fixit || Matchmaker
Motorhead || Baby Daddy

WANT THE FREE EXTENDED EPILOGUE? SIGN UP TO MY MAILING list to receive it as soon as it's ready. If you're already on my list, you'll get this automatically.

PREVIEW: MR. FIANCE

BY LAUREN LANDISH

It's fake, but it feels so good.

Oliver Steele is supposed to be my knight in shining armor. He's tall, handsome, and as cocky as he is rich. With his good looks and charm, no one's going to suspect a thing. No one's going to believe our engagement is fake.

But he's taking this thing way too far. The way he wraps his arm around me like I'm his. The way he kisses me and presses his hard body up against mine. I almost believe that it's real. Almost.

He's doing it on purpose now; he loves that this is getting to me.

Two can play his game, I won't let him win. By the time our week together is done, I'll leave Oliver on his knees and begging.

But the minute we're alone in the bedroom, I know I'm in over way my head. When he undresses me with his eyes, I realize I lost before the game even started. It's only a matter of time

before I lose myself in his touch and let him do whatever he
wants to me.

I know what I want, but I can't tell what's real anymore.

❄

Chapter 1
Mindy

"CAN WE GET SOME SERVICE OVER HERE?" yells a woman who's
seated at one of the tables in the packed coffee house. "You girls
are moving slow as molasses!"

I slap the lids down on a couple of cups and place them in a cup
holder before taking them over to the counter. I pause for a
moment to dab the sweat from my brow with my apron, sighing.
My feet ache from running back and forth during the early
morning rush and I need a damn break.

Jesus, I tell myself as I force a fraudulent smile on my face. This is
the worst morning ever. It's a blistering hot day in July. The A/C's
shoddy, it's like 100 degrees outside, and it feels like I'm working
in the fiery pits of hell. And to make matters worse, it's a packed
house and I'm running behind. I don't know how much more of
this madness I can take.

"We'll be right with you, ma'am!" I call out, flashing her an easy
smile and a playful wink that hides my irritation. I ring up the
order for a man standing at the front of the line and then send
him on his way with his two iced coffees. He's immediately

replaced by another man, who spits out his order so fast I almost feel dizzy, barely catching it all. "We're just running a little behind schedule this morning."

"Bullshit!" the woman snaps, glowering at the line of people in front of me. She's a well-kept, middle-aged blonde with an immaculate short hairdo, garbed in fur-trimmed designer clothes that go along with her snobby attitude. "There's three of you back there, yet I've been waiting for over ten minutes for my frap." She shakes her head, practically frothing at the mouth. "It's ridiculous!"

A lump of anger forms in my throat. I quickly swallow it back, glancing to the sky. *Dear God, give me the strength!*

I grit my teeth, my eyes cutting off to the side where the equipment is. I see Cassie, one of my employees, taking her sweet ass time blending something. She's acting like we don't have customers piling up out the ass. Throwing her long, brown hair back, she takes in a deep yawn as if she's tired from working *so* hard. If she weren't new, I'd chew her out.

I shake my head.

At least she looks nice enough in our new uniform, a blue skirt that shows a lot of leg, with a white V-necked T-shirt with *Beangal's Den* printed over the chest. But looking cute and pretty doesn't mean shit to me if you're not getting work done.

Sighing, I look around for Sarah, my other employee, but she's nowhere to be seen.

Figures, I say to myself. *One disappears on me, and the other is moving slower than a snail. Why did I want to be the manager of this place again?*

"Ma'am," I say as politely as I can manage, turning my eyes back on her. I signal to the waiting customer that I'll be with him in a moment. "I understand your frustration with having to wait, but there's no need for that language. There are kids in here." I pause and add, "However, I promise that once you try our world-famous Tiger Caramel Frappuccino, you'll forget *all* about the wait. It's just *that* good." I flash her another smile and a wink, hoping to defuse the situation.

"Ha! We'll see! But if your service weren't so damn bad, we wouldn't have a problem," the woman hotly retorts, ignoring my peace-making attempt and looking as if she's ready for a fight.

I clench my hands, biting back a sharp response that instantly forms on my lips. Usually, I can handle even the most disgruntled customer with my charm, but this one seems immune to it. And she's testing my patience.

Taking a deep breath, I draw myself up, then speak in calm, even tones. "Ma'am, if you can't watch your language, I'm going to have to kindly ask that you leave."

Steeling myself, I wait for her to challenge me. But surprisingly, she just grumbles, muttering something nasty under her breath as she looks away.

I sigh in relief. I was half-expecting to have to call hotel security to deal with this one.

For the next five minutes, I go back to frantically taking and filling orders. I have to stop three times to tell Cassie to pick up the pace. It does little good. If anything, she moves slower, like she's silently protesting having to work hard.

Dammit. I just don't have the time to get on Cassie's ass right now.

It wouldn't be so bad if Sarah weren't MIA.

It just so happens that as soon as the rush of customers is gone, Sarah reappears from the back.

"Where on earth have you been?" I gasp, setting down a tray I've brought over from an empty table on the counter. "We've been slammed out here! I'm doing three people's jobs!"

The twenty-year-old short brunette with dimples *normally* has a penchant for being overzealous about her job. She shakes her head as her eyes fall on Cassie. "I bet. She was probably up all night screwing Brad's brains out." I hold in a groan. Sarah loves to get digs in against Cassie whenever she can. I ignore responding to the bait as Sarah looks back to me. "I'm sorry, Mindy. I was just having a little trouble back there."

I frown with confusion. "What kind of trouble?"

Sarah tilts her head to the side, biting her lower lip. "Well, uh, my tampon—"

"TMI!" I say, cutting her off and looking around fearfully, hoping no one heard what she just said. "Jesus, Sarah," I hiss quietly, "what are you trying to do, scare our customers away?"

Sarah blushes, her cheeks turning a rosy red. "Sorry!"

I shake my head, gently grabbing her by the shoulders and guiding her toward the dining area. "Never mind that. I need your help. There's like five tables that need to be cleaned off and wiped down, and I need a few supplies from the back."

Sarah nods dutifully, wiping her hands on her apron and making her way over to the messy tables. "On it, Boss!"

I sigh and shake my head as I watch her nearly run into a

customer on her way. A pulsing ache runs down my side as I lean against the counter for support. I really don't know how I'm going to get through the rest of the day. The stress of running this place is getting to me lately. In fact, ever since I became the operating manager of Beangal's Den, I've been overworked and tired. Sure, I'm making more money than I ever have, but I'm beginning to wonder if it's even worth it.

I work so much now that I have no social life. The vibrant small-town girl who wouldn't hesitate to give a wild bull a run for his money has been replaced by an old maid. In fact, I can't even remember the last time I've been with a guy and let him do the . . .

A buzz at my side and a Taylor Swift ringtone of *We Are Never, Ever Getting Back Together* interrupt my thoughts. Grumbling, I pull my cell out of my pocket and glance around the cafe to make sure things aren't getting back out of hand before I answer it.

"Hello?"

"Mindy, my dear!" my mother's voice greets me in a singsong tone.

I hold in a groan. I love my mom dearly, but she's the last one I want to hear from right now. She always gives me a headache with her constant picking. "Mother," I reply cordially.

"My God, Mindy," she complains with a sniff, "we haven't talked in weeks. Can you sound any unhappier to hear from me?"

I knew I shouldn't have answered.

I try my best to keep my tone even. "Sorry, Mom. I'm just working right now. Can I call you back after my shift?"

"No," she replies flatly. "This is important."

I try not to sigh out loud. "Okay, Mom. You have two minutes before—"

A piercing shriek interrupts my words and I jump in surprise. I turn around to see Cassie wiping coffee off her chest at the counter. Luckily, she'd only gotten it on herself and not a customer. I swear, I don't know what I'm going to do with this chick.

"What the hell was that?" my mom demands on the other end of the line.

I pull away from the counter, shaking my head. Then I walk around, grab a towel from a shelf, and hand it over to Cassie. "Nothing," I reply. "Just the background noise of the cafe."

"It sounded like a dying cat."

Can't argue with that.

"There was something important you wanted to tell me," I remind her, getting back on point.

"I'm getting married next week," my mom announces, dropping the bomb on me without warning.

My jaw drops and my heart skips a beat at her words. While I've been expecting this, it still feels like a shock. After the heartbreak of Dad's sudden death during my senior year of high school, Mom swore on her grandmother's grave that she'd never marry again . . . until she met John Wentworth, a multi-millionaire businessman.

Unfortunately, I've heard more about John's status than anything else about him. During their courtship, it was almost all she talked about.

John has this, and John has that. John bought me this and John bought me that. And one of my favorites, 'Do I need to remind you how much John is worth?' It's a line she likes to pull out whenever I dare question the dynamics of her relationship. I swear, I think the only reason she's doing this is because he's loaded.

Still, despite my misgivings on the authenticity of their relationship, now is not the time to voice my displeasure or doubts. This is her happy moment, and whether I like it or not, I need to be supportive.

"Mom, that's wonderful!" I say in the most joyful tone I can manage.

"Isn't it?" Mom says proudly. "It's going to be absolutely gorgeous. He's already rented out the venue too. A grand ballroom that sits on the shore with breathtaking views of the ocean."

"Gee, Mom, that sounds great. I'm so happy for you!"

There's a short pause and my mother's voice drops a few octaves. "And I want you to come."

I pause, glancing around the busy cafe. Cassie's finally gotten most of the coffee off her shirt, although there is a giant stain on it, and is taking a man's order. Meanwhile, Sarah's busting her ass, bringing the sitting patrons their fraps. She's looking pretty worn-out herself.

"Mom . . . I don't know," I say slowly, not wanting to upset her. "This is a little out of the blue. With my work schedule and all, I don't know if . . ."

I hear her sharp intake of breath. "Are you kidding me right now, Mindy Isabella Price? I'm your mother, the most important person in your life and the one who gave birth to—"

"You're right!" I say quickly. If I don't head that off, I'll be here until next week listening to her tell me how she was in labor with me for thirty-seven hours and that I owe her the universe. "I don't know what I was thinking. Of course I'll be there."

"You need to take at least a week off," Mom adds.

"A week—" I began to protest. Dear God, with Cassie and Sarah running things? They'll burn the place down.

"Yes, a week! Everyone's going to be there. Your sister, your cousin, and your aunt. Your grandmother."

I open my mouth to argue but then shut it with a snap. It's a fool's errand. My mother has a head harder than granite sometimes. Shaking my head, I bite my lower lip, thinking. *Damn, she drives a hard bargain.*

But the more I think about taking a week off, the more I begin to like the idea. I haven't seen my little sister, Roxy, in forever. Same for my cousin Layla, Aunt Rita, and Grandma Ivy Jo. It sure would be nice to take a break from this mess to relax and chill with the fam.

"I can do that," I say finally, feeling more at ease. "It'll be so good to see you and the family again."

Heaven help Cassie and Sarah.

"It sure will," Mom agrees. "Roxy has been asking about you non-stop."

A grin plays across my lips as I think about my younger sister. At twenty-one, Roxy's young, dumb, and full of fun. Basically, an even more smartassed and sassier version of myself.

But my Mom's next words take me out of my reverie and hit me like a lightning bolt. "And I expect you to bring your fiancé."

"My fiancé?" I ask with a croak when I can finally find my voice.

"Yes! You know, Harold. Tall. Handsome. Rich. Good in bed. The one you've been bragging to me about for the past year." She lets out a little laugh. "Roxy's been dying to meet him . . . and so have I."

Shit, shit, shit!

I pause, the phone pressed against my ear, my mind racing in panic.

That lie. I should've known it would come back to bite me in the ass. I'm not one for long-term relationships, and I got sick of Mom trying to set me up with some man back at home she wanted me to meet. Knowing her, probably a son of one of John's friends. I got tired of it, so I told her I was engaged to get her off my back.

Stupid me.

I suck in a deep breath, about to tell her the truth, but I stop. There's no way I can admit that I was lying for the past year and show up at her wedding without a man. Absolutely *no* way. By now, everyone in the family has heard about my fiancé, *Harold*, and mom is going to be overly dramatic if I fess up now. Besides, she's getting married. She doesn't need to hear that I lied.

"Mindy?"

"I—" I began to say, not knowing how I'm going to get out of this one. At that exact moment, Brianna Adams, my best friend and ex-partner in crime—and now part-owner of the Beangal's Den—

walks through the door, her adorable little boy, Rafe, balanced expertly on her right hip.

Suddenly, I'm struck by an idea, my face lighting up like a light bulb. "Of course, Harold," I say cheerfully, regaining my composure. "He'll be coming. He's been wanting to meet you for forever!"

I can practically feel my Mom beaming through the phone. "Perfect! I'll be expecting you both. See you soon, love."

The line goes dead, and I'm quick to pocket my cell as I wave Brianna over to the counter. She's halfway there when the disgruntled woman from earlier jumps up from her seat. Apparently, she's finished with her drink and not satisfied in the least.

"You were wrong," she says loudly at me, brushing by Brianna to get to me. "It wasn't worth the wait. I've tasted far better, like the Unicorn Frappuccino they serve at the place on the other side of town." She shakes her head angrily and almost yells, "You guys suck. I'm never coming here again!" Cutting her eyes at me, she spins around and walks off, nearly running into Brianna on her way out.

Brianna's forehead crinkles into a frown as she reaches the counter. "Having a bad day, I take it?" She asks.

My chest fills with warmth as my eyes fall on my good friend. Dressed in a white and yellow flower dress that has a low V-cut with her long brown hair pulled into a lazy bun, she looks absolutely voluptuous. Shit, had I known pregnancy could do that, I would've gotten knocked up years ago.

"Besides the A/C not working and being overrun for over half the morning? Business as usual," I say dismissively. With my mind on my idea, the dissatisfied customer is already old news. "We were a little behind earlier."

"I feel sorry for you. Someone's been called about the A/C," Brianna says. She pauses and frowns again. "And what the hell's a Unicorn Frappuccino?"

I roll my eyes. "It's all the rage right now. What rock have you been hiding under?"

"Have you tried it?" Brianna asks curiously.

I shake my head. "Hell, no! I have a friend who did and she was shitting glitter and rainbows all week."

"Mindy!" Brianna protests.

I shake my head. "I'm serious! It's a real drink."

Brianna looks like she's about to argue and then thinks better of it, shaking her head. "I'll take your word for it."

"Good," I say, reaching across the counter to tug on Rafe's small hand. He giggles as I shake it. He's a spitting image of both his parents, with adorable baby blues and dirty-blonde hair. "How's my little man doing?"

Brianna smiles, her eyes lighting up as she looks at her baby boy. "Good. He's talking even more now and can almost form a full sentence."

"That's awesome." I grin at Rafe and soften my tone into a voice as sweet as sugar. "Can you say a sentence for Aunt Mindy? Huh, Rafey?"

"Hungry!" Rafe says, reaching for his mom's left breast.

"Rafe stop it!" Brianna snaps, grabbing Rafe's little arm before he can pull her boob out in public, her cheeks turning red. "Sorry," she mutters. "He does that all the time."

I shake my head. I know I shouldn't, but I can't help myself. "Takes after his Daddy, and I don't blame him, Jersey Maid. You look like you can feed the village with those milk jugs."

"Mindy!"

"Girl, I'm serious. What are you, a triple-D now? If I ever run out of creamer, I know just the person to call."

"I'm gonna leave!" Brianna threatens.

I let out a laugh. "Oh my God, lighten up, will you? It was just a joke."

Brianna scowls. "Well, you're not funny."

"Yeah, I am." The grin on my face slowly fades as I remember my idea.

"So how's Gavin?" I ask, clearing my throat. Gavin, Brianna's husband, is almost just as good a friend as Brianna is to me. A former football star, he's settled down into small-town life with surprising ease. But I would think it would be hard not to with the beautiful ranch they moved into. "He enjoying fatherhood much?"

Brianna nods, a smile coming to her face. "Very much so. He can't wait until Rafe is old enough to go fishing with him. He talks about it every day."

"What about work?" I ask, leaning in with intense interest.

Brianna gazes at me for a moment. "Well, with the money he made during his football career and his investments, he's not hard up for a job. He's taking it easy right now. The kids love the football camp he runs, mentoring disadvantaged children, and helping local actors—"

Brianna's talking, but I'm starting to zone out, my mind drifting to my predicament.

It seems she notices, and Brianna stares at me suspiciously. As my best friend, she always knows when something is up. "Mindy Price, what is going on in that head of yours?"

"Umm . . . I need to ask you something," I admit.

Brianna arches an eyebrow as I feel sweat begin to form on my brow. "Oh, really? What's that?"

I stand there silently, not knowing how to form my next words, my heart pounding like a battering ram. *Jesus, she's not going to make this easy.*

"Mindy," she presses. "I'm waiting."

I'm unable to part my lips. I don't know how to tell her about the lie that I'm caught up in.

"Mindy!" Bri cracks.

"Mindy!" Rafe echoes, pointing at me.

Just say it!

Closing my eyes, I take a deep breath. And when I open them, I finally ask, "Know any hot guys named Harold?"

Want to read the rest? Get Mr. Fiance HERE or visit
www.laurenlandish.com

ABOUT THE AUTHOR

Irresistible Bachelor Series (Interconnecting standalones):
**Anaconda || Mr. Fiance || Heartstopper
Stud Muffin || Mr. Fixit || Matchmaker
Motorhead || Baby Daddy**

Connect with Lauren Landish.
www.laurenlandish.com
admin@laurenlandish.com